His E

LUCKY
US

USA TODAY BESTSELLERAUTORIN

GENEVIEVE JACK

ABOUT THIS BOOK

Happily ever after is worth fighting for...

Luck was on our side when Seven and I thwarted his father's evil plan to sabotage Dragonfly Hollow. Now all we want is to be together, but to protect my daughter Arden, we agree to keep our relationship secret a little longer. Keeping our hands off each other though proves more of a challenge than we anticipate.

Things are going our way until my friend, a satyr named River, is found hunched over a human victim in front of his restaurant. Turns out danger still lurks in the fairy realm. Soon Godmother has us on the case, and the clues surrounding who framed River just get weirder and weirder.

Solving this mystery is the key to freeing Seven from Godmother's hold and paving the way for us to become a family. Only, our happily-ever-after won't come easily. Lucky for us, we're ready for a fight.

DEDICATION

This book is dedicated to all those who have ever had to make their own luck.

THE DAILY HATTER

SPILLING THE TEA IN DRAGONFLY HOLLOW SINCE 1845.

BOMBSHELL KISS GIVES LESS BANG THAN EXPECTED

Devashire is once again abuzz with rumors about most eligible bachelor, Seven Delaney. In what is being called the bombshell of all kisses, no less than a dozen fairies have come forward to attest that they saw Seven kissing prodigal daughter Sophia Larkspur through the window of the Victory Building in Elderflame on Tuesday. This reporter has it on good authority the two engaged in a bout of tongue wrestling worthy of an Olympic medal.

Despite the purported heat of this public encounter and the enthusiasm their audience had for capturing it, oddly none of the pictures or videos taken are intelligible. If you are equally puzzled at the plausibility that a glare from the glass should occur at every angle in conjunction with simultaneous equipment malfunctions, then you will understand why I sought out Seven for a statement. Clearly luck was at play.

Although yours truly did not score an audience

with the leprechaun, PR spokesperson and sister to the man himself, Evangeline Delaney, offered this:

"Do we have your attention, Devashire? The Dragonfly Casino is pleased to announce that for the first time ever, we will be offering poker lessons to human guests with the potential to expand the program to interested fairies in the future. Beginning later this month, Sophia Larkspur, aka Soho Lane, who made a name for herself as a poker pro while living in the United States, will bring her personal expertise to the table for a fee. Specific session dates and times to be announced. And yes, this partnership was sealed with a kiss!"

There you have it, Hatters! We should have suspected, given the circumstances, that this was a publicity stunt. A public relationship between a leprechaun and a pixie would be shocking, but the unconquerable Seven Delaney choosing a pixie is truly preposterous. Far more logical that the Lucky Enterprises mogul knows how to get your attention!

What do you think about opening poker lessons to fae despite the ban on regular play? Your favorite columnist wants to know. Leave me your comments at DailyHatter.com.

Fairly Goodweather
Columnist

CHAPTER

ONE

E veryone thinks they want a fairy-tale life, but those stories always focus on the wrong things. Cinderella rises above her circumstances when she enchants the prince. No one stops to consider that everything the prince knew about her was a deception. None of it was hers. Not the dress, not the shoes, not the pumpkin carriage. She pulled fictional history's greatest bluff. What happened next? After the wedding in the castle, did she rise to the demands of being a princess? Did the townspeople magically set aside their envy and spite and accept her as a regent? Or did happily ever after come with a dark and dangerous edge? It's possible Cinderella found herself in an equally difficult predicament, simply serving a new master.

I think about that story a lot when I ponder my own situation. Seven and I have known each other since we were children and our love is built on more than just a single night's dancing, but the divide between who he is and who I am couldn't be more complete. And I wonder if we will ever close that gap. Will there ever be a time I don't have to bluff? Will my relationship with Seven ever be accepted as real? I don't know. At the moment, I'm still riding in the pumpkin.

"Tip your head back and to the right, Sophia." Evangeline motions for me to adjust my position and I do, arching over the poker table at an angle that I'm sure makes the best of my figure but is terribly uncomfortable. The elbow I'm braced on prickles as if it's fallen asleep, and I'm starving. I missed lunch because the photographer is in a time crunch. My stomach growls a threat that it might start eating me from the inside.

Still, I smile as the camera shutter releases a series of fast clicks and the photographer, an artsy-looking leprechaun with long silver hair, moves around me. At least my outfit is flattering. With me leaning back like this, the floor-length dress splits midthigh, revealing one gold stiletto and the majority of my right leg. The sparkly red number hugs my waist and gives my breasts a marvelous, strapless boost. There's no room for a bra of any kind. The thing is backless—convenient, considering my wings have to be out for this shoot—but that means my upper half is precariously tucked into a stiff panel of fabric that runs from my sacrum to just above my nipples. Honestly, the fact I'm not spilling out of it is a feat of fashion genius. I'd thank luck or magic, but being fae, I'd feel it if there was any involved. We can sense both even if we can't always see them at work. Alas, my skin does not tingle and my own luck is nestled deep within me, snoring peacefully.

"Okay, darling, turn toward me and look directly at the camera, ankles crossed, both hands on the table on either side of your hips." The photographer squats down, adjusting his lens.

I do as he asks, beaming down at him, but he doesn't take the picture.

"Drop the smile. Look at me like I'm a competitor. I'm the player standing between you and a big win." He makes a few more adjustments while I try to dredge up the right look.

I spent the majority of my sixteen years in the United States supporting myself by playing poker. One of the skills that came with the territory was the ability to hide my actual emotions behind a poker face, the ability to either be unreadable or to telegraph an emotion that is inconsistent with what I'm feeling. The look I give the photographer now is one of supreme confidence and determination. It's an expression meant to intimidate. I'm projecting intensity, telling my opponent that I'm holding cards so good they might as well push their chips into the middle of the table right now. My smile dissolves, but not entirely. I close my lips but keep them slightly upturned at one corner, preserving the tightness in my eyes. When I lower my chin, my dark hair falls over one eye.

"Gods, Sophia," Evangeline says in a low voice. "You look like you're holding the secret to the universe behind your back."

"Maybe I am," I say, sending her a wink.

The photographer stands, studying his screen. "That's it. I think we got it. Thanks, darling. You were a wonderful model." He takes a step forward and kisses me on the cheek, his breath skating over my skin. He's a leprechaun, but up until this point, he's kept his luck to himself. Now I feel it beside me like a large, predatory bird. I give him a nod, and he hurriedly collects his things before kissing Evangeline on both cheeks. "You'll have the comps tomorrow by end of day."

"Thanks, Mac." She brushes her shiny red hair over one shoulder as she watches him leave.

Only a few short weeks ago, I thought the Delaneys hated me, especially Evangeline's brother, Seven. He stood me up at the Yule ball when we were teenagers and humiliated me in front of everyone in Dragonfly Hollow. Turns out Seven didn't want to hurt me at all. He was a victim of his psycho father, Chance, who'd poisoned him with blue iron—the only substance in the world capable of draining a fairy's luck—and kept him locked in a dungeon beneath his hunting cabin.

Weirder still, it turns out Seven is Arden's father. That little revelation is thanks to some serious magical interference by Godmother. I still don't completely understand her motives, but I do know this: Seven and I deserve to make up for lost time. Unfortunately, until we have a chance to tell Arden about her unlikely origins, we've decided to keep our relationship a secret. We want to give her choices. We want to give her a chance to control the narrative about her own life.

Seven's responsible for getting me this job teaching poker, and his sister, Evangeline, the head of public relations for Lucky Enterprises, is leaning into the moment. This photo shoot is just the start. I have interviews with all the major news outlets in Devashire scheduled over the next two weeks, at the end of which I'll be teaching my very first class.

"You did a great job today." Evangeline hits me with one of her ten-thousand-watt smiles. Just like her brother, she's supermodel attractive, the kind of person who walks into the room and turns every head. She's tall, thin, and radiates confidence. But then that's what being a leprechaun does for you. Leprechauns are always beautiful. Their luck seeps out of their pores.

"Thanks. I'm not used to being photographed. I hope Mac can get what he needs from what we did today."

She laughs. "Are you kidding me? Sophia, I don't

think you realize how lovely you are."

"For a pixie," I add in for her.

"For anyone. If it weren't for the wings, I'd swear you were a leprechaun. I think living among humans was good for you." She shakes her head. "That look in your eyes. I've never seen a pixie look like that. You're a badass. And if people knew what you really did for Devashire, they'd treat you like one."

What I did was help take down her father and prove he was imprisoning pixies in his rural sex dungeon. He also murdered a few people for reasons that only he and maybe Godmother fully understand. Together, Seven and I proved Chance was guilty of murder. He's now serving a life sentence in Ashgate Prison.

I try not to think too much about the night we took him down. It still shakes me. I'm not sure if what Eva says is true—if Devashire society knew, would they respect me more? It's a moot point. Godmother took credit for solving the case, and the only people who know my part in it are Seven, Eva, and my friends River and Penelope, all of whom have been sworn to secrecy. One does not challenge Godmother's narrative of events. Not unless one wants to have one's wings broken.

I glance down at my toes. My stomach growls loud enough that I'm sure Eva hears it. "Uh, thanks. Are we done for the day?"

She laughs. "No, I want to introduce you to some

high rollers. But go ahead and take a break. It sounds like you need one. Eat and get changed into something more comfortable, then meet me in my office."

I open my mouth to say okay, but the word never leaves my lips. My breath hitches when the buzz of Seven's luck skates across the back of my neck, over my shoulder, and between my breasts. My nipples tighten at the feel of it, and I have to draw a breath to steady myself. The tingle of it causes the tiny hairs on my arms to stand on end, and everything inside me takes on an electrical charge.

Evangeline's lips quirk into an impish grin. There is no way she can't sense that. "In my office by four, Sophia," she singsongs before striding out the door without looking back.

I adjust my dress and smooth my hair, suddenly filled with a different type of hunger. My heels click on the hardwood floors of the new poker room as I push my way through the gold-plated doors and into the foyer of the Dragonfly Casino. My steps falter when I see Seven standing in front of a poster advertising the latest Cirque du Soleil production going on in the theater.

My very own personal Prince Charming.

His back is to me, which means I have a moment to observe him as my inner world goes topsy-turvy with attraction. The soft shine of his toffee-colored hair picks up the gold reflected off the shiny surfaces in the room and contrasts perfectly with his dark suit, specially tailored to make the most of his broad shoulders. His jacket skims down to his hips in a perfect taper, both professional and somehow sensual, as if the material loves to touch him as much as I do. His long legs end in polished Italian-leather loafers.

As quietly as I can, I sidle up to him, leaving a few feet of space between us. Nothing to see here. Just two people who happen to be reading the same poster at the same time.

"That dress should be illegal," he whispers, his head still tilted as if he's studying the picture of the aerial act in front of him. "I take that back. It should be perfectly legal in the privacy of my bedroom. Outside of it, I'd prefer you wrapped in a hooded cloak."

I lick my bottom lip. "So sad. This dress, with me in it, is about to be plastered all over social media to promote the new poker classes. Evangeline picked it out."

A growl rumbles from his chest. "Is there no justice in this world? If she must flaunt you for all to see, shouldn't I, at least, be the first to enjoy you in it, to touch you beneath the material, to... help you out of it?"

My lips twitch. "Who are you to claim first dibs?"

Only his eyes move, but I see him glance in my direction, his emerald gaze twinkling with his regard. "The one who loves you."

He's said it to me before, but hearing it now still sends a thrill through me and makes my heart thump in my chest. I know what he wants to hear. There is one thing that Seven needs from me more than anything else, the thing I've learned holds his pieces together.

"Be the first then. I'm *yours*, after all. Do with me as you wish." Aside from his sister, I am the one person in his life who knows him, his true heart, and knowing that I accept him, that I want to be his and want him to be mine is a balm to the wounds his neglectful parents left behind.

His throat bobs on a hard swallow, and his chest rises and falls at a faster rate. "Come."

His luck coils around me, nudging me to follow him as he turns and strides through an unmarked door near the banquet hall. I check over both shoulders. No one is watching. Of course not. Not with him concentrating his luck to make sure we're alone.

I duck inside.

Seven's arm circles my waist, and he pulls me against his chest in the darkness. I hear the lock slide into place, and then the light clicks on. We're in some kind of utility room, surrounded by shelves of tablecloths, aprons, and cloth napkins. At the back is a stack of folding tables.

I pivot in his arms to face him. "Classy digs, Seven, but I was hoping for a gas station bathroom."

He gives one breathy laugh, but the heat in his eyes shows me he isn't in a comedic mood. His expression is ravenous, predatory, *feral*.

"Are you done modeling for photos today?" he asks, deep and low.

"Yes." My voice comes out in a squeak, my throat tight from the intensity he's putting off.

The smile he gives me is positively wolfish. "Good."

Luck slams into me like an ocean wave I didn't see coming. Someone has popped the cork on a bottle of champagne and bubbles rush between my legs, through my torso, and to the tips of my breasts. Electric fizz tingles in my blood. My knees wobble but he has me, one hand between my wings and the other in my hair.

When his lips crash down on mine, it isn't gentle. He's claiming me with a desperation that tells me exactly how Seven feels about our clandestine circumstances. Leprechauns aren't used to being denied what they want, and he wants me. All of me.

I melt into him, opening wider for him, his tongue stroking expertly against mine. His thumb braces under my jaw, his fingers wrapped firmly around the base of my skull. The way he's gripping me is almost painful. Almost. Instead, it makes me feel secure. Safe. And completely turned on.

He shifts me back to the tables and lifts me as if I weigh nothing, perching my bottom on the top of the stack. My dress shifts. Despite hours of staying in place no matter which way I moved, my breasts spill out of the top. He catches one in his mouth, sucking hard. I have to flutter my wings to stay balanced in this position, and I dig my fingers into his hair to steady myself.

"You are so beautiful." Emerald-green eyes flash in the dim room, and he smiles wickedly at me, breath skating across my nipple. "I saw that photographer kiss you."

"You were watching me?" Not surprising really. Security cameras record every corner of the casino.

"Only at the end. I wanted to check if you were done."

"Did it bother you when he kissed me on the cheek?"

He laughs darkly. "Only because I have no way of marking you as mine. I wanted to throw open the doors to that room and make it clear as day that you're spoken for. Instead, I'll have to settle for reminding you of the same."

"How do you plan to do that?" I ask breathlessly.

His hands work under the skirt of my dress, bunching the shiny material around my hips. Adroit fingers hook into the sides of my panties and slide them down my legs. Once they're off, he brings them to his nose and inhales. My blood heats at the sight, and my breath comes in pants. He slips them into his pocket, then plants his hands on my inner thighs and shoves them apart, exposing me.

"Seven," I gasp.

He lowers himself to his knees in front of me and

licks up my center with the flat of his tongue.

My cheeks heat. I arch against his mouth, and he flicks and circles my clit before plunging his tongue inside me. His luck follows, filling me with a rush of effervescence that presses against my inner walls even as he worships every inch of pleasure-inducing skin between my thighs. I can't form words.

It takes an embarrassingly short amount of time for my head to tip back in a silent scream of over-whelming pleasure. I'm still blinded by the light of the first orgasm when he rises, hooking one of my legs over his shoulder, and enters me fast and hard, sending me over the edge again.

"Oh. Gods. Sev. En." He's thrusting so hard it feels like my teeth might clack together. The only thing I want is for him to thrust harder, to hold me tighter. I want him so close I can smell him on my skin days from now when we have to be apart.

He grips my hips, his face buried in my neck as he pounds into me until he finds his release, tremors of ecstasy rippling through him in my arms. We're as close as two people can get, all my limbs wrapped tight around him, and I hold him to me.

He runs his nose from my jaw to my ear. "I love you, Sophia."

"I love you too."

Drawing back, he returns my panties and helps me fix my dress, which thanks to his luck hasn't ripped or sustained a single wrinkle, then zips his pants and takes a seat next to me on the tables. Leaning against the wall, he pulls me against his side. I make myself comfortable.

"So tonight's the night," he says.

"Yeah. It took some doing, but my grandmother is playing bridge in Sunnyville, my parents have a date planned, and Arden isn't babysitting for Penelope. We'll have the house and her all to ourselves for at least two hours."

It's taken a few days for me to arrange everything, but it's important to both of us that Arden be the first to know that Seven is her father and that she is the only pixie/leprechaun hybrid in existence. What a heavy hammer to be dropped on her. She's lived her entire life believing she's half-human. She believes it because I believed it, thanks to Godmother's trickery. But it's time she knows the truth. She deserves to know.

"When should I come?"

"Six should be safe."

He nods.

I tip my head back until it clunks against the wall behind me. "I hope she doesn't hate me."

"If she hates anyone, it will be me. You couldn't tell Arden what you didn't know, and I'm going to make sure she understands that."

"You're putting a lot of trust in a teenager to have a logical response to this situation."

He frowns. "Admittedly, I don't have much experience with teenagers. When Evangeline was her age, I was just two years older and still a teenager myself."

I groan. "Let me fill you in on raising teenagers. Arden is an exceptionally responsible, levelheaded, and remarkable young woman with the potential to turn into a hormonal, irrational beast when pushed beyond her limits. It doesn't happen often, but it does happen."

He strokes the back of my head. "Whatever happens, however she reacts, it will be okay." His voice is soft. "We're in this together. I'll do whatever it takes to protect both of you. I promise."

Is that my heart or a warm pat of butter sliding down my ribs? "I know you will."

A shadow passes through his expression, and he glances away from me. "You know it's a lie though. If I was willing to do anything, I'd stay away from both of you. You'd be safer and happier."

I grab his chin and turn his face toward me. "Safe is overrated, and I couldn't be any happier than this."

He sighs and kisses me before glancing at his watch. "I'm fifteen minutes late for a meeting."

"You'd better get going then." I scamper off the stack of tables.

"Before I do, there's something I want you to have."

"Hmm?" I straighten my dress.

He reaches into his pocket and pulls out a necklace with a coin dangling from the end. I recognize it as one from his collection of charms, the magical objects he keeps in a hermetically sealed room in his office. He once brought a coin just like this with us to Shadowvale and used it to distract Yissevel the bone fairy so that I could escape the unseelie's clutches. It's gold with the imprint of a goddess on one side and a dragonfly on the other, and he's mounted it on a matching chain.

"I want you to wear this."

"Why?" I ask hesitantly.

"Because it protects its wearer from harm and because it will make the man who loves you happy you're wearing his gift," he says around a half smile.

"Who could say no to that?" I pivot, moving my hair aside so he can fasten the chain around my neck. The coin rests just below the hollow of my throat. "Thank you."

In response, he kisses me just below my ear. "One day this will all be easier."

I smooth my hair and check my makeup in the bottom of a silver tray, but like everything else, it's fine. Seven's luck has kept every one of my hairs in place.

I replace the tray and turn in his arms. "I'm not sure it will ever be easier exactly." He frowns, and I continue. "But it will be worth it. I know it will be worth it."

His usual lopsided grin comes back in full force. "See you tonight."

TWO

When I was living in the United States, I read somewhere that children come *through* their mothers not *from* their mothers. The idea the author was trying to convey was that although our children share our genetics and are influenced by how we raise them, they come into the world their own person. Back then I laughed at this notion, chalking it up to silly human religiosity. The idea that some greater power had sent Arden through me, as if I were a portal between worlds, was something I couldn't take seriously back then. But as I look at my beautiful daughter now with her auburn hair and those emerald eyes that remind me so much of Seven's, those words return to me and they finally make sense.

I have no idea how she's going to take the news that Seven is her father. Arden and I have never been apart more than a few days. I know she likes avocado toast for breakfast and her bacon must be extra crispy. I know her favorite book is *Little Women*. I know she can't sleep with her closet door open. Before today, I would have sworn that no one knew her better than me, that I could predict exactly how she would react to almost anything. But not this. She's no longer my little girl. She's a woman. A whip-smart, stunningly beautiful young woman.

And I can't protect her from this. I have no idea what the truth will do to her, only that she deserves to know it.

"What was it you wanted to talk to me about?" Arden's voice is a low whisper. We wave goodbye to my parents as they slip out the door dressed in their date-night clothes. Both of them look great, younger than when I first arrived. I despise the thought that the years I spent raising Arden in the US prematurely aged them, but our current situation seems to be undoing some of the damage.

I clear my throat. "I'll tell you in a minute." I haven't seen Seven since our rendezvous in the banquet closet this afternoon. Afterward, we both went our separate ways. But he said he'd be here by six, which means I need to keep Arden busy for another fifteen minutes.

"Why can't you tell me now? We're alone." She shifts from foot to foot.

"I'm just, uh... We have a guest coming."

Her brows crowd together. "Oh my god, is it

Godmother? Is there something wrong with my passport again?"

I hold up my hands. "No. Nothing like that." *Fuck.* That's not exactly true. It might be like that depending on what she chooses. I don't want to lie to her, but nothing I say will make sense until she knows everything. Only, I can't tell her the truth until Seven gets here.

She places both hands on her stomach. "Please just rip the Band-Aid off, Mom. You're giving me anxiety."

Should I tell her? Break the ice before Seven arrives? Make her wait? I'm still contemplating my options when a knock comes on the door.

"Hold that thought," I tell her, then move to answer it.

"I'm early, but I took a chance," Seven says from the stoop. Of course he did. He's lucky and he's been thinking about this all day. I breathe a sigh of relief and invite him in.

"Hi, Seven." Arden's gaze darts between us. If anything, she's even more nervous now. "What are you doing here?"

He gestures toward the dining room. "Sit. We'll talk."

"Am I in trouble with Godmother?" Arden blurts. She looks like she might bolt for the door.

It doesn't surprise me that she might think that— Seven works for Godmother after all. I have to calm her down before she passes out or does something stupid.

"Arden, you're not in trouble. It's nothing bad. Just please sit down." I gesture toward a chair across the table from us.

She sighs heavily but plops herself down, although her expression is nothing short of exasperated.

Seven pulls a coin from his pocket, an ordinary quarter, and slides it across the table toward her. "Has Bailiwick's ever tested your luck?"

Arden looks at him and snorts. "Um, no. I told them I'm human, so..." She licks her lips. "I'm given accommodations. I don't need it for lessons."

Seven taps a finger on the table. "Usually children in Devashire are given a test before they enter grade one. On average, leprechauns are born with more luck than pixies, who are born with more luck than satyrs. But there are exceptions. A few satyrs have tested at the top of the pixie range. More than a few leprechauns have disappointing results and test in the pixie range. Our natural ability to store and wield luck varies greatly by the individual, even among the normal species ranges."

She nods, her brows bunching as if she's confused.

I lean my elbows on the table. "The reason they test children is that luck is like a muscle. Use it regularly and your capacity to use it grows. Don't use it and it atrophies. You're my daughter, and it's possible you have more luck than you realize, it's just you've never tried to use it."

Arden lifts the coin from the table and raises her eyebrows. "Do you want to test me?"

Seven and I nod in unison.

"What do you want me to do?"

"Flip it," Seven explains. "Concentrate. Picture tails in your mind."

Arden places the coin on her thumb and flicks it into the air. When it lands, it's heads up.

I frown. "Did you concentrate on tails?"

Arden laughs. "Not really. I mean, it's not like I can change how it lands. That's ridiculous."

Seven plucks the quarter from her fingers and awakens his power. His luck rises to fill the room, a hot-blooded, long-bodied dragon of energy that slithers and coils around the table. Arden shifts, glancing over her shoulder.

"Do you feel that, Arden?" I ask her.

She nods. "What is it?"

"That's Seven's luck. What does it look like to you?"

Glancing around the room, she frowns. "It doesn't look like anything. It's invisible."

"Is it? You have a picture in your mind, don't you? Based on what you're sensing."

The beast brushes by her again, blowing the hair off her shoulder.

"It's a... It's like a... dragon!" Her eyes widen. "Long and red. Fire-breathing."

I laugh. "Good job. Can you tell mine?"

I concentrate, and my luck rises in the room beside Seven's and pounces across the table.

She giggles. "Tiger. Oh my god, Mom, yours is so much smaller than Seven's."

Teenagers! "Well, I'm a pixie, so..." I frown and pull my luck back inside myself.

To his credit, Seven doesn't laugh at Arden's jab. He holds up the quarter. "Observe." He launches the silver disc straight up off the tip of his thumb, where it flips over and over again in the air. He locks eyes with Arden as it drops, landing perfectly on its edge. Seconds pass, but it does not fall over.

"Holy shit!" Arden gapes.

"Language!" I can't really blame her. It's fucking incredible.

Seven knocks the coin over and pushes it across the table toward her. "Try again, and this time concentrate."

With Seven's luck still circling Arden, she places the quarter on her thumb. My lips twitch into a smile as I realize what he's doing. He's using his luck to draw hers out, focusing his power on her. If there's any luck in her, he'll coax it out.

She tries again, her face tightening with concentration. There! Another presence pops into the room with a small, bouncy energy. Raccoon, I realize. Its ringed tail waves as it holds its tiny hands out to catch the coin. I want to squeal in delight, but I can't break her concentration. The quarter lands.

"Tails!" I clap my hands together.

Arden chews her lip. "Holy crap. I think I did that!" She rubs her chest. "I... I felt it."

I nod vigorously. "What did you picture in your mind when you felt your luck working?"

A blush colors her cheeks. "Well, it wasn't a dragon."

Seven chuckles. "I once knew an old woman with luck that manifested as a mouse, and she was ten times as strong as me."

That seems to encourage Arden because she blurts out, "It was a raccoon."

I straighten. "That's what I sensed too."

"Try again," Seven says. "We can measure the strength of your luck by how many times in a row you can flip tails."

Arden eagerly picks up the coin and flings it into the air. This time Seven's dragonish luck disappears from the room and only the sweet and bright energy of Arden's raccoon remains. She squeals when it lands on tails.

"You're doing it, sweetheart. Keep going!" I clap my hands.

Seven holds up two fingers. "That's two. Go for three."

An hour later, Arden is visibly fatigued and I can

barely feel the raccoon in the room anymore. She's flipped tails successfully 175 times, but this time it's heads. She slumps in her chair, forehead hitting the table. "That's all I got."

Seven and I beam at each other.

"What? How did I do?"

I rest my chin on my threaded fingers. "Do you want to tell her, Seven, or should I?"

"Oh, I'd love to," Seven says. "The probability of a human being flipping tails one hundred and seventy-five times in a row is almost zero. It's possible but so unlikely we might as well consider it impossible. The average satyr can reach twenty-five flips regularly, although it's not unusual for exceptional satyrs to near the one hundred mark later in life."

Arden's fingers go to her lips. "Mom, I did inherit your pixie luck!"

"The average pixie can manage sixty-five flips, but an exceptional pixie might hit 145 on a good day," I say. "My test was 105 as a child."

The grin fades from her face. "That doesn't make sense. It's genetically impossible," she says. "I can't be luckier than you. Not with a human father."

Seven rubs his jaw. "The average leprechaun can reliably make 150 flips as a child. I've managed five hundred myself as an adult, and the only reason I stopped was because I didn't have time to continue. The test was taking too long."

She stares at him as if he's not making sense. "So then how did I do 175 if I'm half-human?"

This time Seven turns to me and waits. I made him promise to allow me to be the one to say the words. Here we go. Please, gods, help her take this well.

"Because, Arden," I begin slowly. "You're not half-human after all. It turns out I made a mistake in assuming that. You're half-pixie from me." I press a hand into my chest and take a deep breath. "And half-leprechaun... from Seven."

Arden stops breathing, and the smile fades from her face. She tips her head, her eyes swimming with unshed tears. Confusion and betrayal war in her expression, and I want to explain but I can't find the words around the lump that's formed in my throat. Thankfully Seven rises to the occasion.

"Your mother never lied to you," Seven adds quickly. "She didn't know. Neither of us did until recently."

I hadn't thought it possible, but Arden seems even more confused. "I think she'd know who my father was!"

I shake my head. "Godmother changed his appearance and there were circumstances..." I sigh and look away. "I didn't know until very recently, but it's true. Godmother changed Seven into the form of a human man, and I didn't know who he really was the night we conceived you. I thought he truly was a human man."

"The three of us and Godmother are the only ones who know," Seven adds.

The moment Arden realizes the ramifications, I watch fear chase the other emotions from her expression. "Wait... I'm not human. Not at all?" She stands, sending her chair tumbling backward across the wood floor.

I shake my head, eyes locked on hers. "No one has to know, Arden. You have the choice. You can either keep this a secret, and so will we, or—"

"Or you can take your rightful place in leprechaun society." Seven's body language tells me exactly what he feels about keeping this a secret. He wants to shout that Arden is his daughter from the rooftops.

Arden snorts. "My rightful place? You make it sound like I'm in one of those movies about a teenager who finds out she's a secret princess." Her eyes rove between me and him and she snorts.

Seven brushes invisible lint from the sleeve of his jacket. "We have no royal title, although you do have a family crest and are currently the sole heir of my portion of the Delaney family fortune, currently estimated at approximately thirty-five billion dollars."

All humor drains from Arden's expression, followed by all color as she looks to me and realizes that this isn't a joke. That what Seven says is true.

"Mom?" she squeaks. "What does this mean?"

As I suspected, there's no immediate joy in learning she's extremely wealthy. Arden isn't like that.

The money won't in and of itself mean much to her. Like she always has in the past, she's waiting for me to frame this up, to help her make sense of it.

"It means you have options. You can pretend to be human and go to medical school as planned. Once you graduate, you can work in America. As far as the US government is concerned, you are human and a natural-born citizen. But you'll have to be careful. You should probably come here for medical care, and you can't overuse your luck no matter how badly you want to. If anyone determined that you were fae, the Fairy Immigration and Rehabilitation Enforcement agency would come knocking on your door. Also, you won't age like other humans, which means that at some point you'll have to return here."

Seven clears his throat. "Or we can take this public. Every year on the summer solstice, leprechauns throw a ball called the Gilded Gala. It's basically a coming-out party where all the young leprechauns of marriageable age are introduced to society. If you decide before then, I will introduce you to Devashire's elite. Everyone will know you're my daughter. You could attend university and medical school here, and of course you'd have plenty of resources to start your own practice."

I almost gape at his mention of the Gilded Gala. It's more than just a ball—it's an exclusive, televised event. All the attendees dress in gold, although how much gold and to what shiny degree is open to interpretation. The *Daily Hatter* puts out a special edition each year covering the best dressed, and designers clamor to outfit the wealthiest families. Although pixies and satyrs rarely attend the ball unless they're working at it, humans and fae alike line up to watch the procession of leprechauns down the rainbow-colored carpet that leads into the Dragonfly After Dark hotel where the ball is held each year.

Seven must really want Arden to stay to pull out the Gilded Gala, but it's important she understand the cons as well.

"But Arden, once it's announced that you're not human, it will invalidate your passport." I shoot Seven an apologetic look for popping his gold-plated balloon. "If you go public with this, there's no going back. Devashire will be your home... forever."

She blinks at me. "I can never leave."

Seven shifts uncomfortably. *Back to you, good cop.* "Lucky Enterprises' employees are sometimes granted special temporary visas in order to conduct business in the United States. I've been there twice this year. But no, I can't stay without permission, and if they know you're my daughter, you won't be able to stay either."

Arden rubs her face with both hands. "But if I go, I'll have to be careful not to get caught. I'll have to live like we lived before. No one can ever know who I am."

"It wasn't so bad before," I say defensively.

"Mom, you never had a real relationship my entire

life. Anytime someone got close, you'd push them away."

"To keep you safe."

"And I'll have to do the same to keep myself safe."

I nod. "I liked our little life before I was arrested, Arden, but what you say is true. Now that I'm back here, I realize there is nothing more valuable than the freedom to be who you truly are."

Seven locks eyes with me, what I leave unsaid passing between us. One day *we* will be *us*. If all goes as planned, the two of us will live here, in our truth, come what may. We've agreed to spare Arden the burden of knowing about our relationship for the time being. Whatever she decides, I want it to be for her, not for me, and telling her would feel too much like pleading our case for her to stay.

My heart breaks when I turn back to her and she buries her face in her hands and slumps in her chair. No one wants to hurt their child like this. For a second I question whether we should have told her at all.

Seven reaches over and places a reassuring hand on my arm. Bright emerald eyes flash with his intense emotion. How could I miss how similar they are to Arden's for all these years? His expression isn't happy exactly, but he seems resolved.

"Arden." Seven's voice is low but certain. "You don't have to decide now. You have time to think about this. While you're thinking over your options, we can meet and I can help you learn to use your luck. I can answer your questions."

She lowers her hands. Here face is wet with tears, and I give her my most reassuring smile.

"Seven mentioned the Gilded Gala. That's June twenty-first. That's also right around the time we have to confirm with Chapel Hill. Why don't you take until then to decide?" Releasing a deep sigh, I reach across the table and grasp her hand. "In the meantime, you can put graduation behind you, enjoy some of the summer here in Dragonfly, and practice controlling your luck with Seven. You have time to process everything."

I glance at Seven and see weariness return to his expression. His fingers slip from my arm where I realize he's been resting his hand the entire time. Arden doesn't miss it. She darts a questioning gaze between us but doesn't say a word.

She takes a deep breath before wiping under her eyes. "Okay. Before the Gilded Gala is fair. And I'd like to meet with you, Seven, for practice."

"How does Saturday afternoons sound? Down by the lake."

She nods. "I can do that. I also want to visit the university here. I'll need to apply... make sure I actually have an option."

Seven's smile turns smug. He probably knows the admissions people. She'll have no trouble getting in. I have to hand it to him for not saying anything.

Knowing Arden, she might insist on doing it without help. By not offering, he has more freedom to do as he pleases.

She leans back in her chair, looking exhausted. "Thanks for telling me," she mutters. "Thanks for giving me the choice."

"You deserve it. The truth is something Godmother never gave us a choice about."

Arden's eyes narrow. "Godmother knew, and she kept it a secret my whole life."

My hand curls into a loose fist. "She did. It's a fact of life here, unfortunately, and something you'll have to accept if you stay. Godmother doesn't play fair, and you can't trust her to do what's best for anyone but herself. Not ever."

She stands and crosses her arms over her chest. "I'm going to go lie down."

Before I can think of anything to say, she flees the dining room, leaving two possible futures in her wake. In one future she stays, and along with Seven and me, we become a family. In the other she goes, and we make do with stolen moments and vacation memories. I squeeze Seven's hand, reminding myself that I'll be fine either way so long as Arden's happy.

CHAPTER

THREE

Five weeks later...

"Why did you raise on that hand, Mr. Tannenbaum?" I squint at the elderly human sitting to my right. I've been teaching this class for three weeks now, and he still doesn't seem to be getting it, although he's a pleasant enough pupil. He's got to be at least eighty years old, and I suspect the only reason he's here is to spend time with his wife, who's an absolute shark.

"Just mixing up the play. Gotta keep these suckers on their toes." He gestures vaguely at the rest of the table.

Mrs. Tannenbaum bursts out laughing. "Harold, they won't need to be on their toes. They'll just need to lean forward in their chairs a little to rake in your chips. You have a seven and a two, nonsuited, for cripes' sake!"

Harold shrugs and holds up both hands. "I was bluffing. That's part of poker."

I hold up a finger to get everyone's attention. "This is a great opportunity to enforce a point I've made before but perhaps you didn't catch. It's important to understand not only the cards you're holding but..."

"Your position at the table," they say in unison.

I nod reassuringly. "Exactly. Harold has the big blind, which means..."

A young woman named Margaret lifts her hand, and I call on her to answer. "He had to ante up in full before he saw his first two cards."

"Exactly. So as the last to bet before the flop, bluffing isn't a bad idea. He's already put his money in after all, and he has the advantage of the most information anyone at the table can have this round. But because he has very bad odds of actually winning with a seven and a two, his only strategy has to be to get the other players to fold. The best way to do that would be to signal a strong hand. In other words, to raise before the flop. There's a good chance that if he does that, other players with weak hands may fold rather than meet his bet. Winning small pots like that by bluffing can be a great way for a poker player to increase their bankroll."

"See, Janice? I know what I'm doing!" Harold harrumphs.

I can't help but chuckle. "Where you went wrong though, Mr. Tannenbaum, is to keep up the charade once Margaret raised significantly post flop. She's played conservatively the entire time we've been together. Chances are she has something with that sort of a bet. So at that point, knowing you've got nothing, folding would have been the more prudent option."

Janice crosses her arms over her chest and looks at him smugly. Harold isn't happy.

I check the clock. Saved by the bell. Clapping my hands together twice, I say, "Great job, everyone. I'll see you Tuesday for more tips and practice!"

"What about Monday?" Margaret asks.

"I'm sorry, I have the day off. My daughter is graduating from Bailiwick's Academy on Sunday, and we're taking Monday to recover from the festivities."

Margaret laughs. "It's so weird to think you have graduations here."

I grit my teeth. I get that a lot, little comments that show how humans really see us, as if our lives exist for their pleasure. As if we don't have lives of our own and an existence that doesn't involve them. Sometimes it's hard to swallow.

"Thank you for understanding," I force out.

Thankfully all eight of them get up from their seats and filter out into the casino without any more questions. I lock up the poker training room and head for the door, anxious to get back to the Wonderland theme park. There are a million things I need to do before tomorrow, and the character shuttle takes a long time.

"Ms. Larkspur?" Saul, Seven's head of security, is waiting for me near the front entrance. I've gotten to know him fairly well over the past few weeks. He often drives me to and from Seven's place after our many private meetings, and although we've never shown affection toward each other in front of him, I imagine he must suspect our relationship. That said, I've never felt a hint of judgment from Saul, and he's always been discreet. Plus Seven trusts him, which is saying a lot.

A woman passes us, and she turns her head to give Saul another look. The security guard makes an immediate impression. Unlike Seven, who has the build of a man who works out but spends most of his time in an office, Saul clearly spends a lot of time at the gym. He's a leprechaun but is as broad-shouldered as a satyr with a gun peeking from under his dark suit jacket and a gleam of alertness in his eyes that telegraphs "don't mess with me." I immediately feel safer in his presence.

"Hi, Saul. What's up?"

"Mr. Delaney would like me to drive you back to Wonderland. He told me to tell you he'll meet you there."

Sweet of him. It's Saturday, which means Seven is in Wonderland at the beach, giving Arden her luck lesson like he has every week for the past five weeks. "Lead the way."

Saul ushers me toward the elevators. I found out about the garage under the casino a few weeks ago. Only a select, privileged few have spaces there, which includes the officers of Lucky Enterprises. The existence of the garage is top secret, likely for security reasons. All the other employees have to park in the front lot and walk in each day with the guests.

Seven introduced me to the garage once we resumed our relationship and he decided he hated the thought of me riding the character shuttle. The revelation was eye opening. Secret passages exist between theme parks. It's how Godmother moves from place to place securely and quickly and how Seven and Eva and their personal security team travel as well.

The fact that Saul is taking me this way today makes it impossible to forget just how big the chasm between Seven's life and the regular existence of most fae in Devashire actually is. Because he loves me, I get a glimpse of this world, but I can't shake that this is not real life, at least not my life.

I climb into the back of Seven's Mercedes Maybach, the car he prefers when he requires a chauffeur. Saul slides behind the wheel and starts to drive. The concrete blocks that make up the tunnel create the illusion of collapse as he picks up speed, and I close my eyes to stop the overwhelming claustrophobia that sets in.

"You're the only one Seven has ever allowed down here," Saul says.

I open my eyes, and he's watching me in the rearview mirror. Why do I sense this conversation is to distract me? I like Saul. "I guess I'm lucky then."

He smiles. "The first time I learned these passages existed, I found it upsetting."

I can't hide my look of surprise, and he doesn't miss it. "You didn't know either?"

"You think because I'm a leprechaun that I have a life like Seven's?"

"Sorry if that's offensive. I know all leprechauns don't have the same upbringing as Seven, but I thought you had more exposure to this type of lifestyle than I did as a pixie."

Saul grins. "I can understand why you'd think that way, but I was born to a more humble family than the Delaneys. My dad was a security officer before he retired. My mom is a property manager. A good life for sure, but even we didn't know this existed until I got this job. This belongs in a Batman movie."

I laugh at that. "Well, Seven is a brooding billionaire."

We travel in silence for a few minutes, until the tunnel widens and we ascend, circling another parking garage.

"If you don't mind my saying so, Ms. Larkspur—"

"Call me Sophia."

"—he's not done as much brooding as before you

came to work for the casino, and I don't think it's the poker lessons."

Uh-oh. My relationship with Seven is a strict secret. It has to be for now. The only person who knows about us is Eva, and that was necessary for her to help us.

"I don't know what you mean," I say breathlessly.

He pulls to a stop in front of a set of elevators and looks over his shoulder at me. "He told me you were friends as children. I think Mr. Delaney needed a friend. Someone who likes him for him and not all this, you know?"

"Since we were six." I nod. "And you're right. I don't care about any of this."

"Everyone should be so lucky to have that sort of friend." He exits the vehicle and opens the door for me. "You want the fourth floor. It exits into the Wonderland Security building."

"Thanks, Saul." I tap him gently on the shoulder with my fist.

"Anytime, Ms. Larkspur."

"Sophia."

He gives me a wave goodbye and climbs behind the wheel again.

I follow his directions and make my way quickly to Glaive Beach where I find Seven and Arden playing poker at the same flat-topped rock where he taught me all those years ago. Arden lights up. "Mom, you've got to see this."

I pad to her side and take a look at her cards. "A royal flush. Very lucky."

She hands her cards to Seven, who is smiling like the Cheshire cat. He shuffles them into the deck. "Show her how it's done, Arden. Remember to shield."

Arden nods.

As Seven raises the deck to deal the cards, his luck rises in the air around me, a red-hot beast. I feel Arden's rise too. Raccoon energy weaves in and out of Seven's, a faster, more playful vibration that blocks the dragon from reaching the cards while also tapping them with its little paw. All of that happens in my mind. How we perceive luck as fairies is hard to explain to anyone who isn't fae. I don't see a dragon and a raccoon; I sense them, and it's as real as anything else around me.

Seven deals the cards.

Arden anxiously swipes them from the rock and then beams up at me. She laughs and fans them out. Royal flush.

"Wow, Arden. I'm impressed." I hug her around the neck.

"She's done it fourteen times in a row." Seven's expression is brimming with parental pride. "I'm not throwing all my power into it, but she's shielding against a significant attack and waging her own counterstrike. She's very clever."

"Of course she is." I press a kiss to her temple.

"That's more than I can do, Arden. I can't split my luck that way. You're really talented."

The smile she gives me tells me everything I need to know. Arden loves this. She climbs to her feet. "Thanks, Seven. Will I see you next week?"

He rises and glances toward me. "You'll see me tomorrow. At graduation."

"You're coming?" Arden looks excitedly between us.

"I wouldn't miss it."

She launches herself at him and throws her arms around his neck. "I can't believe this is real."

He pats her back, the craziest look of satisfaction on his face. "It's as real as you want it to be."

Our eyes lock over her shoulder, and under-standing passes between us. Something has shifted. For the first time, I feel like Arden might actually choose to stay. A new warmth sparks in my heart. Is it too much to hope we could one day be a family?

CHAPTER

FOUR

"Closer to the front, Sophia! My eyes aren't what they used to be." Grandma shoves me in the middle of my back. Her bony hands are surprisingly strong. I walk faster up the aisle between the rows of white folding chairs, stopping at the third row of seats reserved for guests. We're early but already the first two rows are completely full.

"This is as close as we're going to get without wrestling someone for a seat," I tell her.

Grandma's eyes narrow. "I could take 'em. I'm stronger than I look, Sophia."

"You're going to get us thrown out of here if you keep staring like an axe murderer." I nudge her with my elbow.

She shrugs. "Well-behaved women rarely make history."

"Instead of quoting Laurel Thatcher Ulrich to me,

why don't you grab a seat? It's the third row, Grandma. Any closer and you risk a sprained neck." I gesture for her to go in first.

"I want to be on the end."

I love my grams, but I have to put my foot down. "I have to be on the end to take pictures."

"Pictures, schmictures. You just want that seat because it's the best view of the stage." She fists her knobby hands and rests them on her hips.

"Caught me. I'm pulling the mom card."

My mother saves me from Grandma's comeback, tugging her down the row after my father. "Come on. Sophia gets to choose this time."

Reluctantly, she moves into the row and sits in the seat directly next to mine, arms crossed. "Not sure what a shorty like me is supposed to do in this seat. How am I supposed to watch people from here?"

My mom gives Grandma side-eye and spreads her hands. "You'll just have to ask your friends to spill the tea after the event."

"Oh, all right." Grandma's voice quivers. "But I hope you know you're seriously injuring my gossip potential right now."

Mom sighs and takes the chair between her and Dad.

"Is their room for one more?" I look up from my seat to find Seven standing beside me at a respectable distance. He could be anyone just asking about a seat, but his eyes are filled with longing. I see his fingers twitch. He wants to touch me. He wants to experience this with me. I can read him as if he were saying it out loud.

"You want to sit here? With us?" I love that he's here, but this is going to be too obvious. My gaze jumps around the crowd.

He stares down at me. "Yes. We should watch this together. It's important."

As much as I'd love to sit next to Seven to watch our daughter graduate, this isn't the time or place to draw attention ourselves. People are already turning to stare, wondering why a Delaney leprechaun is talking to a pixie.

"If you sit with me, it will be a distraction," I whisper. "These kids deserve undivided attention."

"Back here then." He steps into the fourth row and takes the seat on the end, directly behind me. I give him a nod of thanks, but he doesn't look happy.

I'm about to lower myself into my seat when two burly arms sweep me into the aisle and against a chest that might as well be a concrete wall.

"River!" I smile up at my friend and satyr, trying my best to breathe through the crushing hug.

"Congratulations! Graduation day. You did it!" His smile is bright enough to make my heart leap.

"I think Arden had something to do with her success," I tell him.

"Don't underestimate the importance of a doting parent." River is the type of person who has never met a stranger and has to touch everyone he greets. He keeps his hand on my shoulder as he speaks to me, and I can practically feel Seven's gaze burning into the side of my head as he seethes with jealousy.

"Thanks, River. Do you have a seat yet? There's one open next to Dad." I gesture with my chin down the row. Out of the corner of my eye, I catch the annoyed twitch of a muscle in Seven's jaw.

"Can't. I'm catering the after-party. I just wanted to drop this off for our Arden." He hands me a box about the size of a small book wrapped in brown paper and tied with string. "Tell her congratulations for me. I expect a full play-by-play the next time she comes into the restaurant."

I take the box and slide it into my purse. Lifting on my toes, I place a kiss on River's cheek. "Thank you. Sweet of you to remember her."

He says his goodbyes and then gives Seven a nod before striding toward the restaurant. I do a double take when I see Seven's face. Shit, he looks like he wants to kill someone. His foot taps.

I lift an eyebrow.

He lifts one right back.

I wave a hand in the air dismissively and take my seat.

Around us, beyond a red velvet rope, humans are lined up to watch the festivities. A family near the front is eating a bowl of green, gray, and white plaid ice cream—Bailiwick's plaid—a Twinkleberries graduation-day exclusive. Magic gives the dessert its char-acteristic pattern, but the flavors are common enough —a combination of mint, vanilla, and lavender. One of the humans catches me staring and waves. I look away like I didn't see him. This is a ticketed event that makes loads of money for Dragonfly, but damn if it's not like being in a fishbowl.

"Ice cream looks good," Grandma mumbles. "So does Seven."

"Grandma, shhh."

She giggles.

The steady tone of a bow being drawn against the string of a cello meets our ears, and I squeeze Grandma's hand. "They're starting."

A band of satyrs seated on the corner of the stage starts to play. The music is nothing like human music. Although I remember this tune from when I was young, it never fails to move me. Along with the cello, one of them plays a gold violin, another a piccolo, and another something like a xylophone made of bones. The music is bright but somehow haunting, like a child's music box in an empty room.

I dig a Kleenex from my purse and dab at my eyes as everyone stands and turns toward the head of the aisle. A collective gasp rises from the crowd when they see Godmother leading two rows of robe-clad students. The students stop at the head of the aisle, but Godmother proceeds forward.

Everything about her is larger than life. She's tall

49

and curvy, her larger size packed with luck and magic. Today she's wearing a deep purple dress with a black corset and a skirt that looks as if it were built from stringing together thousands of cicada wings. It's dark and delicate and flutters as if it's alive when she walks. Peacock feathers fan behind her head and perfectly complement the rest of the dress and her deep mahogany complexion. Pixies garbed entirely in silver manage the train of her gown.

Once she reaches the top of the dais, she raises a jeweled scepter. "It is my pleasure as Godmother and queen regent of Devashire to give you this year's graduating class!"

Two by two, the students parade toward the stage to the sound of thundering applause. Dressed in deep green robes and crowned with laurel, the pairs diverge at the end of the aisle and ascend staircases at either side of the stage. When I see Arden, I whistle and Grandma whoops like she's a frat boy at a football game. Arden's smile warms me. I worried this event wouldn't mean as much to her what with her having only attended Bailiwick's for a few months, but she seems genuinely happy and proud. She catches my eye and places her hand over her heart.

Once the students have all filed onto the stage and to their assigned seats, the music stops. Godmother nods her head, and they all sit down at once. She steps to the podium. There's no microphone, but her voice projects over us, laced with magic.

"Each year, I stand before the graduating class and am called on to speak about the future, the world these young people are graduating into, and their prospects for a better tomorrow. Each year I say something about opportunity and hard work. I wax poetic about how with the right attitude and enough courage, anything these students want can be theirs."

The crowd has gone silent, and I can't tell if it's because they are riveted by what Godmother is saying or appalled at the lie. A satyr will never run Dragonfly Casino. Most pixies won't own their own home until they are over one hundred years old. She might say it every year, but it's all drivel.

"Each year, I say those things," she continues. "But not this year. This year I want to focus on today. Because every day we wake up in Devashire is a good day."

Grandma coughs into her hand, and I swear it comes out "Bullshit!"

Godmother spreads her hands. "We live in a world of magic and love. We are a community of fae with the honor of sharing our gifts with the world." She gestures toward the humans watching the event. "What you do from today forward isn't half as important as who you are. Being fae means being part of something larger than yourself, whether you're sweeping the streets of Dragonfly Hollow or teaching in the education center. Every position is important and equally valued."

"But rewarded at completely different levels," Grandma murmurs. "Gods, this woman."

"Today, my dear students, as you traverse the river between adolescence and adulthood, worry not about what the future brings. As long as you are here, your future is bright, as it is for all fae. Now I am pleased to honor you, the next generation of fae who have demonstrated through your studies your commitment to upholding the values Devashire holds dear. Today you commit yourselves to keeping the magic alive for all. It's important work. We alone have the power. Without further ado..."

She starts calling names, and one by one the students move across the stage, receiving the scroll that memorializes the day. I mop my face when they call Arden's name. Seven's luck coils around me and then threads between my fingers. It's as close to holding my hand as he can get. I glance back at him. His eyes glint, and he smiles proudly.

Once the last student, Blossom Zolder, is announced, Godmother brings the festivities to a fast close. We stand up as one, and the crowd lumbers toward the reception tent.

"Can you believe that nonsense," Grandma says on the way. "As if we're all living in some utopian paradise."

"I think that was for the human audience's benefit, don't you?"

She shrugs. "I hope so. She can't possibly be that cut off from reality."

"Oh, there's Arden!"

Arden plows into me, spinning me around with the force of her hug. "I did it! I'm a high school graduate!" My parents pat her back and she hugs each of them with equal gusto. When she turns back to me, she asks, "Where's Seven? I saw him sitting with you."

"He's right—" I thought he was behind me but he's not. I turn around and scan the crowd, finding him in close conversation with a gorgeous leprechaun with sleek black hair and oversized hazel eyes.

"Who is that?" Arden asks. I don't say so, but I'm wondering the same thing.

Grandma's head pops up between us. "Oh, that's Alicia Faust of the Armon-Fausts. She was once engaged to Seven."

"Huh?" Surprise and jealousy fight for control of my brain, and I turn toward Grandma, desperate for her to spill the tea.

She raises a finger. "It all started when—"

A loud pop interrupts her, and the crowd turns as one.

"Was that a firecracker?" Arden asks.

Seven appears beside me in a heartbeat. "No, that was a gunshot."

A few seconds later, a scream cuts through the afternoon festivities. The crowd scatters, some moving toward the sound and others seeming to rush to the safety of the nearby buildings.

Godmother appears before us out of thin air and grabs Seven by the arm as if she owns him. "Come with me."

I move fast to keep up, but with Arden, my parents, and my grandmother with me, we lose them in the crowd. By the time we reach the sidewalk in front of River's Tavern, a crowd has already gathered. My stomach lurches at what I see at the center of that circle of onlookers.

River is on his knees, and he's covered in blood. It's with some relief that I realize it's not his. He's pressing on the chest of a stranger, whose blood spurts between his fingers. On the ground beside him lies a gun.

FIVE

Breathless, as if someone has punched me in the gut, I turn back to Arden and look between her and my family standing behind her. Around us, things have turned to complete pandemonium. Someone shoves my mother, and she huddles into my father's side.

"It's not safe, Sophia," my dad says.

I lock eyes with him. "Take Arden home. I'll meet you there."

"Mom?" Arden clings to my arm.

"It's all right. I'll meet you there. I just need to—" I gesture toward Seven. What do I need to do? I'm not beholden to Godmother anymore. This isn't my job.

Arden studies me for a moment, then says, "Okay. I'll meet you at home."

My father wraps his hands around her shoulders and, together with my mother and grandmother, moves through the crowd in the direction of the house.

Once they're gone, it takes me a second to process what's happened. Although I'm too far from the scene to distinguish every detail, I can tell by his build and manner of dress that it's a human man who's been shot. River is covered in blood, his hands still pressed to the wound. A gun rests next to River's knee—a black handgun. Guns aren't allowed in Dragonfly but from my time in the States, I'd guess it was a Glock or maybe a SIG based on size and shape.

The scene is total chaos. Humans are screaming and gathering up their children. Fairies are rushing in every direction. Godmother looks livid.

With a wave of her hand, a purple shimmer casts through the crowd and two things happen at once. A rope goes up, the fairy equivalent of police tape, and a team of uniformed security personnel arrive in a rush.

Godmother and Seven approach River and the victim, but when I try to join them, a large hand shoots out in front of me.

"Sorry, ma'am. Only authorized personnel."

From behind the rope, I watch River, Seven, and Godmother exchange heated words, and then with a snap of Godmother's fingers, River rises from the cobblestone as if lifted by an invisible force. Two leprechaun security guards rush forward and clamp blue-iron cuffs around his wrists.

I can't read Seven's expression from this angle, but he's not smiling.

"Gods, they're arresting him," Penelope says from beside me.

I hadn't even noticed her arrive. Her kids are young, so she wasn't at the graduation today.

"Pen! When did you get here?"

"Only a second ago. I was having lunch in River's when I heard the shot."

"What the hell is going on?" I press the tips of my fingers into my temples. "Did you see what happened? Was there some sort of altercation?"

Penelope leans in to whisper in my ear behind a curtain of her platinum hair. "I didn't see. No one seemed to. After it happened, everyone went wild talking about it and watching through the windows, but the incident itself... No one saw."

I stare at her for a beat. "That's... odd."

She nods.

"Why did they cuff him? River's not capable of causing someone intentional harm. Not unless he was defending himself or someone else."

An emergency vehicle cuts through the crowd, and a team of paramedics rushes out with a stretcher. In no time, the stranger is wheeled into the back. River, still in handcuffs, is also helped into the back of the vehicle. In literally seconds, the gun and all signs of blood have been wiped from the walkway as if the incident never happened.

"Wow, that was fast," I mutter.

"Shhh. I think Godmother's going to speak." Penelope points her chin toward the center of the crime scene.

"If I could have your attention please," Godmother booms in that larger-than-life voice that reverberates in my bones. Her skin glows with power, as do her eyes, bright amber and intense. "Take heart, my dear guests—no one is in any danger. What happened today was a quarrel between two men that ended in an unfortunate accident. The injured party is being rushed to Elderflame Hospital as we speak, and the shooter, River Foxwood, will be held until this incident can be fully investigated and charges brought. Thank you for your patience and please know that we in Dragonfly Hollow do not tolerate any violence in our theme parks. Crime within our borders is so low as to almost be nonexistent, and guns are strictly prohibited. Please know this was an isolated incident and we will be taking steps to ensure it never happens again."

I bristle at the lie. Only recently, Seven and I helped solve two murders that occurred in the park. But this *is* the first act of violence where Godmother hasn't been able to hide the crime scene from the public. It's broad daylight, and the man responsible for the previous murders is in Ashgate Prison. Whoever did this—and I know it wasn't River—wanted this to be seen. And that's terrifying, because if I'm reading the situation accurately, River just became a very convenient scapegoat.

"Poor River. What can we do?" Penelope presses a hand to her chest.

My gaze drifts to the nearest security camera, and I point up at it. "Everything here is recorded. We'll know soon enough exactly what happened. The faster we can pull the footage, the sooner we can clear River of suspicion and refocus the investigation on the actual perpetrator. I'll ask Seven to do it right away."

She makes a face. "Are you still working with him? I thought that was over?"

"It is, but we're still... on speaking terms. I'll ask him nicely."

Penelope chuckles. "Good luck with that. I'm going to go talk to some people inside again. Maybe someone saw something." She strides off toward the restaurant.

Seven makes eye contact with me and has started walking in my direction when he's swarmed by security officers. He's Godmother's head of security. Has been since the night he bargained with her for a second chance with me. It looks like he might be a while. I'm sure the officers need a debrief, especially when it's clear Godmother is spinning this.

I find myself itching to know exactly what River said before he was hauled away. I'm not a detective or anything like it. I'm a poker pro and I'm a pixie. Does that make me qualified to investigate a crime? Hades, no. But it does make me an expert at reading other people's body language and a damn good liar when I need to be. That and my archery skills were enough to put Seven's father, Chance Delaney, away in Ashgate Prison for murder. So if there's anything I can do to save my friend River from being prosecuted for a crime he didn't commit, you bet I'll do it.

"Gods, Sophia!" Evangeline appears in front of me, her usually composed persona visibly flustered. "This is a complete disaster. Have you seen Seven?"

"He's over there with the other security officers and Godmother. I think they're trying to contain the situation."

"This is a fucking nightmare." She frowns and shakes her head.

"You're a PR genius. I'm sure you'll find a way to spin this just like Godmother did. I'm just worried about River. There's no way he's responsible. Can you get your hands on the surveillance video?" I point toward the dark orb under the streetlight that houses the security camera.

"No." She fists her hands at her sides. "I don't have access. Just Seven." She looks me in the eye and drops her voice. "It would make my job far easier if River didn't do this, Sophia. Unless we can blame this on another human, Dragonfly is going to take a hit."

This is why Evangeline is so good at what she does. She understands how precarious our relationship with the outside world actually is. Humans shoot humans all the time outside the parks. Out there, no one would blink twice over this incident. But in here, our ability to draw people into the park is predicated on them feeling safer within our borders than outside of them—safe among beings they believe are *other*. They don't think of us as people. Some call us creatures or even monsters. They have no idea what a monster truly is.

I glance in Seven's direction. "I'll find a way to get his attention. The video will prove River's innocence and show us who's really responsible. Once the victim recovers, we can ask him to fill in the details. Meanwhile, you can use your luck to smooth things over."

She closes her eyes as if she's truly relieved that I've agreed to help. "Thank you, Sophia. After everything we went through to manage what happened with our father, this is just exhausting. At least in that case, Godmother was able to conceal his crimes. No one outside the family knows exactly what he did, especially not the humans. This... It's too late. People saw. We can't hide it."

I lean in and give her a quick hug. "So we'll roll with it. I have faith in you. It's going to be okay."

Her green eyes lift to meet mine, shiny as if she's trying not to cry, and she tucks her deep red hair behind her ears. "You're a good friend."

She kisses both my cheeks and then strides away from me, looking exquisite in an indigo dress with ruby pumps. Only a leprechaun could be as stressed as

Evangeline is right now and still look as fresh as if she'd just walked out of the salon.

As soon as the security team breaks and the rope is lowered, I head straight for Seven, who's now in a heated conversation with Godmother. When he sees me, his lips press into a straight line and his eyes crease at the corners. He isn't happy, but he seems resolved about something. Godmother, on the other hand, is vibrating with cool assurance, as if she is entirely in control of her every thought and emotion and knows exactly what needs to be done to address this disaster.

"Sophia Larkspur, unless you've come to offer some additional insight into what happened here today, I'm going to ask you to move along." She lifts her chin, her gaze sliding down her nose at me from her superior height.

"Just that I'm sure River didn't do this," I say nervously. I don't like the way Godmother is looking at me. "I came to ask Seven to check the security footage."

"Oh, you're sure, are you?" She taps her fingers in front of her. "Are you certain you want that to be the case? You know, if River isn't responsible for that guest's death, the most likely suspect is the person who committed the last two murders. Since that person is supposed to be in Ashgate, I must question whether we imprisoned the right man. Should I remind you what happens if he is not?"

"Excuse me? I'm not sure I know what you're getting it. You caught Chance red-handed."

"Imprisoning pixies, yes, but there was no hard evidence linking him back to the murders. Those were technically committed by Yissevel, and as that creature is dead, he could not be questioned. Needless to say, if you were wrong, and there was someone else involved, our previous bargain was dissolved on the basis of false assumptions. If it turns out that what happened today is in any way related to the first two murders, you will be beholden to me to find the murderer."

I look between them both. "Murderer? But you said he was merely injured and being taken to Elder-flame Hospital. Isn't there a chance he'll recover?"

Seven frowns. "That was for publicity reasons. The man is dead."

I gasp. "What about River? What did he say when you asked him what happened?"

"He denied shooting the man, of course," Godmother said. "Claimed he found the human on the walkway bleeding when he came upon him, but without any witnesses, I'm afraid anyone might claim such a thing."

I hug myself against a sudden chill. So the ambulance was just for show. I glare at Godmother. "There's no way River did this, and you know it. He's not capable of it."

"And if you find proof of such a thing, I'd be happy to examine your evidence, Sophia. Until then, I'll be holding River until we know for sure it's safe to release him."

"But—"

Seven steps between us, cutting me off. "There's a simple way to settle this. I'll go pull the security footage."

Godmother rests a hand on her corset and purses her lips. "You do that, Seven. But until we prove otherwise, as far as I'm concerned, River is our perpetrator."

SIX

"It should be right here." Seven rubs his temple, looking as frustrated as I feel.

We're in the Wonderland Security office, staring at the recording of the spot in front of River's Tavern where the shooting happened. Seven scans backward second by second. Several minutes are missing. At two p.m., all we see is the brick walkway in front of River's, but then the video skips forward to 2:15 p.m. and River appears in the space, hunched over the dead man.

"Someone's tampered with the video," I say breathlessly, pressing a fist to my forehead. "Again! How is this possible?"

"It shouldn't be." He grits his teeth. "Our system keeps track of everyone who accesses these recordings. Very few employees have the clearance to delete video." He navigates to a command prompt and types a few lines of code. The system returns a string of characters around a single name we both recognize.

I brace myself on the desk, my heart pounding with the implications. "Chance Delaney? How?"

Seven scowls. "This says the change was made from the IP address of Chance's desktop computer."

"How? He's in Ashgate Prison." No one has ever escaped from Ashgate. Then again, has any prisoner ever been as powerful as Chance? My stomach aches at even the thought that he might be free again.

"It's *not* possible that he did this himself." Seven runs a hand down his face. "After he was arrested, his office and everything in it was sealed off. We plan to demolish it eventually but didn't want to destroy any evidence Godmother might need."

That made sense. The legal system in Devashire works similarly to the one in the US. The difference is that our regent, Godmother, can sentence criminals to Ashgate without a trial in extreme circumstances like murder or treason. In those cases though, her verdict can be challenged up to a year following imprisonment. It's supposed to allow for a check on Godmother's ultimate power. In reality, she uses the privilege so rarely that her judgment has never before been questioned. In Chance's case though, with him telling us he wasn't working alone, I can see where Seven would want his bases covered.

"What if he wasn't bluffing, Seven?" I whisper. "What if someone was helping him back then and is still helping him now? Someone with access to his things." I wrap a strand of hair around my finger and pull it tight, anxiety rising in me like a swarm of insects and crawling across the inside of my skin. The base of my neck prickles with it.

"There's no way into that office. The only two people on the payroll with access are me and Eva."

"What about remote access? Maybe someone hacked it?"

He frowns. "Possible but unlikely. I'll get one of my tech guys on it." He fires off a quick email.

"Seven, did River say anything about what happened?"

Seven leans back in his chair. "There wasn't time for him to tell us much. Godmother couldn't wait to get him and the victim out of there. He said he heard a scream and ran toward it to find the victim lying on the sidewalk with a bullet wound in his chest. At that point, he knelt next to the body and tried to keep him from bleeding out. Godmother didn't buy it thought. Not with the gun right beside him."

"He admitted to touching the gun?"

"Not exactly. He said he didn't remember seeing it before but it's possible he moved it out of the way. He was focused on the victim. Godmother believes that he made it up to explain why his fingerprints will be on it."

"Aargh!" I grab the sides of my head. "How is it that no one else saw this?"

"Half the park was at graduation. There were people in the restaurant, but no one will admit to seeing anything."

"Fuck. What are the odds that that patch of sidewalk would be completely abandoned aside from River? It's almost like—"

He catches my gaze. "Like a leprechaun was involved. Someone wanted River to take the fall for this."

I groan. He turns back to the video and reverses it again. For a good twenty seconds before the skip, no one is visible in the camera's range. "I don't like this. Someone uses my father's computer to tamper with the security cameras, and then the scene is cleared in a way that screams leprechaun. If I didn't know he was in Ashgate, I'd think he was behind this."

"What if he escaped somehow?"

Seven shakes his head. "It's impossible. Trust me on this, Sophia. He's there."

I take a deep breath. "He told me he wasn't working alone." Our eyes meet. Gods, Seven looks exhausted. "We need to find out who the victim was. Maybe that's the clue to all this."

"Already on it. We didn't find any identification on him, but I have someone down the hall going through the Wonderland admissions logs and comparing pictures."

"Good." I push my chair back and stand. "I'm going to visit River wherever Godmother is holding him. Maybe he knows more than he was able to share given the circumstances."

He shakes his head. "You can't. They're holding him in Ashgate."

"Ashgate! Why? Godmother knows he didn't do this, Seven. She all but admitted she knows."

"She also told you that he did it until we can prove he didn't." Seven rubs the back of his neck. "The politics around this is bigger than any of us. She needs a scapegoat. She will never let him out of that cell unless we have someone else to put in it."

"I'll just have to go to Ashgate then."

He blinks at me as if I just said I planned to cut off my wing and donate it to science. "You can't just walk into Ashgate. You have to petition Godmother, and then they give you a specific time. There are procedures."

"I'll go to her office and fill out the forms now."

A muscle in Seven's jaw dances wildly, and his body tenses like a loaded spring. "No, Sophia," he finally blurts. "You absolutely cannot go out there. I'll go." He pulls out his phone and stares down at a calendar that has no white space.

I spread my hands. "Even if you went instead of me, it wouldn't be the same. River and I are friends. He'll share things with me that he won't share with you. The two of you have never exactly been chums."

Seven rubs his jaw as if remembering the time

River slugged him. "He'll answer my questions if he wants to get out of there."

I tip my head to the side and shoot Seven a disappointed look. "Isolation is torture for a satyr. River thrives on in-person contact. I can't just leave him in there. He's my friend. I need to go to him and tell him that he's not alone and that we are doing all we can to get him out."

"Right. Because he's your *friend*."

"That sneer isn't attractive, Seven, and you're acting childish." I place my hands on his chest and lean in until my face is close to his. "Are you jealous?"

He shrugs. "Why would I be jealous of a man who can walk down the street holding your hand without everyone and their brother losing their shit over it?" His emerald gaze drills into me, brutal in its intensity. I guess when he puts it that way, it makes sense. He's the luckiest man in Devashire. I'm the thing he wants most, and yet he can't have me. It's making him crazy.

I take his face in my hands. "River was there for me the night of the Yule ball. He was a friend to me before that, but he truly supported me then in a way no one else could. And he's been a good friend to me since I returned to Dragonfly."

"Yeah, River's an all-around great guy." His tone is wooden, and he blinks up at me slowly.

"I'm not interested in River and never will be. I'm in love with you."

The corner of his mouth tugs upward. His hands

land on my face, and he kisses me gently. "I know why you want to go," he says. "But this isn't about jealousy. Ashgate is a dangerous place. We should go together."

"I don't think so. I think River will be more open with me if you're not around. He doesn't trust you the way he trusts me."

He squeezes his eyes closed. "You're not going to be talked out of this, are you?"

"No."

"Can I convince you to take my personal security with you?"

"Would it ease your mind?"

"Yes."

"Then yes."

"Fine." He flashes me a disarming smile. "Will you join me tonight for a late dessert?"

"I do like to end the day with something sweet." I kiss the corner of his mouth. "I might be able to stop by after graduation dinner, but it will depend on Arden. She's probably freaking out after everything that happened today." I give an exaggerated sigh.

"That reminds me. I have something for her." He reaches in his pocket and pulls out a jewelry box. "Something from my collection."

I balk. "Not your secret collection? A charm?"

He nods. "Tell her not to use it until I have a chance to talk to her about its... properties."

"Is it safe?"

"For her? Yes." The intonation on that *yes* holds a

slight question, as if he's not entirely sure about his answer.

I shoot him an exasperated look. "What are you giving our daughter, Seven?"

He leans back in his chair. "Hopefully one more reason to stay in Devashire."

THE FORMS TO VISIT ASHGATE PRISON ARE FIVE PAGES OF bureaucratic hell. They ask for my name, address, income, and highest level of education, and there are no less than fifty questions about why I want to visit the prisoner. As the cherry on the shit sundae, they must be completed in triplicate, each form only slightly different than the last. Mercifully, the pixie at the window of the administration building is a friend of River's. She speeds my application through. My phone rings before I even reach home, and she informs me she's cleared me to visit in two days' time.

Poor River. Two more days seems like a long time to be locked away without a friendly face. But it's the best I can do.

"Mom!" Arden meets me at the door, still dressed in her gown and laurel. I hug her and kiss her cheek.

"I'm sorry it took so long. River is in real trouble, and I'm trying to help him."

"I can't believe he killed that man." Arden's eyes widen.

"That's because he didn't."

Mom chooses that moment to walk into the room. "Sophia! Oh good. I wouldn't let Arden change until you got home. We need a family picture."

I push all thoughts of the tragedy aside. Today is Arden's day, and she deserves far better than what's happened. "Great idea," I say, hooking my arm around Arden's shoulders. "No more talk about the incident that shall not be named. For the rest of the night, it's just us and our pride over this amazing girl."

"Hear! Hear!" Grandma yells from the living room.

I peek at her around the corner. She's knitting something that looks like a sweater for a hamster. I don't ask.

I use a little illusion to spruce my hair and makeup and then follow my parents to a spot in front of the fireplace where Dad has the camera set up on a tripod to take our picture. We time a photograph, all of us smiling as the flash goes off again and again. Afterward, we huddle over the screen, laughing about who has their eyes closed or is making a face.

Mom claps her hands together. "Dinner will be a few more minutes. Let's do gifts first."

"Yes!" I squeal, excited to give Arden the gift I am sure will be her favorite.

I sprint upstairs and retrieve the giant box I've had wrapped for her from my desk and bound back down the stairs to present it to her.

"For the girl whose every dream I pray comes true."

She grins and pecks me on the cheek. Carrying the huge box to the dining room, she rests it on the table before pulling off the bow and lifting off the top. "Oh, Mom!" She draws the cobalt dress from the box and holds it against herself. It's strapless with a formfitting waist and a full, floor-length skirt embroidered with crystals that deepen the color depending on the light. It sparkles under the glow from the dining room chandelier.

"When you first came here, you asked about my dress. I realized you've never had a fairy dress of your own. And since you're half-pixie, that had to be rectified. No matter where you go in life, you should always have a princess dress in your closet. And there's a tiara, necklace, and shoes in there to add to the ensemble."

Only the two of us know how accurate my description of her as a princess is, or how when I mention where she might go in life, it includes fairy society. But Arden knows. And whether she wears this dress here in Dragonfly or in the human world at some future event I can only dream of, she'll always know what it means. Deep down, she's lucky. She's fae. She's the only person like her on the planet. And she deserves this dress to prove it.

"Oh, Mom, I love it." As she hugs me, I feel wetness where her face touches mine. She pulls back, and I wipe away her tears.

I reach into the box, grab the tiara, and replace the laurel leaves on her head with it.

"Beautiful," my mom says.

We all bask in the glow of my perfect gift for a moment, and then Mom pulls a box the size of a coffee mug from the china cabinet behind her and places it in front of the dress box. It's all wrapped in green paper with silver cords to match her school colors. I have no idea what it could be. "The rest of us went in together on this. Happy graduation."

Arden repacks the dress in the box but leaves the tiara on her head. "Thank you all," she says sweetly, then rounds the table to hug Mom, Dad, and Grandma before she even opens their gift. My heart swells with pride. She's a good kid. I've done my job.

Returning to her seat, she unwraps the box. Inside is a metal toy car—a blue Kia Soul. She laughs. "It's adorable!"

I look between the car and my mom, who is wearing a devious grin. "There's more. Look in the wrappings. It's in there."

Arden digs her hand into the tissue paper and pulls out a key.

"You didn't," I mutter.

"We did!" Mom's eyes twinkle impishly .

Grandma squeals.

"What is this?" Arden shakes her head, her eyes expanding to the size of saucers. "Did you... Did you buy me a car?"

"We did," my dad says proudly. "It's used and you'll have to wait until after dinner to see it because it's parked in the guest lot, but it looks just like that one." He points at the toy.

I'm speechless. I glare at Grandma, who flutters her eyelashes at me. "We just hope you like it," she says. "I knitted you a steering wheel cover too, but it wouldn't fit in the box. I'll give it to you later."

"I don't even have a car!" I toss up my hands.

Mom shrugs. "So get a car, Sophia. You're making enough now."

True. I should get my own car, but that's not the issue here. I focus the full weight of my stare on my three elders sitting across the table. "Oh. My. Gods. You did this so that you'd win at graduation gifts!" I point at each of them. "You intentionally one-upped me with the car."

"Don't be silly, Sophia. You can't *win* at gifts," my mom says, but Grandma is nodding her head, mouthing *we won* through a wicked smile.

Arden laughs. "I like both your gifts equally," she insists. "Thank you so much."

I give an exaggerated sigh and straighten her tiara. "Who would take a car over a crown anyway," I mumble. "Oh! I almost forgot." Grabbing my bag, I dig out the brown-paper-wrapped box from River and the small jewelry box from Seven. I hand her the one from River first.

"River made sure I had that this morning before

everything happened. He wanted me to tell you congratulations."

The mood in the room sobers, but she tears into it. It's a framed photo of her and a bunch of kids her age in their Bailiwick's uniforms, in front of River's Tavern. All the teens have their arms around each other, but the handsome dark-haired boy who might be a leprechaun next to Arden is kissing her temple. She's beaming, her eyes shifted in his direction. Three dark-skinned girls, one with gorgeous bright red hair that matches her wings, are on her other side. All pixies. A satyr stands behind them all, hands on Arden's and the redhead's shoulders. It's a fun memory of what must have been a memorable moment.

"This is so sweet," Arden said. "I forgot about this day."

"When was that taken?" I ask.

"About a month ago. We had a half day at school and went there for lunch." She sets it on the table. "This is the only picture I have with my new friends. It's gone by so fast. I never thought to take more." Another tear slides down her face, and I rub her back.

"We'll make sure to thank him for it when he's back among us," I say, forcing cheerfulness into the words. I follow it up by handing her the jewelry box. "One more gift, from Seven."

Grandmother's brows shoot up. "How thoughtful of him."

"He's a friend of the family, Grandma. Friends of the family give gifts."

"Sure they do," she says through a tight smile.

Arden tears into the paper and lifts the lid.

My dad leans forward a little to see and gives a quirky smile. "A gold acorn? Hmm." He shrugs.

Beside him, Mom is squinting at the charm. "You just never know with leprechauns."

Grandma scratches her neck. "I'm sure it's valuable, and the folklore says they're lucky."

Arden takes it from the box by the chain and stares at the charm. "Well, I love it. Put it on, Mom." She hands me the chain. Our gazes lock. I can sense the power in the tiny object from a half foot away. This is no ordinary acorn.

As I hook the chain around her neck, I whisper in her ear. "He said not to use it until he has a chance to talk to you about what it does."

She nods once to indicate she understands.

"Thanks, everyone," Arden says. "This is the best graduation day I've ever had."

Grandma laughs. "It's the only graduation day you've ever had."

"Not true. I graduated from eighth grade," Arden says. "Mom watched as I walked across the stage and shook my principal's hand. No robes though, and Rudy Fenton kept nudging the back of my chair. Also, the gym smelled like Fritos."

"It was a moment." I fold my hands on the table.

A buzzer goes off in the kitchen, and Mom pops out of her chair. "That would be dinner. Arden's favorite lasagna."

"I've got to change before we eat. I'm supposed to return this robe to the school, and I don't want to get sauce on it." Arden heads for her room.

I glare across the table at my father. "I can't believe you bought her a car without talking to me first."

The dad stare slides right down his nose at me. "You're surprised we splurged on our one and only granddaughter when this might be our last time to be a family with her? When she goes away to school, we want her to have something to remind her of us."

The sound of Arden jogging down the steps from her room meets my ears and it hits me. Dad's right. This is it. This might be the last time we're all together in this house, living under the same roof. Even if Arden decides to stay, she'll go to Elderflame and sleep in the dorms at the university there. Since the day she was born, we haven't spent more than a night or two away from each other, only for the occasional sleepover or camp. Now only a month or two separates us from her crossing the abyss into adulthood.

I swallow down a seed of anxiety that rises in my throat and cough into my hand. My face feels cold, like all the blood has drained from it.

"Ah, it's just caught up to you." Dad reaches across the table and squeezes my hand. His eyes fill with tears. "It'll be all right. We're all under the same moon after all."

Grandma blots the corners of her eyes with her napkin and taps the table. "You people are a barrel of laughs tonight. Stars above. Should I knit us some Kleenex? I haven't cried this much since Antoine left Juanita on my favorite telenovela."

Arden breaks the tension when she sails into the room in jeans and a T-shirt and plops into the chair beside me. "I've got a great idea of what we can do after dinner."

"What's that?"

"Trivial Pursuit. I saw it in the cabinet next to the fireplace."

"It's the fairy edition."

She shrugs. "Maybe I'll learn something."

Grandma rubs her hands together. "I'm totally going to win." She leans toward Arden and whispers conspiratorially, "I know everything."

Once Mom arrives with the lasagna, I pull out my phone and text Seven.

> Sorry, can't work tonight. Important family stuff.

> Understood. See you tomorrow.

> She loved your gift.

THERE'S A LONG PAUSE BEFORE HE RESPONDS.

> Someday.

I know Seven well enough to know what that someday means. All the thoughts I just had about running out of time, about this being my last chance at experiencing Arden's childhood... He feels the same way. Only he's already missed most of it.

A lump forms in my throat. It's not fair. She's his, and no matter what, he doesn't deserve to miss this night with her. I swallow hard and steel my spine.

> No. Come. Bring the papers you need me to sign.

We both know there are no papers.

Twenty minutes later he shows up at our door with a stack of documents that have nothing to do with me. I have no idea what they say, but I sign them anyway. Then I politely ask him to stay and join us for the game, and Arden enthusiastically demands his participation. My parents have no choice but to duplicate my invitation.

To my delight, he stays and for three glorious hours, we are a family.

When we play Trivial Pursuit, he's the blue piece.

Grandma wins.

SEVEN

S aul arrives at my parents' door two mornings later, ready to escort me to Ashgate. "Ms. Larkspur, if you'll follow me. I have a car waiting."

"Let me grab my bag." I slip my feet into my shoes and my purse strap over my shoulder, yell my goodbyes to Arden and my parents, and follow him out the door.

We're halfway to the parking lot when Saul looks down at me from his considerable height and asks in his deep, serious voice, "Can you run in that outfit?"

Per Dragonfly policy, I'm wearing a dress—a strapless, tea-length light blue ball gown and silver heels. All pixies and satyrs have to appear in character anytime we might be seen by humans, which we definitely will be while leaving the park. Leprechauns run everything, which means they can appear in regular clothing, usually suits for the guys. Since I've been back in the fold, I've gotten used to living in princess dresses. It's as comfortable as anything else to me now, and that includes the shoes.

I flutter my wings in a devil-may-care sort of way before responding lightheartedly, "Pixies are light on our feet." Not that I haven't tripped and landed on my face before. It's happened, usually when I'm too distracted to remember to compensate with my wings, but it's rare.

He points his chin at me. "Good. Ashgate is a dangerous place, Ms. Larkspur. I can carry you if I have to, but it's good to know you can run."

"Call me Sophia. Why is Ashgate so dangerous anyway? The criminals are sealed inside the mountain. They can't get to me."

He frowns. "It's not the criminals you need to be worried about."

"Then what?"

He opens the door to the Mercedes for me, and I climb into the back seat. "The cells are guarded by unseelie creatures."

"What sort of unseelie?"

He looks at me in the mirror and grins. "Does it matter?"

I shake my head. There isn't a single unseelie creature I'd want to meet in person. For the first time, my stomach gives a fearful twist at the thought of visiting Ashgate, but I push it aside. River's a good friend and he needs me.

It takes us about an hour to reach the mountain and another twenty minutes to pass through three modern security checkpoints. But when we arrive at the prison itself, it feels like we've gone back in time. No sliding metal gates or video technology is anywhere in sight, just a cave-like opening at the top of three flights of stone steps.

"What now?" I ask Saul.

"We visit the gate warden. She'll tell you what to expect."

"You don't know?"

"No. I've never been."

"But you told me it was dangerous and guarded by unseelie. How could you know that if you've never been inside?" My words come fast and furious, that niggle of fear in my gut now a raging anxiety that threatens to expunge my breakfast.

He turns to me at the base of the stairs. "Jules Strickland, a fellow leprechaun, visited in 1985 and was never seen again. Went in but never came out. By the time anyone tried to investigate, all they found was a pile of bones and his signet ring. It's dangerous."

My stomach churns. "Great. I wish I didn't know that."

He cuts a judgmental glance in my direction and shrugs. "I tried to keep things vague. You insisted on details, Ms. Larkspur."

"Call me Sophia."

I follow Saul up the stairs to the entrance. The gate

warden is a satyr with tattoos covering all her exposed skin and a wild mop of curly gray hair. Silently she hands us both a flyer with instructions.

"Only one visitor may enter at a time—" I begin to read aloud, but she grabs me by the arm and holds a finger to her lips. I continue reading to myself. *Remain absolutely silent until both feet are in the circle outside the cell of the prisoner you wish to speak with. You will be given a maximum of ten minutes with each prisoner you wish to visit. When you are finished, place an offering on the platter beside the door and step out of the circle. Remain silent until you reach the exit.*

"I didn't bring an offering," I say to the woman.

She answers me in sign language.

Oh, so she's mute. I shake my head. "I don't understand ASL," I whisper.

She frowns and points at a bowl of fruit on the table, then at a cup for donations. I dig in my bag for a few dollars and exchange them for a shiny red apple.

"I'll be here if you need me," Saul says, backing against the wall across from the gate warden.

I stare into the dark passageway, fear turning my hands cold as I cradle the apple in front of my chest. I can't get my feet to move. Saul said the guards are unseelie. Is that what eats the apples? I take a deep breath and let it out slowly. I've now been standing here so long things are getting awkward. Saul is watching me with a suppressed smirk, like he's just waiting for me to yell "oh hell no" and head for the car.

But River is down there. He's shown up for me on more than one occasion when I really needed him. As frightening as it might be to visit him, it must be exponentially more frightening to be imprisoned here.

With that thought held tightly in my mind, I start forward in the only direction I can go. The stone walkway slopes down and curves until the natural light is snuffed out, leaving only flickering illumination cast by candles that burn in wall sconces lining the tunnel. I've walked for a good five minutes before I reach the first cell and realize I have no idea which one River is in. Worse, there aren't bars on the doors like a human prison. The openings are blocked by giant stones. You can't see in or out.

However, the circles referred to in the instructions are outside each stone, and when I step near the first one, a name scrawled in blood across the stone glows to life—Crawfoot Gallery—a rather infamous unseelie fae who was responsible for a mass killing before I was born. I shudder to think how long he's been in there.

I move forward, my gaze drifting over each name as it surfaces with my nearness. My skin pebbles from the cold, solemn atmosphere. It feels like I'm in a crypt, and I realize why. This isn't so much a prison as a place where fae are buried alive.

My heart aches for River. The restaurant isn't just his livelihood. He lives for social interaction and thrives on physical touch. This isn't just prison for him

—it's torture. The longer I think about that, the faster I walk. I've got to get him out of here.

A familiar name flashes on the stone to my right, and I pull up short. Chance Delaney—Seven's father. The leprechaun kept six pixies prisoner in his own personal sex dungeon and ended up murdering one of them along with two humans. Just seeing his name brings back horrific memories of the night I confronted him. He deserves to be behind that stone.

I hurry on, relieved when I see the name River Foxwood nearby. Drawing a deep, fortifying breath, I step into the circle and wait. Almost immediately, a beam of light with no clear origination surrounds me. The stone melts away. River is sitting on a lumpy-looking cot with a thin blanket wrapped around his shoulders. He lifts his face, and I can tell he's been weeping. I've never seen him like this before. My heart pounds. I decide right then that I will clear his name no matter what it takes.

"Sophia?"

"I'm here, River."

He stands and rushes toward me, stopping when he reaches the invisible barrier between us. "Oh gods, it's good to see you. You have no idea—"

"We don't have much time, Riv. You need to tell me about the murder."

"I didn't do it."

"I know. I plan to prove as much and I'm going to

get you out of here, but I need you to tell me exactly what happened."

He shakes his head. "I don't understand. Shouldn't there be video? There's a camera right outside my restaurant."

I lower my chin, hating to tell him. "It's been tampered with. Fifteen minutes are missing. It goes from empty walkway to you hunched over the victim."

He tips his head back and curses. "Damn it. Who the fuck is messing with me?"

"Help me find out. Tell me exactly what happened."

He sighs heavily. "After I left you, I went to the restaurant to make sure everything was handled for the after-party. I helped my staff get all the food to the tent. But a burner on one of our warmers went out, so I headed back to the restaurant to get a replacement. That's when I stopped to talk with a... friend."

I analyze the way he says *friend* and draw some conclusions. "Friend with benefits?"

He nods once. "One who'd left for home directly from my place that morning, along with another friend who sometimes joins us."

"Oh!" I'm not sure why that surprises me. River's never hidden the fact that he's pansexual or occasionally entertains multiple partners. I just didn't think his sex life would be relevant to this case.

"I heard a shot and a scream and ran toward the sound. There was a hole in the victim's chest, and he was covered in blood. I yelled for help, then went to his side to put pressure on the wound. I held his hand while he died." River's eyes glaze with unshed tears, and I can see the memory deeply affects him. "I never even knew the human's name."

Hand on my heart, I say, "That must have been horrible, River, but we don't have much time. Tell me the name of who you were with that morning. If the victim was already shot before you entered the empty walkway, you were likely still with them at the time of the murder. Maybe they can vouch for you. I'm surprised you haven't already brought this up with Godmother."

River balks, his eyes shifting to the side. "I can't... reveal who it is."

"What? I understand wanting to be discreet, but this person could prove your innocence!"

He runs a hand over his face. "The person in question would suffer greatly if it was widely known they participated in a threesome with two satyrs. I promised to keep our affair a secret, and I won't break that confidence."

My hands ball into fists. "This is the exception. Whoever this person is, if they cared for you at all, they'd want you to tell me their name."

He swallows hard. "You don't understand. I *can't* say. I... bargained. I'm *bound* to keep their confidence."

"Fuck! Can you tell me who the other participant was then? The third."

River smiles excitedly. "Yes. It was Patrick."

"The satyr? Patrick Fawnear?" Patrick was always the class clown in school and is a brilliant musician. I hadn't expected he was River's lover.

"Yes. The three of us were together all night. He can confirm that."

"But he wasn't with you before the murder."

"No."

"Can he tell me who was?"

River's face falls. "No. He made the same bargain."

"For fuck's sake! Give me a clue. Work around the bargain. This person isn't worth protecting if they left you in here!"

"You don't understand, Sophia. We *all* made the bargain to hide our arrangement. They can't come forward. They are also bound."

It feels like I've been punched in the gut. "Are you telling me that even if the person wanted to help you, they couldn't?"

"If it involves admitting that we were... together with that person, that's exactly what I'm saying. I can say I was with Patrick. Patrick can admit he was with me. Our third's identity can never be revealed, not even by them." Suddenly unsteady on his feet, River stumbles back and sits back down on the cot, dropping his head into his hands.

"I'll talk to Patrick. I'll figure out a way, River. It just might take me a few days."

He stares at me, and his hands start to shake. His voice sounds tight and raspy as he says, "A few days..."

I check my watch. "We only have a few minutes more. Do you know anything at all about the victim?"

"No," River says firmly. "I'd never seen him before. Nothing odd about that. He was human. They come and go."

"Right. But he didn't say anything to you in his last moments?"

River shakes his head. "He had a bullet hole in his heart and was bleeding out. I think he had a lot on his mind."

"I'm just trying to help."

His eyes narrow and he lifts his chin to look at me, a memory sparking behind his eyes. "He had a rock in his hand."

"A rock?"

"Yeah. It might not mean anything, and I only noticed it because he was gripping it in his fist and I knew the moment he died because his hand went slack and it rolled off his palm."

"What kind of rock? Like a jewel?"

He shook his head. "An ordinary gray rock."

I glance at my watch. We're out of time. "You'll be okay, River. I'll find a way to get you out." The words have to squeeze around the lump forming in my throat.

He raises his red-rimmed eyes to meet mine, and his voice is strained as he says, "The food appears,

Sophia. No one comes in, not ever. You are the first living person I've seen since—"

The stone snaps back into place, cutting him off. It startles me and I jump. The light shifts from engulfing me to shining on a silver platter beside the stone. Only then do I remember the apple in my trembling hands. Careful not to drop it, I place it on the platter. My throat is dry and my heart pounds.

River is still in there. He's alone. Truly alone.

A shiver runs through me, and then my breath stops altogether when a pale hand extends from the darkness above the silver tray. Yellow nails tapered to sharp points jut from bony fingers wrapped in pock-marked skin. Round suction cups like sores honey-comb the palm of the hand, and as it wraps around the apple, I hear each of them bite into its flesh like tiny mouths. Juice dribbles from the fist, and then the hand, and the fruit, is gone.

I cover my mouth to keep from screaming and hurry toward the exit. But I slow my steps as I near Chance Delaney's cell. Thinking about Chance twists my gut, as if I've swallowed a worm that's gnawing my insides, wriggling dark and deadly somewhere I can't reach. If he'd had his way, I'd be in a cell in the base-ment of his hunting cabin, starved, beaten, and likely raped. He's the rot on the underbelly of a diseased snake, and the last thing I want is to see him again.

But I can't shake the thought that this murder has something to do with him. Someone used his computer to tamper with the security cameras. Leprechaun luck cleared the area before the murder. One of the last things he said to me before I put an arrow in his shoulder was that he was working with others to sabotage Dragonfly Hollow. He'd never told me who, just that it was bigger than me. Bigger than all of us.

And then the horrifying suspicion I had before comes to me again. What if he's not behind that stone? He is considered by most to be the most powerful leprechaun alive. What if he figured out a way to escape and he's responsible for the murder? It would be the perfect crime. Everyone would assume he was still here.

I have to know. I have to see for myself that he's in there.

My eyes fall on the platter. I only brought one apple, and I used it for River. Reaching for my purse, I wonder if I could just leave money. That seems like it would pass as an offering. I dig in the center compartment, and my hand falls on a square container of cubes of berry-flavored gum. Hmm. Gum or money. If I had a dozen mouths on my hands, I'd want the yummy gum, not the filthy money.

Gum in hand, I step into the circle. The light turns on, and the stone melts away. What I see inside makes me thankful I haven't eaten today. Chance is there—I take some comfort in that—but he stands at the wall, writing something in his own blood. Gibberish. I can make out letters but no coherent words. His fingers are raw, gripped around a pointed chip of stone. Blood drips from a gash in his arm—his ink.

He stops and slowly turns his head. I'm once again disgusted by his resemblance to Seven. Aside from graying temples and smaller eyes that remind me of a rat's, there's no question they're related, although he's gaunt compared to the last time I saw him and a short beard covers his jaw. His hair is longer too.

"Well, well, well, little bird. How nice of you to visit my cage. If only you could step inside, we could have such fun together."

Eww. Everything about this moment makes me feel sick, but I have ten minutes with this asshole and maybe he knows something that can help us. "Who is responsible for the murder in Wonderland, Chance?"

A dark and wicked laugh bubbles from his chest. He lowers his chin and stares at me like a wolf stalking its prey. "I told you it wouldn't end with me, little bird. The hydra has many heads."

"Give me a name. Tell me who you were working with. Who might have done this?"

He steps closer. "Why would I tell you anything?"

"Because you have nothing left to lose. Maybe if you contribute something useful, Godmother will show you mercy." There is no way in hell Godmother would ever let Chance out of here, but I have nothing else to offer.

"You truly are an accomplished liar," he says

through his teeth. "I'm not even sure you realize what a rare and valuable talent that is for a fae. Some of us can't lie at all. We can deceive, we can mislead, but lying like you are to me now, as you look me in the eye —by the gods, I'd say that's as rare as being able to resist a bargain."

I don't bother denying it. I'm running out of time. "Then what do you want?"

"You'd bargain with me?"

"Within reason."

He hesitates, his gaze sweeping down my form in a way that makes my skin want to peel off my body. "Make Seven come and visit me. Don't deny you have power over him. You've had your filthy pixie stinger in him since he was a child. If you tell him to come, he'll come."

"And in return, you'll tell me who's responsible for the murder."

He chuckles. "I've been here, little bird. I don't know who committed the murder you speak of."

"But you have a guess. Someone you were working with who wanted to pick up where you left off."

"Yes."

"You tell me who that is, and I'll ask Seven to visit." I will ask. He'll never come.

"Do more than ask." He sneers. "I want him here."

"We're running out of time, Chance."

"Deal," he says quickly.

I make the gimme motion with my hand.

"Mirror, mirror on the wall, the one you seek isn't *one* at all, but he whose crown is in his bones, and they whose hunger has grown and grown, and she whose hatred is cast in stone. Blood shed by one is blood shed by all."

"What the fuck does that mean?" Based on his earlier comments, I knew more than one person was involved in his scheme, but this poem is utter nonsense.

"You have my answer. You asked who was responsible for the murder, not for a specific name. I told you the truth."

I scoff. "Fine. I said I'd ask Seven to visit. I didn't promise when."

He hisses. "Filthy bird." He pulls his shirt over his head, staining it with blood. "Let me show you what I do with your kind." I cringe as he runs his palm down his swollen stomach and it slithers under his waistband and into his pants. Mercifully, that's when the stone slams into place. My time is up.

The light shifts to the silver tray, and I empty the gum onto it. The only sound is the pounding of my heart in my ears as the pale hand reaches for my offering. This time I don't wait to see what happens. I start for the exit, walking as fast as I can without breaking into a jog; I don't want to call attention to myself or make too much noise. But when a head-splitting screech comes from behind me, I launch into a full-out run.

I'm not fast enough. The creature rushes me from behind, that pallid hand snatching my ankle. I fall, my wings flapping uselessly as I hit the ground hard. My elbows and forearms sting where they slap the stone, but remembering the warning of the warden, I don't make a sound. What will happen if I scream? Will more come? I don't want to find out.

Circular mouths suction to the skin of my ankle, digging in, hurting. I kick at it, freeing myself long enough to flip over. Above me, a faceless thing seethes. At least I think it's seething. It has no mouth and only two indentations where eyes should be. Its nostrils, however, flare angrily. Its body is humanoid but strange, light gray and too long with multijointed limbs. There are holes on the sides of its head but no ears.

It reaches for me with one hand, fingers formed into claws, and I see that the mouths on its palms are lined with tiny sharp teeth. I smell berries and realize my "offering" is stuck and strung between several of the orifices, forming a sticky mess that lowers toward my face. I hold my breath to keep from screaming and turn my head, trying to put distance between me and it.

Out of the corner of my eye, I see the hand stop just a centimeter from my face, and a soft golden glow forms a barrier between us. The thing screeches again in frustration, leaving my ears ringing. Slowly I shift my head and see that the coin around my neck, the one Seven gave me, is the source of the glow. It pulses gently in the hollow of my throat.

For protection. Thank you, Seven! I crab-walk backward, away from the creature.

My foot extends beyond the coin's glow, and it grabs my ankle again. I wince from the pain and pull the coin away from my skin by the chain, directing the glow at the unseelie and trying to get my feet under me.

That's when I hear a thump and another thump. Something red bounces near my hip and rolls toward the creature. An apple. Another one rolls on the other side of us. The creature sniffs like a dog, turns on its haunches, and pounces, taking the apple into its hungry grip.

I use my wings to help me to my feet then half run, half fly for the exit. I'm winded and shaking by the time I reach Saul, who is pointing his gun toward the darkness behind me and holding the empty basket the apples had been in. The gate warden is signing angrily at him.

"I hope you have what you need, Ms. Larkspur," Saul says, "because we've been strongly encouraged to leave the premises."

I nod breathlessly, and we head for the car. My ankle is throbbing, and I have a stitch in my side that makes it hard to breathe.

Once we're inside, I tell Saul what happened.

"How was I supposed to know that gum wasn't an appropriate offering?"

Saul hands me the flyer and points at an asterisk at the bottom of the page.

It simply says No Gum.

EIGHT

"I need you to take me directly to Godmother's," I tell Saul. I've thought about what to do from the moment we left Ashgate. I can't leave River in there. Not for another hour, let alone another day. It will break him. He's too good a friend. "It's important."

"Seven's orders are to take you directly back to his place to debrief." Saul keeps his eyes on the road as he answers me in a tone that's not exactly dismissive but holds a note of resolve, as if the decision is out of his hands.

"Do you need me to call him and have him tell you it's an emergency?" I sit up straighter. "Every minute I don't speak to Godmother is an extra minute that River stays locked up in that hellhole, and let me tell you, Saul, it is the very definition of hell."

His eyes slide to me and then he pulls his phone from his pocket. His thumb flies over the screen while his eyes remain on the road. I'd chastise him to not text and drive, but he's a leprechaun. The chances of us getting into an accident are almost zilch.

His phone dings. Dipping his gaze to the screen for a split second, he frowns. "He says he'll meet us at Godmother's."

I smile smugly and lean back in my seat. Seven trusts me. We've been there for each other since we were children, aside from the time I spent in America, and that was because of his megalomaniac father. I know he's got my back.

At my direction, Saul drops me off under the Wonderland Security office before parking, and I beat feet to Godmother's Tearoom, giving me a few minutes head start ahead of both Saul and Seven. I'm going to need it. A few human patrons are having tea in the gingerbread dining room, but a word with the host and I'm escorted into Godmother's backroom office. To my surprise, it's light and airy, all white wood and delicate furniture. Fuzzy pink throw pillows decorate the white turned-leg sofa. A shiny gold paperweight on her desk reads Boss.

"Sophia Larkspur, to what do I owe the pleasure?" Her deep voice resonates between us, and then her gaze locks on the coin at the base of my throat. Her eyes narrow slightly, but if there's a question in her gaze, she doesn't voice it.

I pretend I don't notice her interest in Seven's gift

to me and jump into why I'm here. "River Foxwood is innocent. You have to let him out of Ashgate."

She braids her fingers together and rests her chin on them. "No. I don't have to do anything, Sophia." She points at the Boss sign on her desk, but her gaze shifts back to me.

"Why are your arms all scraped up?"

"I had a run-in with one of the guards at Ashgate."

"Why?"

"Someone tampered with the video surveillance."

"Seven informed me."

"River did not murder that man. The only reason he was covered in the victim's blood is he was trying to help him. The man had already been shot by the time River came upon him outside his restaurant. No witnesses saw what happened because someone used luck to clear the area—likely a leprechaun. You saw that on the video. Who else would be strong enough to do that?"

She drums her fingers on her desk. "Just because a leprechaun cleared the area does not mean they committed the murder. What proof do you have that River didn't do it?"

"I don't need proof." I take a deep breath. "Patrick was with him. He didn't leave his side until he heard the man scream."

Godmother sneers. I can almost feel her scanning me like some sort of lie detector, but I hold my ground, making my expression at once genuine while also showing a hint of shame.

"If that's true, why didn't River mention it?"

"Everything was too... public. Patrick's being with River that morning was a secret because they were discussing something private." I lower my chin. "You see, the only reason that I know about it is because I was with the two of them the night before. But neither of them will be able to tell you it was me specifically. They bargained with me and promised discretion. After everything that's happened since I've been back, I needed it. But it was me who asked Patrick to speak to River, to tell him I was breaking off the affair. That's how I know they were together at that time. I visited Ashgate and River so he could release me from our bargain and I could speak to you about it."

Godmother leans back in her chair and studies me. I get the sense she knows I'm lying, although I'm doing my best to make it believable. Ancient magic nudges me, attempting to taste the lie in whatever I'm made of, or maybe that's just my nerves. She rings a bell on her desk, and a hidden door opens at the back of the room. A redheaded pixie I've never met runs in. Godmother whispers in her ear, and she scampers off again.

"This is a dangerous game you're playing, Sophia," Godmother says softly, only for my ears. "I could give you something to force the truth from you."

A chill runs through me. "You could. I'm sensing you won't."

"I don't think River did it any more than you do." Her dark lashes blink at me, and she toys with a quill on her desk.

"Then why is he in Ashgate?"

She taps the pads of her fingers together. "The safety of our guests is my top priority. If River didn't do this, who did?"

I swallow hard, not at all sure how much I should share with Godmother about what Chance told me. I choose my words carefully. "I have reason to believe that Chance Delaney wasn't working alone and that this murder is part of a master plan that is still being carried out in his absence."

Godmother's brow rises. "And what would give you that idea?"

"I spoke to him in Ashgate, and he admitted it. He is working with others, perhaps fairy or maybe a human." *Maybe both*. At least that's my interpretation of the riddle Chance told me.

The redheaded fairy runs back in and whispers something in Godmother's ear, and her mouth spreads into a wide smile. "It seems Patrick has corroborated your story, although, as you warned, he was not able to identify you. But when presented with your version of events, he was able to affirm them. I have to hand it to you, Sophia. If you are lying, it's a very good lie." She grabs a piece of parchment from a pile on her desk, signs it, and marks it with her seal. It sparkles as she rolls it up and hands it to the pixie. "Have River Foxwood removed from Ashgate Prison and delivered to the safe house in Sagewick Forest."

The pixie nods and rushes from the room.

"Safe house?" She's up to something. I can see the twinkle of some devious idea in her eye.

"I'm going to do you this favor and release your lover, Sophia." I bristle when she says *lover*, then correct myself, shoring up my defenses for whatever comes next. "Mind, it may take up to forty-eight hours to complete the necessary paperwork and procedures."

I cringe at the thought of River enduring that place for two more days, but it can't be helped. "If that's the fastest it can be done."

Godmother points her chin at me. "There is a condition of his release."

"And that is?"

"I cannot allow the general public to know River's been freed, you understand, until this case is solved. So in return for my generosity, I expect you to find the real murderer. The sooner you do, the sooner River can return to his regular life."

My breath halts in my throat. This is beginning to sound a hell of a lot like a bargain, and I never signed up to make another deal with Godmother. All amiability drains from my expression, and I glare across the desk.

"Is this how you did it to Seven?" I ask through my teeth. "Gods, a person might agree to a bargain with you without even trying, without even understanding the consequences."

"Careful, Sophia." Her eyes spark, and power gathers in the small room.

"He came to you, a child—"

"He was almost eighteen—"

"Abused by his father, poisoned with blue iron, he came to you for help—"

"And I helped him." One eyebrow jerks upward derisively.

"Not to escape his father's influence."

"He didn't ask to escape. He asked for you."

"Then you never upheld your side of the bargain."

She gives a wicked laugh. "Oh, I did. Your daughter is proof of that."

"Proof of sex. Nothing more."

"Who do you think you're kidding?"

My lips peel back from my teeth, and I can barely contain my rage as I ask, "What exactly was his side of that bargain? How long does Seven have to serve you until he's free of your control?"

Her nails win over her interest, and she draws the tip of one across the cuticle of another. "Until I release him."

"That's not fair."

"Not fair? Nothing about a bargain need be fair, Sophia. Stars above, you're starting to sound like one of those humans you spent so long living among. Seven was remiss in his terms. He never specified how long he'd have to work for me. I could have taken more. He offered *anything* to be with you. Never specified what that anything was or what being with you entailed. I took his servitude as the head of my security team for as long as I desire it, but I could have demanded far more. So don't test me now, pixie. It's not my fault you can't recognize mercy when you see it."

Mercy. Only a fool wouldn't fear Godmother, but this is the first time in my memory that she disgusts me. From the roots of repulsion, I promise myself right there and then to grow strong enough to force her to free Seven, and I don't wait a single moment to try.

"I'll solve this murder if you free Seven."

She laughs. "I've already done you a favor by freeing River, whom you say is your lover. If that's not enough for you, I can call back my assistant and tear up my order to free him from Ashgate."

I blow out a breath. "Fine. I'll do it, but no bargain. You have my word, nothing more."

"Fine." She grins as if this was more than she was hoping for and points a perfectly manicured fingernail at me. "Your word is all I need. After all, unless you want Fairly Goodweather to feature your threesome with Patrick and River in the *Daily Hatter*, you will do as I wish."

I scoff. If I don't do what she wants, she'll further

ruin my reputation and hurt Seven in the process. *Bitch.* "You have my word if I have your silence."

"Done." She brushes her hand across her desk.

No silver threads bind me, but they may as well have. I'm knee-deep in Godmother's crap once again, and River's future and my happiness with Seven are at stake. *Fuck.*

"For future reference, Sophia, that coin around your neck won't work against me. If I wanted to bind you, I could bind you." She looks at her nails again, and I feel the tiniest twinge in my stomach. *She's bluffing*, my instincts tell me, and I try to hide my surprise.

"Now go. I'm sure you have better things to do than take up my time discussing your tawdry personal affairs. I'll text you the address of the safe house. I'll leave it to you to break the news to River about my order that he remain there until the case is solved."

Fuck.

CHAPTER
NINE

I'm leaving Godmother's Tearoom with my phone in hand when the love of my life meets me in the street with a folder under one arm. Both of us light up when we see each other, drawn together like magnets until we realize where we are and stop a reasonable distance from each other. It hurts not to reach out and touch him.

My phone dings, and I look down as a text from Godmother streaks across the screen with the address she promised me.

"Looks serious. Why is Godmother texting you an address?"

"It's a safe house—"

"Why do you need the address to a safe house?" Seven steps in closer, lowering his voice and looking as if he's a hair's breadth away from throwing me over his shoulder and locking me safely within his tower.

"Because that's where she's sending River in two days," I whisper. I glance around me. We're alone, but perhaps not for long. This is a public place. "We should go somewhere private."

He gestures with his head toward the Cast Members Only door, and I follow him back there, through the woods and onto our beach. We used to come here all the time as kids. I fell in love with Seven on this beach.

His luck rises around us like a dragon, the heat from its long body brushing against me and making the leaves on the branches shimmy. "We're alone. Tell me everything."

I do. Everything. I am completely honest, not because I'm forced to be but because I want nothing to come between us. I tell Seven every detail about what River and Chance said, even the promise I made to try to get him to visit. I hold back nothing.

Seven takes it all in stride until I tell him how I got River out.

"You told her you were the third," he grits out. "Is it true?"

I glare at him. "No! But River said he and Patrick made a bargain with this person not to reveal their identity. It could be anyone, and it was faster to tell her it was me than to waste time trying to find the person."

He grunts his understanding but continues to sulk.

"Are you upset I lied?"

"No."

"Then why do you look like someone stole the prize out of your cereal box?"

"I just don't like thinking about you with him... or *them*."

I step in closer. "Then stop thinking about it. You do realize it never happened. I lied."

"I'm trying. I can't help it, Sophia. I'm jealous of every second another man gets to be with you even when it happens in my imagination." His crooked smile tells me he knows it's ridiculous, but he pulls me into his arms anyway and brands me with a deep, hot kiss. I melt into him and only pull away when I need to catch my breath.

"The coin worked, by the way," I say against his lips. "It saved me from a run-in with one of Ashgate's unseelie guards." I tell him about my mistake with the gum.

"Fuck, Sophia! Thank the gods it worked, but did you have to put it to the test so dramatically? How exactly did you think you'd escape?"

I shrug. "Who doesn't like gum? I took a chance."

He tucks my hair behind my ears and touches his forehead to mine. "Can you take fewer chances? After all this is over, I want us to be together. That can't happen if you're not in one piece."

"I promise whatever's left of me is all yours," I joke.

He growls and kisses me again.

"Any leads on your dad's computer?"

He groans. "I confirmed it was still there, in his office. And that the tampering happened from that device, not remotely."

"What? How is that possible?"

He shakes his head. "It isn't. No one keyed into the room. Unless someone has learned to walk through walls, I have to believe a very talented hacker has covered his tracks in the data."

"Great. Sounds like a dead end. Did you ever hear back about the identity of the victim?" Last I heard, his team was still working on it.

"Just today. It took longer than usual because his passport wasn't processed through tickets or park admissions."

"Huh?"

"He was a guest of Bailiwick's. His name is Adam Barker. He's a geology professor from a public university in Illinois." He opens the folder and shows me Adam's picture. "He came last week to do a presentation to the grade one students on the geology of the Appalachian Mountains and decided to tack on a short vacation since his entrance into the parks and accommodations were taken care of."

"Geology? I guess that explains the rock in his hand."

"Rock? What rock?"

"River told me that when the man died, a gray rock rolled out of his hand. He'd been gripping it in his fist."

Seven snorts. "Odd."

"So who would want this guy dead? Did he piss someone off at the Dragonfly Club or something? Did you get any footage on him?"

"Hours. My people went through it all. The guy was as exciting as wallpaper. Didn't drink alcohol or gamble. Talked with very few people. Spent a ton of time by the pool and reading on the balcony of his room."

"What else? Who was this guy? Did he have any known enemies?"

Seven closes the folder and pulls out his phone. He brings up Adam's Instagram and hands it to me. I stare down at a handful of pictures of a man with... rocks. Some are of him holding a rock. Others are of him standing in front of a rock with some geological feature. I thumb through his feed and it's more of the same.

"That's it?" I wasn't aware anyone like this guy existed.

"On every social media channel. And I checked Flutter and Puckers. He didn't have accounts on either of them." Flutter is the app humans use to be matched with pixies. Puckers is the one for humans and satyrs. So Adam didn't have a fae fetish. Going off these accounts, it seems the only thing he was interested in was rocks.

"Gods, he really did have a singular interest, didn't he?"

"His Twitter feed is full of geology one-liners."

I stare at Seven like he's speaking a different language.

"Don't take geologists for granite," he deadpans. "Be patient with geologists, they all have their faults."

I groan. "This man is probably the least notable or controversial person who has ever existed. Why would anyone want him dead?"

He rubs a hand over his mouth. "Maybe they didn't. Maybe he was just in the wrong place at the wrong time."

"Unlucky bastard. But if whoever did this chose Adam randomly, how do we find the killer?"

"Tell me again what my father told you."

I recite the verse again for him. "Mirror, mirror on the wall, the one you seek isn't *one* at all, but he whose crown is in his bones, and they whose hunger has grown and grown, and she whose hatred is cast in stone. Blood shed by one is blood shed by all."

"Hmm. That mirror, mirror part could refer to the passage to Shadowvale."

"I thought so too."

"He whose crown is in his bones sounds like Vissevel, but the bone fairy is dead."

"Any ideas on the rest of it?"

He looks out over the water, then shakes his head. "Not a clue. I have an entire library of books on the unseelie though. I'll do some research."

I move in closer and run my hands up his chest. "I can come by tonight to help."

He heaves a beleaguered sigh. "Can't. We have somewhat of a crisis on our hands at Lucky Enterprises. I need to put out a few fires, and after all this"—he holds up the folder he still needs to share with Godmother—"I have a long night ahead of me."

"Crisis? What's going on?"

He smiles and tugs on the cuff of his shirt. "Nothing interesting enough to talk about. A supply chain issue. How about tomorrow night?"

I check my phone. "I'm supposed to meet Penelope for dinner and drinks."

Seven's eyes turn a brighter shade of green, and his lips curl into a wolfish grin. "Excellent. I'll take advantage of your drunken and lecherous state."

"I'm Penelope's night away from the kids. It will be late and my parents will definitely be suspicious if I stay out all night. Rain check?"

He steps in closer, the electric current between us building. "I waited for you for sixteen years, Sophia. What's a few more days?"

LATE TUESDAY AFTERNOON, I GET THE CALL THAT RIVER IS finally being delivered to the safe house. After the week I've had, it's a breath of fresh air. Seven and I keep missing each other, and there hasn't been a single new clue on the case. We made a date for seven o'clock tonight at his place though. I can't wait.

The safe house is a simple but relatively large log cabin nestled in the woods in a remote section of the Appalachians on the border of Devashire. It took me over an hour to drive here, and the closest neighboring house is fifteen miles away. I scoop the groceries I brought for River from the back of Arden's Kia and think again that I need to get myself a car. I shuffle to the door and give it two hard knocks with my knee. When it opens, I almost drop the groceries. Instead, I close my eyes.

"River! Why are you naked?" Satyrs in their natural form have hooves and a shaggy coat of hair from the waist down that does an excellent job of concealing their, um, considerable members, but they can shift to look human. That includes the ability to mask their horns. For practical reasons though, such as ease of finding appropriate clothing, keeping their fur groomed, et cetera, most choose to appear as River does now, human from the neck down, satyr from the neck up. Which means that before I closed my eyes, I got a clear view of the full monty, and River's monty is incredibly, er, full.

Eyes still closed, I jerk when the groceries lift from my grip and he says, "I just got out of the shower. I was trying to find a towel. Does it bother you?" He sounds genuinely surprised.

I open one eye to see he's in the kitchen, his bare ass mooning me as he sets down the groceries. I avert my eyes, but they catch on his wet hair and the way droplets of water stream in rivulets down his spine. I refuse to follow them and instead fasten my gaze on the tattoo of a phoenix on his left shoulder. I never knew he had a tattoo. "Um, I know it's common for satyrs to embrace nudity, but I'd prefer if you—"

He turns around to look at me, exposing himself again. I wince on behalf of all his former lovers. Every single one of them must have left River's bed with a limp.

My eyes flick toward the ceiling. "*Pants*, River! Could you put some pants on?"

"Sure. All you had to do was ask." He sounds as if the thought never occurred to him before now. I hear him walk from the room, and a moment later he returns in board shorts and a T-shirt.

"Thanks."

"Don't mention it." He looks me in the eye and then at the groceries on the counter, and his expression grows serious.

River is an imposing presence, at least six foot four inches of corded muscle just shy of bulky. Horns of impressive size curl like a ram's from the sides of his head. Usually his cheerful disposition acts to balance out his hulking exterior, but when his face morphs like it does right now, I almost take a step back.

"Thank you, Sophia, for getting me out of Ashgate. I wouldn't have survived much longer in that place. But... how did you do it?"

I scratch the back of my neck, wondering if I

should tell him. This is River. He'll understand. "I told Godmother I was the third and it was Patrick with you that morning, and Patrick was smart enough to back me up."

His big brown eyes blink incredulously. "You *lied* to Godmother? You told her that you were our third?"

"I had to. If I'd waited to find your actual alibi, it might have taken weeks."

He peers at me with something close to reverence. "Fuck, Sophia. Thank you. You are an amazing friend and much braver than most, but you shouldn't have done that. What do you owe her for getting me out?"

I grimace. "You might want to hold off on singing my praises for a beat. My price was promising to solve this murder, but I didn't exactly get you out, like in the full sense of the word. There's something I have to tell you."

"What do you mean, I'm not out?"

"Did they tell you anything about this place when they brought you here?"

"Not much. They said I'd have to stay until I got the final okay from Godmother to return home. It sounded administrative." Glancing toward the kitchen, he turns sullen. "You brought enough groceries to last... awhile."

I grimace. "You have to stay here until we find the real murderer."

He balks, then tilts his head as if he doesn't quite

understand. "But I have a restaurant to run and a cat to feed—"

"You have a cat? Who's been feeding your cat?"

"Sophia, she can't mean to keep me here indefinitely. I have a life." Sudden horror widens his eyes. "Do people still think I did this?"

Silently, I curse Godmother for making me break this news to River. "She wants them to think you did it until we catch someone else. She's afraid if the public knows the killer is still out there that it will impact park revenue. Godmother released you from Ashgate based on my confession, but she'll return you there if you leave this house or tell anyone you're here."

He scrubs his face with his hands and turns a circle as if he's looking for something to punch.

"I'm sorry, River. I promise you that Seven and I will solve this case—"

"Seven? Godmother is making you work with that asshole again?" Oops, River doesn't know about my relationship with Seven. He still thinks I hate him. I shouldn't have brought that up.

I pick at the side of my thumbnail. "Uh, I'm over it. He's all right. The important thing is that we catch the murderer and get you out of here."

He studies me for a second. "Gods, you're involved with him again, aren't you?"

My brows shoot up. "What makes you say that?" I giggle nervously. Did he just look straight into my soul or what?

"Sophia, you're blushing." He grimaces. "When did this happen? After what he did to you? I thought you hated Seven."

I drop down onto the sofa, and he sits down next to me. "I was wrong about him, River. He wasn't responsible for what happened to me at the Yule ball. That was all his dad." This is where I have to be careful. No one knows how abusive the Delaneys were to their kids, and it's not my secret to tell.

River shakes his head. "He had to be at least partially responsible."

"Well, it was a long time ago. We've... been talking... uh, spending time together."

"Fucking..."

"River!"

"Oh come on, Sophia. We both know leprechaun sex is the stuff of legends. There are hearts floating above your head every time you say his name. You're getting some."

I send him a soft smile. "Well, for reasons I don't need to explain to you, please keep this to yourself."

"Who am I going to tell?" He gestures vaguely around him.

"Seriously, River."

"Your secret is safe with me. But you should give a message to Seven for me."

"Oh?"

"Tell him that if he hurts you again, I'll make him

hurt seven times as much, and all the luck in the world won't stop me."

I smile. "You're a good friend, River."

"I'm serious. If I ever have to pick you up off the ground again, that guy is going to pay."

I nod. "I heard you. I'll let him know." I rise from the couch. "I should go. It's getting late."

He stands and wipes his hands on the sides of his shorts, then pulls me into a hug that feels like he's wrapped himself around me twice. His lips press into the top of my head. "Thank you, Sophia, so goddamn much. I can never repay you for this."

"It's enough that you'd do it for me. And I'm sorry you're stuck here."

He snorts. "I'll take the bedroom of this place over that cell."

"I'll come back and visit whenever I have an update or a free minute. Text me on the burner phone they gave you if you need something. Stay strong, okay?"

"You too. And I'm always here for you if things go wrong with the asshat."

He levels a whiskey-colored stare at me. I've started for the door when I hear him say, "Sophia" softly behind me. His voice is choked with emotion.

"What's wrong?"

He glances at the grocery bags. "I hate to ask this. I know you're busy, and you've done so much for me already."

"Ask, River."

"Can you stay for dinner? I don't want to eat alone." His voice cracks, and he swallows hard before adding, "In there, I was always alone."

Days and days he was in that place without seeing another face aside from my short visit. I'm here, and for now I'm all he has.

"You're the chef. What are we making?" I head for the kitchen and start unloading the groceries.

CHAPTER

TEN

After a night of laughter and a delicious meal with River, I finally feel he's in a good place with a positive mental state where I can leave him. I promise to check on his cat, then race to Seven's. I've texted him throughout the evening, and he knows I'm going to be late, but his responses have become more and more terse.

I arrive at his penthouse just after nine and am whisked into the elevator by a very high-strung security guard. I'm not sure what his problem is, but he fidgets in silence all the way up to the penthouse. I've been here before and don't need an escort. Weird.

When the doors finally open on Seven's floor, the security guard who's stationed at a desk outside Seven's penthouse is out of his chair immediately. "You can go right in, Ms. Larkspur."

"Thanks, Lucas." There are five men who work on this floor at various times. Lucas is by far the nicest.

I push through Seven's door and immediately feel his power in the room. It paces like a hungry animal, pulsing against my skin with an almost erratic tempo. I stride through the magnificent foyer, over the custom fish tank that creates a river of koi fish through his floor, and into his living room. All the lights are off, but I can see Seven's silhouette on the sofa from the light of the moon through the window.

"You're late," he says gruffly.

"I'm sorry. It took longer than I expected." I flip on one of the lamps, casting the white-on-white decor in a cool glow, and my breath catches in my throat. Seven looks like hell. He's cast off his suit jacket and is nursing a bourbon. "What happened?"

He tosses back the rest of what's in his glass, his emerald eyes focused on me with an intensity that steals all the oxygen from the room. Rising from the sofa, he sets the glass down and stalks toward me until his chest brushes mine. "What happened is I've been denied your company for close to a week."

"You saw me at Arden's graduation."

"Your physical company."

I spread my arms.

He reaches around me, his fingers finding the zipper of my dress. It's off me in seconds. I'm just happy he didn't luck it off me. Seven is capable of making fabric tear or a zipper malfunction with nothing but intention. I've had bras deteriorate right off my body. I like this dress. I'm glad he didn't ruin it, although the way he's looking at me, I'm surprised he didn't.

He lowers his nose to the side of my neck and brushes his lips along my skin. "You smell like him," he says darkly.

I scoff. "I don't see how. I hugged him goodbye. Nothing more."

With a flick of his fingers, my bra comes unhooked and I let it drop on top of the dress. I reach for him but he backs away, leaving me standing alone in my panties. I give him a slow, taunting smile. "Well, Mr. Delaney, what do you plan to do with me now that you have my physical company?"

The corner of his mouth lifts, and the world tilts on its axis. Luck rushes through me, an effervescent geyser that leaves me breathless and dizzy. He catches me before I can fall and whirls me behind the sofa. With a hand at the back of my neck, he bends me over the back until my chest falls against the plush white fabric, and I instinctively plant my hands on the cushions.

His hand rubs a circle over my ass. If he didn't know I was turned on before, he knows now. I'm soaking wet.

"Mmm, Sophia, is this for me?" He moves my panties aside and strokes along my wet slit. A low, carnal sound rumbles from his chest. Heat bubbles through me again, a rush of sparkling luck that makes my body feel as light as air.

"Always," I rasp. It's hard to think, hard to breathe, around the luck he's feeding me. My blood fizzes with it.

He leans over me, pulling my hair gently so he can whisper in my ear. "But you were late, bad girl. You kept me waiting."

I turn my head and flash him a slow, smug smile. "You would have waited longer."

His hand leaves my backside and then smacks against my ass. The momentary sting is dwarfed by a massive amount of pleasure as luck and heat rush between my legs. I moan and spread my feet a little wider.

"I bet you would have waited all night," I say breathlessly.

He spanks me again, then drags his fingers through my wetness and circles my clit before pinching it just short of pain.

"Let's see who's willing to wait." He removes his hand.

I try to stand up, but he grabs my hair to hold me in place and spanks me again, then sends a rush of luck to ease the sting. I moan and try to push into his hand, but he removes it and my panties in one swoop, leaving me cold.

"Seven," I say breathlessly.

"I bet you'd wait all night," he says, throwing my own words back at me.

I most certainly do not want to wait all night. I'm aching with a need that seems to ratchet up by the minute.

I don't say a word. His hands land on my ass and spread me open right before his tongue licks up my center. I cry out from the current of desire that shoots through me. He pulls away.

Frustrated, I try to stand and reach for him, but his hand lands gently on the back of my neck, holding me in place. Palming my breast, he tugs at my nipple while his other hand strokes down my spine and between my legs. He massages my folds, circling, teasing. My legs start to shake.

His finger dips inside, and I try to buck against his hand, but he moves away, never deep enough, never hard enough. It's a torturous tease. And when his thumb presses gently against my asshole, I find myself panting with need. He's still fully dressed behind me, looking cool and collected, and I'm naked and so hot I might incinerate into ash if he doesn't do something about it quickly.

I crack. "Please, Seven. I can't wait. I need you in me."

He leans over me, placing a kiss to the top of my spine. Luck dances across my skin, sending all my tiny hairs standing on end. "Are you begging?"

"Yes," I say enthusiastically.

"Thank the gods," he murmurs.

The sound of his belt and then his clothes hitting the floor has me breathing a sigh of relief. He grasps my hips and jerks me against him. My breath hitches.

He leans over me again, his lips brushing the shell of my ear as he says, "I'm going to fuck you so hard you'll spend every minute away from me thinking about it."

I turn enough to touch my lips to his, my voice heavy with emotion as I say, "I already do."

A strangled sound exits his throat as he fills me in one rough thrust. I take a deep breath, adjusting myself to accommodate the size of him. He barely gives me a chance before he's pounding into me. I grip the couch cushions and unfurl my wings, the feeling heavenly after having them tucked in all day.

"Beautiful," he mumbles between thrusts.

One of his hands strokes along my spine and pets the sensitive base of one wing, making me buck harder against him. He gives me what I need, unleashing himself until I cry out as my body hums like a struck tuning fork. The orgasm hits me, but he doesn't let up. At this point, I'm saturated with his luck. Even my fingers vibrate with it. I keep climbing, another orgasm slamming into me, this one stronger than my first. My entire body clenches around him.

He moans but doesn't stop his assault. One hand wraps itself in my hair, tugging gently, as the other finds my breasts, kneading them, pinching my nipples.

I gasp and then scream as the most intense pleasure is wrung from my body like the last drops of liquid from a wet towel.

Hot jets fill me as he gives in to his own ecstasy. *Fuck.* My bones have turned to noodles. I don't fight it but go perfectly limp over the back of the couch.

Still buried inside me, he grabs my ass cheek. "You're mine. Only mine."

"Yes," I say over my shoulder. "Just so you know, there is no way I can walk after that. I'm now a permanent fixture in your living room."

He strokes my hair and nuzzles my neck, threading his fingers into mine where I hold myself up on the cushions. "Nothing would make me happier than having you as a permanent fixture in my life." His lips press against my pulse. "One day I'm going to put a ring on this finger with a diamond the size of the iceberg that sank the *Titanic.* It's going to be large enough to see from space. Even visitors from other galaxies will know you're mine."

I smile sleepily at him. "A simple band will do."

He kisses my temple. "Wait here. I'll get a towel."

When he lifts off me, a waft of uncomfortably cool air takes his place and I wish we were in his bedroom so that I could snuggle under the comforter. He returns quickly with a wet towel.

"Thank the gods for birth control." I used to think that pixies and leprechauns couldn't procreate. It sounds ridiculous now, especially since I learned that

Arden was Seven's, but in fae society, cross-species relationships are rare and it stands to reason that leprechauns who take pixies as lovers would use their luck to make sure a pregnancy doesn't occur. Pixies open to such a relationship are also usually on birth control. In any case, I'd never seen or heard of a leprechaun/pixie baby until Arden. Godmother has confirmed she's the first. Until Seven and I take our relationship public, we're not ready for a second.

He sighs. "I can use luck to stop you from getting pregnant if I remember. The problem is, deep down, I'd love to see you round with our baby. I hope we have five more of them."

"Five?" I ask, alarmed.

"Unless you'd prefer six?" He winks.

"Let's start with having a relationship we can tell the world about and then decide." I place a kiss along his jaw. "Hey, that was sex games, right? You weren't really angry with me for being late, were you? I did text."

He barks a laugh. "Sex games. I like that." He studies me for a beat, toying with the ends of my hair. "No, I wasn't upset with you, but I was anxious to see you."

"Obviously." I bob my eyebrows.

His eyes drift from mine, and he snags his shirt from the floor, wrapping it around my shoulders. I slide my arms in, and he starts buttoning it up. He's still naked, and my heart warms to know he's putting my comfort first.

"There is something I need to tell you."

I can tell by his voice it's serious. "What's going on?"

He takes me by the hand and leads me into the bedroom where he pulls on sweats and a T-shirt. "After you left, I went to see Godmother. She told me about your agreement and that you refused to bargain with her."

I scoff. "Oh, I bargained, just not magically. She promised not to ruin my reputation, and I promised to keep River in the safe house and solve Adam's murder."

"The thing about Godmother is she always has a plan B. She told me something, something I think you and I both suspected."

A heaviness gathers in my torso, and I brace myself.

"When you first arrived here, I suspected I was Arden's father, but Godmother told me not to tell you."

"I know. We've talked about this before."

His lips thin. "Until today, I didn't know for sure that I *couldn't* have told you even if I'd chosen to." My blood turns to ice. "When I bargained for you, Sophia, I was desperate. I didn't specify the terms specifically enough. I am bound to Godmother for life, and if she orders me to do something, I can't deny her. She hasn't used that power before, not until it came to Arden, and the scary part is, until she told me, I wasn't even aware that I didn't have a choice. I thought I simply desired to follow her wishes."

"But you did tell me eventually."

"She released me after we solved the murders even though she discouraged it."

I narrow my eyes. "Because she knew I'd find out anyway."

He nods.

"And now she's told you about this because she knows that she can use you to control me. She knows about us, Seven. We may have kept our relationship secret from the general public, but she made damn sure I knew she wasn't buying it for a second. She knows I love you and that all she has to do is command you away from me and I'll do anything she asks."

He tips his head back and closes his eyes. "Of course. That's exactly it and why she chose this moment to reveal it. She wants us both to know we're under her thumb."

My fingers toy with the coin around my neck, remembering how she'd looked at it. "We have to find a way to break her hold over you."

He snorts. "Breaking a fairy bargain without being released from it is nearly impossible. Breaking a bargain made with Godmother has never been done."

I fold my hands in front of my stomach. "Then we get her to release you."

He laughs and shakes his head. "She's not in the business of being forgiving."

"No, but maybe we can find something she wants and convince her to release you in exchange."

"If you figure out what it is that Godmother wants and doesn't have, you are a smarter fairy than I am."

I cross my arms. The chance that we will ever break Godmother's hold over Seven are close to nil. Even with all his luck and all his riches, he's not even close to as powerful as she is. Clever of her to trap him like she did, at a time when he'd been drained by his father and was at his most vulnerable. If she hadn't tricked him then, she never would have succeeded later. She knew what she was doing, and now he's her own lucky charm. *Bitch.*

"Sophia... I know you don't want to consider it, but it's dangerous for you to love me. As long as she's in control, you can't trust what I do. What if she commands me to do something really awful? What if she commands me to leave you and never return?" The weariness I saw on his face when I first arrived is back again. So it wasn't about me being late. It was about this... guilt over the consequences of his bargain with Godmother and the strong feeling that he was roping me into those consequences by loving me.

"Why would she do something like that?"

"Why does Godmother do anything?"

"Right now she needs me. I'm doing what she

wants, and someday we will find a way to convince her to break the bargain. Have faith in that."

He kisses me soundly. "I'll try."

Drawing a deep breath, I blow it out slowly. "Have you spent any time trying to decipher your father's riddle yet?"

He rubs his forehead. "No. And about that... it's going to have to wait a few days."

"Why?"

"That problem I mentioned with our supplier, it's bigger than I thought it was. I have to go to the US for a few days to meet with the CEO and see if we can come to an agreement."

My heart thumps heavier, missing him already. "No one else can go for you?"

He shakes his head. "This was one of the few vendor relationships my dad always handled himself. The CEO is old-school, likes the personal touch. It shouldn't take long. I'll go there for a few days, finish negotiating the new contract, seal the deal, and be back here before you know it."

I can't hide my disappointment, but I can't be unfair to him. His responsibilities have multiplied since his father was imprisoned. He has a company to run. I know Seven wouldn't do this if it wasn't absolutely necessary. "When do you leave?"

"First thing in the morning."

"On a Friday? You'll be there all weekend?"

"This can't wait."

"I'll miss you," I say. "And you'll miss your Saturday lesson with Arden."

He closes his eyes as if my words sting. "I'll text her. Tell her I'm sorry."

"She'll understand, Seven. You have important work to do. No one is blaming you."

"Thanks."

"Will you text me?"

"Of course."

"Will you send me dick pics?"

"Definitely. Does it have to be *my* dick?"

"Yours is the only one I want to see."

He pulls me against him. "Would you like an early-access preview?"

I wrap my arms around his neck and lean the full length of my body against him. "Definitely."

CHAPTER

ELEVEN

The next morning, I wake to the blare of my alarm and slap the machine with one lazy hand. I'm due at the casino in an hour to lead my regular class. Evangeline wants me to stop by her office beforehand to discuss something. It promises to be a full day. Only problem is, I can hardly keep my eyes open. Seven and I stayed up most of the night, making love and talking in between. It's becoming harder and harder for me to leave at a reasonable hour each night, and our late-night interludes leave me feeling like a zombie.

"Need coffee," I whisper, rolling myself off the bed and using my desk to hold myself up while my feet hit the floor. I drag my robe from the back of the chair and wrap it around me. Dressing will have to wait until my worship of the goddess caffeine is completed and her celestial gift of alertness is bestowed.

I'm halfway to the stairs when a sniffle from Arden's room interrupts my zombie trudge toward the kitchen. Backing up a few steps, I peek through the crack of Arden's partially closed door. She's still in bed, but her hands are covering her face. It looks like... she's weeping. Although she's trying her best to remain silent, her chest and shoulders shudder with her muffled sobs.

I push the door open. "Arden?"

She wipes her face with her hands and then tries to hide beneath the covers. "Mom, I'm sleeping. What do you want?"

I cross to her bed and sit beside her, rubbing her shoulder. "I want to know why you're crying, and if there's anything I can do to make it better."

The blanket slides from her features and she blinks wet green eyes at me, the same shade of emerald as her father's. All those years I thought her father was human and that those green eyes had come from some ancestor on his side when the truth of her lineage was right in front of me.

My heart gives a painful squeeze. "I think I know what this is about, Arden. Nothing you say to me will ever make me love you any less. Whatever you decide about your future, I have your back." I stroke her hair from her face. "Is this about you deciding you want to leave Devashire? It's okay if you do. You've known what you wanted to do your whole life. You can still follow your dreams. I would never hold you back." I can feel myself start to ramble, but I can't stop. "We'll still see each other. We'll FaceTime and you'll come here to visit—"

"Mom, stop!" Slowly she draws back the blanket and reveals her left wrist. My breath catches in my throat. A crisp Yule ball red ribbon is tied there. I flash back to the day Seven tied a similar ribbon around my wrist. That ribbon has meaning here. A boy had to rent a sleigh for the Yule parade to get it, and he had to choose her to be his date. Choosing this early in the year is a serious commitment.

"Arden, where did you get that?"

She chews her lip. "His name is Edmund. Mom, he's a leprechaun, and he asked me to the Yule ball."

"The Yule ball is in December. It's June. Will you even be here in December? Are you planning to come back for the event?" My skin feels too tight, and my gut is telling me the other shoe is yet to drop.

Her eyes never leave mine, but a stack of books on her desk falls over and the pen that rested on the top rolls across the floor and stops near the bed. She reaches down and swipes it from the floor.

"You did that?" I look at her with pure awe.

She nods. "I have luck, and I can use it. Edmund has been helping me practice some of the same things Seven is teaching me. We were friends before, but we've grown close the past few weeks. He asked me to the ball yesterday."

Suddenly uneasy, I shift and hold up a hand.

GENEVIEVE JACK

"Wait. Did you tell him what you are, honey?" My voice sounds high and tight. Leprechauns do not normally ask human hybrids to the ball. Seven and I were the exception, and that was a disaster. But we'd known each other since childhood. Seven and I have spent so much time and effort protecting Arden's secret. What if she hasn't protected it herself?

"He doesn't know who my father is," Arden says. "He doesn't even know I'm part leprechaun. All he knows is that I just discovered I have luck. I'm sure he assumes it came from you. My teachers did."

"Your teachers know?"

"Before I graduated, I used it in class with the other kids. Anyway, I'm going to need all the luck I can muster if I'm to have any chance of getting into Elderflame University." She hands me the pen, and I stare at the Elderflame logo on the side. "I've already talked to an admissions councilor."

My mouth works like a fish's. "It... it sounds like you've made up your mind already. Are you sure about this? You're not just doing this for some boy, are you?"

She snorts incredulously. "No. Mom, please. I'd never."

"It just seems... sudden."

She shakes her head. "Not really. I was already considering staying before I knew about Seven."

My eyes narrow. "What? Why?"

She pushes herself up in bed and rests her back

142

against the wall. "You don't get it, do you?" She wipes under her eyes. "This is why I was worried about telling you. You hate it here and you think I should too."

"That's not true! I just want you to know you have options."

"But I don't. Not really!" She spreads her hands, her tears coming faster.

I shake my head. "Has something happened?" All my organs clench, and a desperate whisper in my head says, *Please don't be pregnant.*

She tips her head and looks at me. "Yes, something happened. I found out that I have a family. I have a father I hardly know and I desperately want to change that. I have a mother and grandparents and even a great-grandmother. I have a home. And the best part is that I belong here because I am fae. I know you wanted me to be a doctor in the human world—"

"You wanted that. You've wanted that since you were twelve—"

"I'm not twelve anymore!" She scoffs. "I don't want to go back to pretending. I don't miss it. I want to be part of a family. I want to be surrounded by people who know exactly who and what I am and love me anyway. I don't want to worry about disguises or identities ever again. I'm fae. That's what I am. And here, people will love me for it. I'll have you and Grandma and Grandpa and Great-Grandma and all my new friends at school. And I'll have Seven." A wistful smile lights up her features. "I have roots. Do you have any idea how good that feels? How loved I feel here?"

"But what about your friends in Nevada? What about Jayden?"

She sighs. "We were already going our separate ways. She got into a college on the West Coast. We'd likely never see each other anyway."

Everything about her—the bright clarity in her eyes, the square of her shoulders, the way she leans slightly toward me—tells me she genuinely believes every word of what she said to me. Arden wants to remain in Dragonfly. My heart does a little leap. "You want to stay."

"I do." She laughs.

"So why were you crying?"

"Honestly?"

I nod.

"I was afraid how you would react to this. I was afraid you'd be angry." She plays with the ribbon on her wrist.

"Why?"

She looks away as she admits, "I know what happened between you and Seven, Mom. The Yule ball? I know it probably bothers you that I'm going with a leprechaun. It must be hard enough for you, being forced to spend all this time with Seven after what he did to you. This is what I want, but I am truly sorry if it makes you unhappy."

I shake my head vigorously. "No, Arden. Things between Seven and me are better now. We're... friends. Really, really good friends." Our eyes meet, and I see the moment she suspects there may be something more. "I'm not unhappy at all. Just surprised. In fact, if this is your choice, I'm ecstatic."

"Mom, is something going on between you and Seven?"

My cheeks feel hot. I made a vow when Arden was a baby to always try to tell her the truth. I want her to trust me, and that means I want to be a good source of information for her. And I can tell by her face she knows. "It's supposed to be a secret."

A long gasp fills the room. "I thought I sensed something between you, but I thought I must be seeing things. Before, when we first came here, you seemed to hate him."

"I was wrong. About many things. I love him, but we want to wait to reveal our relationship until the right time."

"The Gilded Gala!" she says excitedly. "Seven can announce you as his girlfriend at the same time he announces me as his daughter."

I smile sheepishly. "If that's what you want. I don't want to steal your thunder."

"You wouldn't be stealing anything from me. Just making more thunder."

"So when do I get to meet this Edmund?" I ask. "Do I know his parents? Please tell me they don't own

Grandma and Grandpa's store or something. That would be awkward."

"No!" She rolls her eyes. "His dad died when he was younger, so it's just his mom, and she works with her parents at some car place. I wasn't really listening." Maybe his family are drivers like Saul or work at the dealership selling cars. Grandma knows all the leprechaun families, but I don't. "Anyway, he wants to meet you too. I was thinking of inviting him to dinner."

"That sounds like an excellent idea."

She lets out a deep breath. "I'm relieved you're taking this so well. I thought you were going to explode. You've been talking about my leaving since I got here."

"Only because I thought it's what you wanted." I can feel tears pricking my eyes as it all settles in. When Seven gets back, we can talk about going public. We can move forward as a family. My lips twitch into a smile. "I'm glad you're staying, Arden. The only thing I care about is that you're sure, because there's no going back on this one."

She looks me straight in the eye. "I'm sure."

I hold out my arms, and she dives into them. "Then welcome home, sweet girl."

I can't wait to tell Seven about Arden's revelation, but I'm running so late by the time I leave her room that I barely have enough time to get dressed and make it to After Dark. Saul is with Seven, acting as his personal security while he's in the States, which means I'll need to take the character shuttle. Everything feels like I'm moving through quicksand. Plus, after my talk with Arden this morning, I've added a layer of emotional exhaustion to my already-painful physical fatigue.

When I reach the circle in front of Wonderland, there's a man I've never met before standing in front of Seven's black Mercedes. He's holding a sign with my name on it.

"I'm Sophia Larkspur."

The man holds his hand out. "Jericho. I'm a driver for Lucky Enterprises. Mr. Delaney sent me in place of Saul."

"Oh! I didn't know you were coming."

Jericho smiles. "I got the call around two a.m. Mr. Delaney was concerned about the shuttle's reliability. He said the class you're teaching is essential to the casino's operating plans this year and he didn't want to leave it to chance."

How sweet. "Who am I to argue with Mr. Delaney?"

Jericho opens the door for me, and I slide into the back. Once he's behind the wheel, he turns in his seat. "Mr. Delaney also gave me strict instructions to deliver to you the following." He hands me a venti Starbucks cup, and my heart pounds with gratitude. "One fairy-spice latte, oat milk, no whip."

"Oh, thank you, the gods, and all that is good in the world."

Jericho laughs. "It's from Mr. Delaney. I can't take the credit. And I'm not done. One slice of River's famous quiche lorraine." He hands me a compostable cardboard box that smells of bacon and eggs, and I practically swoon. I take it along with the fork he hands me.

"I'm speechless. This is possibly the nicest thing anyone has ever done for me," I murmur. I sip the coffee and moan.

Jericho stifles a laugh. "One more thing." He hands me a sealed red envelope. "I don't know what's in this, but he handpicked it very early this morning. Almost made him late for his flight."

I tear into the envelope and pull out a card with bunnies on the front. Two extra-strength Tylenol slide from between the folded halves. I pop them in my mouth and chase them down with a swig of the sweet elixir of life, coffee.

Inside, the card reads: No BUNNY LOVES YOU MORE THAN ME. On the opposite side is a personal note from Seven.

Sophia, Sorry to keep you up so late. I think we put Devashire's rabbits to shame. I hope the coffee and break-

fast help you get through the day. Get some rest. I expect to make up for lost time when I get home. Love, Seven.

A deep contentment passes through me as I close the card and slide it into my bag. I am possibly the luckiest pixie on earth. And soon we'll be a real family. I know it won't be easy for us. People here have their prejudices, and I don't expect anything will change just because of Seven's position, but after my talk with Arden this morning, I'm convinced this will work. We'll be okay as long as we stay together.

I snatch my phone from my bag and shoot him a text.

> Thanks for breakfast and for the bunnies. I can't wait for you to make good on your promise. Talk soon? I have news about Arden.

Once I press Send, I dig into my quiche in earnest. It's delicious. I'm glad to see that the management and staff of River's is carrying on well in his absence. I've licked the last crumb and polished off the coffee by the time Jericho parks and helps me out of the back seat. He reaches for the box and cup in my hands.

"Oh, I'll take care of these," I say.

"It's no bother, Ms. Larkspur."

"You're right, it isn't," I say with a laugh. "You have enough to do. And please call me Sophia."

He nods. "Have a good day, Sophia."

I stride toward the entrance, recycling the remains of my breakfast gift on the way in, and check my phone for the fiftieth time. My text has been delivered but not read. He must still be in the air. I should have asked exactly where in the US he was heading. I was too eager to say goodbye in every physical way I could think of.

I make it to Dragonfly Casino just in time to slide into Evangeline's office with a half hour to spare before my class. To my surprise, she looks as rumpled as I felt before Seven's gift. Her usual flawless appearance is gone, replaced by makeup that looks rushed and a messy bun. Her face is splotchy too, like maybe she's been crying. I'm filled with concern at the sight of her. Leprechauns rarely get flustered. Something must be terribly wrong.

"Are you okay?" I ask. "Is this a bad time?"

Eva blinks rapidly, as if just realizing I'm here and wipes under her eyes. "Ah, that obvious." Her shoulders sag. For several long moments she stares at me as if trying to decide what to say. "This... *murder* has really gotten to me. I'm not sleeping well." When she says the word *murder*, it comes out like she can hardly force her lips to make the word. As if she still can't believe it's true. "I thought when they caught my father doing what he did, this would be over."

Odd. Adam Barker's murder happened almost a week ago. Working in public relations might mean she's exceptionally hard hit by the event, but I've never seen her this shaken about anything before, not even her father's arrest.

"It's terrifying that something like that could happen here, but Seven is a genius when it comes to security. We're working with Godmother, and we are going to make sure it never happens again." This is one of those times when I'm happy to know how to bluff. I have no idea if what I'm saying is true or not. I hope it is. But if there's one thing I've learned since I've returned to Dragonfly Hollow, it's to expect the unexpected.

She closes her eyes and gives her head a slow shake. "To think that the killer is still out there some-where... It's chilling."

I stop, my morning brain grinding on that thought. "You don't believe River is the killer?"

Her lashes flutter and she inhales deeply, collecting herself. "Do you? He hardly seems the type. I know he was over the body and everything, but what motivation could he have for killing that man? He counts on humans for his business."

"I don't believe he did it either. I guess that's why Godmother assigned me to help investigate what happened."

She sighs. "I'm glad you're on this, Sophia. I trust you. You'll sort it out."

"I'm not a trained investigator. I've never shot a gun or served in a security capacity. Even what went down with your dad wasn't completely my doing. I'm not qualified for this really, but Seven and his team are, and I'll do what I can to help."

She leans back, her mouth a straight slash. "You are exactly qualified for this," she says. "You've always underestimated yourself, even when we were children. You have an uncanny ability to read people. You may not be a detective, but you can see right through a lie like no one I've ever met. What is solving a crime anyway but deconstructing the lies around it?"

Great. Eva is the third person to nudge at the idea that my ability to lie and to smell a lie are my superpowers. I don't want to be known as a liar, not anymore. I thought I'd escaped all that when I came back here. Especially now, with Arden deciding to stay in Dragonfly and the life I've always wanted so close I can taste it, all I want is to be seen. I want my life to be genuine.

I glance at my watch. It's almost time for my class to start. "Speaking of bluffing, what was it you wanted to talk to me about?"

She rubs her eye. "This actually. Have any of your students asked about what happened last weekend?"

I shake my head. "None. I'm pretty sure the humans see it as an isolated incident. Honestly, when I was living in America, shootings happened every day. Comparatively, Dragonfly Hollow is incredibly safe, and Godmother did a great job spinning it as a personal squabble between River and the victim even though we both know that's not true."

She frowns, her gaze drifting. "Let me know if it becomes an issue. I can give you talking points."

"Okay," I say, slightly confused as to why this warranted a personal meeting.

She gives me a dismissive smile. "Thanks for stopping in."

TWELVE

"Mr. Tannenbaum, you had a question?" I brace myself. He hasn't won a hand yet, and none of my lessons seem to be sinking in. He's playing the same way he did on day one.

The elderly man scratches his ear. "You keep telling us to assign a range to each of our opponent's hands, but how is guessing what cards they have helpful? How should we know what they're holding?"

"It's true that unless you're psychic, you don't know for sure what cards are in your opponent's hand until you see them, but you can assume a range based on what's in your hand and what's on the table. There are only four aces in a deck. If two are in your hand and two are on the table, how many does Marjory have?"

"None. But that kind of thing doesn't happen very often," he grumbles.

"No, it doesn't. But keep an eye on your opponent's behavior and you'll have another clue. Do they glance at their chips? Are their fingers trembling? Did the corner of their mouth twitch when they first looked at their cards? Every player has their tell, you just have to learn to watch for it."

He leans back in his chair and narrows his eyes on his wife. "What's in your hand, Janice?"

She laughs. "You can find out at the end of the game or if you pry these two cards from my cold, dead body."

A chill runs through me at the turn of phrase, and Adam Barker's last moments flash through my mind. Adam guarded that rock with his fist until it rolled from his cold, dead body. I wonder if it's still there. Did anyone but River notice it? Why would they?

I'm relieved when class is over. I promised River I'd check on his cat, Jinx. Apparently he's an indoor/outdoor beasty, and River was certain he could fend for himself, but he asked me to change the litter and refill his food and water. Now that I know the creature exists, I plan to stop in every other day and make sure he's okay.

His cottage is just past his restaurant, and the only way to get there is through a winding, wooded trail. I've never been there before, but I find it easily enough. Wind chimes strung from the porch ceiling play a tune welcoming my arrival. Nestled within a grove of oak trees, the yard is a collection of clover and wild violets.

The home itself is stone with a chimney running up the south side and a dark purple door with a moon-shaped window.

Before I left him, River mentioned a key in the mouth of a toad near the front porch. I find the statue readily enough and stick my fingers into its laughing mouth. They hook on a key ring, and soon I'm inside.

Cozy. The main room has a fireplace, a plush sofa, and two recliners. A suspiciously misshapen knitted blanket on the back looks vaguely familiar, and I wonder if it was a gift from my grandmother. A driftwood coffee table is weighed down by stacks of books. There's no TV, but there's a four-foot-long fish mounted to the wall where one might go.

A galley kitchen runs along the back of the place. I find two empty bowls there and fill them with water and kibble from a full bin right beside them. I haven't even stood up yet when Jinx appears in the open window behind me, his black fur shining in the sun. He leaps to my side and weaves between my ankles, his purr filling the room as I scratch his back and behind his ears.

The cat's belly is round and his eyes bright. "River wasn't exaggerating. You seem to do just fine on your own."

He meows and arches his back into my hand.

I stand and leave him to his meal, making my way to the bedroom on the north side of the cottage and the bathroom off it where the litter box is supposed to reside. I pause when I see River's bed. It's unmade and there are three wineglasses on the bedside table. River, Patrick, and the mysterious third were here, together, right before his world fell apart. I narrow my eyes on a smudge of red on one of the glasses. Picking it up by the stem, I inspect the perfect bow-shaped print.

Lipstick. So the third is a woman. Good to know. If I can find her, I might be able to coax more information out of her about that day.

I take care of Jinx's box, which is remarkably clean considering how long River's been gone. The cat's likely been doing his business outside. I tie off the bag and head for the door to throw it away in the garbage can on the side of the house.

When I return to the cottage, I notice a coat stand that I walked right by my first time inside, tucked behind the door. A long purple trench catches my eye. A woman's coat. I close the door to get a better look.

The fabric is high quality, a European brand with complicated stitching at the cuffs. But it's the buttons that draw my eye, unusual in their craftsmanship. I turn one over to find VS carved into the back and drop the coat like it's on fire. VS is Valentine Sullivan, a satyr who designs custom accessories for the elite of Devashire. Elite meaning leprechauns—they're the only ones who can afford them at hundreds of dollars a pop.

River wasn't just with a woman. He was with a leprechaun woman. Holy shit! No wonder she required that bargain. If anyone found out a leprechaun was carrying on a sexual relationship with two satyrs, it would be a scandal. A male leprechaun with a female pixie would spark a certain level of social outrage— Seven and I are prepared for that. But a female leprechaun with two male satyrs? The fairy world would go up in flames. Devashire would be shooketh. All other gossip would pale in comparison. And if she was a married leprechaun? Why, the *Daily Hatter* might not report on anything else for the rest of the year.

But who? I check the size. Small. A younger leprechaun then. Luck filled the older ones out over time, giving them powerful curves. I'd have to ask Seven who the most likely candidates were next time I talk to him. I check my phone again, but he still hasn't texted me back. Must be busy.

My mind grinds on the question as I lock up the cottage and then head back toward the restaurant. So a female leprechaun met with River to talk about the night before outside his restaurant. I pause on the pathway behind the tavern. It was here, or around here. River said he couldn't see where the man was murdered, only heard him scream. But this wasn't an overly private place. If the wrong person passed by in front of the restaurant, they might see the two lovers together.

A sudden thought causes my breath to hitch. What if River's lover used her luck to cause the area to empty? If she was the reason for the lack of witnesses, the murderer might not be a leprechaun at all. It could be anyone.

I grit my teeth as I put together the implications. It actually makes sense. The person who messed with the security videos didn't edit out the empty sidewalks because they weren't responsible for them. Which means our search for a leprechaun murderer is way off base. It's someone else, someone who was after Adam Barker.

I round the corner of River's Tavern and revisit the spot where Adam was murdered. Unlike that day, the sidewalk is packed with people coming and going from the restaurant. Concentrating hard, I let my luck bubble in my blood, a tiger that rises at my side. I focus it on one thing, the single clue that River shared with me and the thing that made my blood run cold when I thought of it during my poker lesson.

Why was Adam Barker so protective of the rock he was holding in his hand?

Pouring on the luck, I inspect the cobblestone side-walk, looking for the gray rock River described. My luck tiger sniffs along the pavers. The man held it firmly until the moment of his death. No one would do that unless they were desperate to keep it a secret. *Why* did he want to keep it a secret?

I spiral out from the area where the murder took place, searching and feeding my luck until my head starts to throb. And then there it is, tucked between a strip of lawn and the cobblestone. River is right—it does look like an ordinary stone, only I know this is what I'm looking for because there're no other stones like this here. The wall is cedar. The grass is thick and green. The cobblestones are red granite, and this rock is different. It's gray, yes, and veined with silver, but unlike any other material in the vicinity. I reach down and pick it up, surprised at the weight of it considering its size.

"Why was he hiding you?" I whisper.

"Sophia?"

I look up to find Penelope staring at me with a funny look on her face. I smile and slide the rock into my pocket. "Hey, Pen! What's up?"

She laughs. "I think I should be asking you the same thing. You were staring at that strip of grass like you might be ill. Did you eat something bad?"

I shake my head, casting a wide smile in her direction. "No." I lower my voice. "Just taking one more look. I'm helping Godmother again."

"You mean to solve the murder?" she whispers, making a face. "Godmother roped you into working with Seven again! Gods, I thought you were done with that."

"I was, but I volunteered myself to help River. We all know he's innocent."

"Yeah, but isn't it hard for you to work with Seven after everything?"

The look of concern on my friend's face is enough

to make a ball of iron form in my chest. I can't do this anymore. I can't lie to her, not about this, not now, not when her friendship has become so important to me.

"I like working with Seven," I mumble. "I like... Seven."

"What?" She's looking at me as if she can't quite hear me.

"In fact, I love him, Pen," I say a bit louder. "And he loves me."

"But... he was cruel to you." All the muscles around her mouth tighten and she scowls.

"No. That was his father, not him."

She shakes her head. "It can't go anywhere, Sophia. He's one of *them*."

I nod. "A leprechaun, yes. It doesn't matter to me at all. It never did."

Maybe this was a mistake. Penelope glares at me like an alien's tentacles are flailing from my mouth. I don't even think she's breathing.

"Say something, Pen."

"How long has this been going on?" she blurts.

"Since right after the hospital."

"Six weeks?" she rasps. "You kept this a secret all that time?"

"I'm sorry. I was afraid of how you might react. And I wanted to be sure. We're keeping it quiet for now. No one else knows."

"I'm the first to know?" She points at her chest, and I see pride flicker across her blue eyes.

Technically she's not the first. River and Arden know, and it occurs to me I haven't done a very good job keeping this secret recently. But then what does it matter? It's not going to be secret for long.

She blinks three times and then grabs me and pulls me against her chest in a relentless hug. A deep breath slowly escapes her lips. "I'm happy for you, Sophia. Truly... *And* I hope you know what you're doing."

A tiny spark of elation ignites inside me. She knows. My best friend knows. And she's accepted it. Accepted us. I hug her back. "You know, I think I finally do."

THIRTEEN

By Saturday afternoon, Seven still hasn't responded to my texts, and I'm beginning to worry. Worse, Eva hasn't heard from him either. I talk to her after my last session of the day, and she reassures me that it's probably nothing to worry about.

"Our cell carrier occasionally has problems with roaming outside Devashire's borders. We're supposed to have coverage, but sometimes the calls don't go through. I'll have my assistant call his hotel and make sure everything's okay."

"Thanks, Eva."

I haven't slept well since he left. Part of it is that I desperately need to talk to him about what I found at River's. A bigger part has everything to do with our past. For over a decade, I thought Seven abandoned me at the Yule ball, intentionally not showing up and humiliating me. Although I now know that isn't true, my body remembers that grief. The memory resides somewhere in my cells, lurking in the deepest portion of my subconscious. And although I know Seven hasn't abandoned me this time, my unconscious mind keeps telling me he has. Tension in my shoulder muscles leaves my neck and back sore, and I catch myself gritting my teeth.

Checking my phone for the thousandth time, I barely look up as I walk through the door of my family's house and almost run smack into Grandma.

"Finally!" Her bony fingers wrap around my shoulders and squeeze. As fabulous as ever in a tea-length ice-blue ball gown, she's wearing her silver hair twisted up the back of her head today. She looks at me over navy-blue specs. "I thought you'd never get home! Have you heard?"

"I didn't know you were coming over tonight. How are things in Sunnyville?" Grandma lives in a beautiful home in a retirement community outside the park. Still, since I returned to Dragonfly Hollow, she's been here more than she hasn't. I'm pretty sure that if my parents invited her, she'd move in in a heartbeat.

"Boring and irrelevant." She shakes me by the shoulders in a surprisingly strong grip for a fairy of her advanced years. "This is big, Sophia."

I narrow my eyes. "Is this about the murder?"

"Pishposh!" She waves a hand as if something smells. "That happened ages ago, Sophia. Live in the now! No, this is about—"

"Thank the gods you're here!" My mother runs into the room and grabs my hand. "I need your help in the dining room."

"Okay." I'm utterly confused. We normally eat in the breakfast nook.

Once we reach the dining room, I'm even more confused. The table is decked out. My family doesn't have a lot of money, but my great-grandmother on my father's side, gods rest her soul, left us some silver and fine bone china. Normally we keep the place settings packed away in storage, but Mom has pulled them all out and polished everything to a high shine. Gold chargers are topped with navy-blue-patterned plates with a gold edge. The shiny silver candelabra are draped with multicolored crystals that reflect the swag of flowers and greenery arranged on the table runner. She's done an expert job. It looks like a scene off the cover of a Pottery Barn catalog. "What's going on?

"I've been trying to tell you," Grandma says. "Arden's new boyfriend is coming to dinner, and he's a *leprechaun*!" Grandma's fingers fly to her mouth, and she inhales sharply.

I laugh. "I know she's dating a leprechaun, Grandma, I just didn't know he was coming for dinner tonight."

Her eyes grow to the size of saucers. "You knew about this?"

"I saw the ribbon on her wrist this morning and she told me."

"Stars and lightning, I'm always the last to know these things."

I scoff incredulously. "What are you talking about? You're always the first to know everything. You know exactly when ninety percent of the people in this town are due to go to the grocery store for milk."

"It's a very regular occurrence, Sophia, if you pay attention." She smiles broadly.

"I've made Cornish hen. Do you think that's fancy enough, Sophia? You work with leprechauns. Do the Delaneys eat Cornish hen?" Mom worries her hands and chews her lip.

My laugh is high, sharp, and completely beyond my control. "At least once a week, Seven eats a burger from that cart off Main Street that always smells like muskrat. And he gets it with imported government cheese."

"What's government cheese?" Grandma wrinkles her nose.

"It's this cheap processed cheese from the United States. Sometimes it comes in individually plastic-wrapped slices. It also melts like plastic and has a slight chemical aftertaste. I think it's awful. He loves it. It's not exactly gourmet."

Mom smooths her hair. "I just want to make a good impression."

I pull her against me and kiss her temple. "You will. This is gorgeous, and dinner smells amazing. Besides, Arden would never like a boy who would turn up his nose at anything you put in front of him."

Grandma grips the back of the chair. "Well, I for one am going to position myself in the living room where I have a good view of the door. I want to be the first to see who it is."

"She didn't tell you?" I can't believe Grandma doesn't know the name and family history of this boy by now.

"No! To be fair, I asked her not to. I want to be surprised." Grandma's eyebrows bob, and she takes off toward the family room at a bit of a skip.

My mom squeezes my hand. "She lives for this kind of thing."

I giggle. "Yes, she does. Gods bless me with something to be as excited about as Grandma is with gossip."

We both laugh.

"Are you okay with this, darling?" Mom asks. "After everything that happened to you, it wouldn't be wrong for you to feel some trepidation—"

"I'm fine, Mom. Arden has a good head on her shoulders." She also has a lot more luck than my mother knows about. I wish I could tell them about what Arden is and that her father is actually Seven, but he would want to be here for that conversation and the one where we reveal that we're together again. I may have let the truth slip about our relationship to Penelope, but Seven would want to be part of telling my family about us and Arden. It can wait until he gets back.

"Good." She tugs at my wrist. "Then come help me in the kitchen."

An hour later, the hens have been baked to golden-brown perfection, Arden is wearing a gorgeous green dress that would be at home on either a pixie or a leprechaun, and we're all trying not to stare at the door as the clock clicks past six p.m., the time Arden told him to come.

At 6:05 I have to go into the kitchen and pour myself a glass of wine. If this kid stands Arden up, I will personally go medieval on his ass. I will sit on him and pluck his damn nose hair out one by—

The doorbell rings. I raise my head and set my drink down. Arden's welcoming voice fills my ears as she introduces Mom and Grandma. I turn the corner and see her new boyfriend for the very first time.

"Mom, come meet Edmund!"

I approach, my smile widening in what I hope is a welcoming way that conceals the nasty thoughts I was thinking about him only moments ago. "I'm so glad you could join us. I've heard so much about you."

"Likewise." Edmund radiates politeness. "It's good to finally meet you."

I can picture the pupils of Arden's eyes changing from circular to heart-shaped in my imagination; she looks at him with such devotion. It's easy to under-stand why she's smitten. Edmund has that inky, dark black hair that takes on blue highlights in the right light. His eyes are an intense royal blue that matches the shirt he's wearing, a fashionable thing with a logo on the pocket I don't recognize. His jeans hang on his tall, athletic form as if they were tailored just for him.

"Come back to the dining room, and I'll get us all something to drink," my mother says.

Arden takes Edmund's hand and leads him toward the table while Grandma and I fall in behind them.

"He's a looker, Sophia," Grandma whispers.

"As long as Arden thinks so." I shrug.

"And a strong name. Edmund is a family name you don't hear too much anymore. What's his last name?"

"You should ask him," I whisper. I want to get this kid talking, and who better to loosen his lips than my adorable grandmother?

I arch an eyebrow when Edmund pulls out Arden's chair for her. *Two points*, Grandma mouths.

My father chooses that moment to reveal himself, and I wonder where he's been all this time. Introductions are made, and we all sit down as my mother fills the water goblets and then brings out a tray of brown-sugar-roasted chestnuts wrapped in bacon. Dad pops one of the hors d'oeuvres into his mouth.

"Matthias!" My mother slaps his hand and glares at him, but he just chews obstinately. "I'm sorry, Edmund. We usually have better manners around here."

"I'm glad you told me, or I might have done the

same," he says, then charmingly spoons a few onto his plate before tossing one between his teeth. "Delicious."

"Thank you, Edmund." My mother preens.

"Ms. Larkspur," Edmund says suddenly, and I realize after a few seconds that he's addressing me.

"Oh, you mean me. The only one I think of as Ms. Larkspur is my mother, although I suppose she's a Mrs." I laugh awkwardly, then sit up straighter. "Yes, Edmund, you have my full attention."

Arden curls her lip in a silent plea for me to be more normal. I try my best.

"Arden tells me you're working at the casino. My family is terribly curious. Can you talk about it? Or has the Delaney family sworn you to secrecy?"

I stymie my surprise at his immediate interest in what I do and answer honestly. "No, I can talk about it. I'm teaching poker classes to humans. It's the first time they've tried anything like this, but so far it's extremely successful. All my classes are full."

"If you don't mind my asking, how did you learn?"

The truth is that Seven taught me, but telling Edmund that would reveal far too much. For one, I'd be admitting to a crime back then and also letting on to a romantic connection between Seven and me. That's no one else's business but my own and could possibly cause more trouble in the wrong hands. Sadly, my newfound flirtation with honesty must be short-lived.

"Self-taught." Not a complete lie. Is there any knowledge we attain that isn't in some way acquired through our own devices? "I developed my skills when I was living in America," I add through a shallow smile, also not a lie. "Although I don't recommend that route. Much safer and closer to family to learn here if you can find someone to teach you."

"Exciting though. It's an incredible opportunity..."

Our eyes meet over the table as he trails off, and I get the distinct impression he was about to add "for a pixie." While I admire him for cutting himself off before he said it, I'm fairly sure he thought it, and my impression of him falls a few rungs. Or maybe I'm putting words in his head. I tell myself to give the boy the benefit of the doubt and snag a bacon-wrapped chestnut from the tray, filling my mouth with it before I can say something I might regret.

Grandma chooses that moment to swoop in and take over the conversation. She smiles sweetly. "Edmund, I didn't catch your last name."

"Faust," Arden answers for him, her fingers threading into his.

Grandma's eyes widen and I lean my chin against my fist, wondering what's going on in that pretty gray head of hers. "You're Alicia and Gregory's son?"

Edmund nods. "Yes... but my father died when I was two. It's just my mother and me now."

Grandmother smooths the cloth napkin in her lap. "Of course. Please forgive an old lady. I think I remember your father, you see, as well as your mother's parents, Vivian and Felix *Armon*, right?"

"Armon?" my father chimes in. "Your family owns Armon Trucking?"

I straighten and dart a glance between Edmund and Grandma. Arden had said his family did something with cars. I'd thought maybe his father was a driver like Saul or owned the Elderflame dealership. Never did I guess Arden was dating an heir to an empire! Armon Trucking is *the* commercial transportation company in Devashire. We have an airport, but all the planes and helicopters in it are privately owned. Trains exist in Dragonfly Hollow to take humans from place to place within the theme park, but because most of our population outside the parks is concentrated in and around Elderflame, there's no need for train service there. Which leaves shuttles and buses to transport people, and trucks to transport goods inside and outside Devashire. The Armons own and run all of it. Every apple, every vehicle, every bolt of fabric in Devashire, with rare exception, has traveled at some point on or in an Armon vehicle.

Edmund takes a drink of water, his lips curling in a proud smile. "Yes, they do. My mother runs it now. Grandma and Grandpa retired some years ago, leaving everything to her."

The table turns strangely silent for a beat, probably just a second or two, but it feels longer. I narrow my eyes on Grandma, who is suspiciously eating a chestnut with tiny bites and lots of chewing like she's trying to keep her mouth busy. She does not look at me.

A niggle starts in my gut. Something bothers me about Edmund. I'm not sure if it's just a prejudice against rich people leaking into my opinion of him now that I know just how wealthy he is or if it's something else, but there's something familiar about him. Something I want to protect Arden from, although I can't put my finger on it.

"Did you play any sports at Bailiwick's?" I ask cheerfully, filling the silence.

"Bowbin. I was a right wing."

My father claps his hands. "It's been ages since I watched the Bailiwick's Basilisks play. I'm sorry I missed this year."

Arden shakes her head. "Wait, I never knew this about you. What's bowbin?"

I try to explain it in human terms she'd be familiar with. "It's like a cross between football, dodgeball, and archery. Instead of a football, the marksman, who is like the quarterback, throws a bright red mark at a player on the opposing team."

"What kind of mark?"

"Like a bright red burr that sticks to their clothing. The marked player then runs for the end zone while the right and left wingmen on the offensive team try to shoot him down with bows and arrows. If he's hit, he leaves the game. The winning team is the one with the most points when the last remaining player of one team or the other is removed from play."

Arden gapes at Edmund in disbelief. "Like real bows and arrows?"

He grins. "The heads are flat. When you're hit, you might suffer a bruise but more likely a bruised ego."

My father laughs. "We'll have to go this fall," he says to Arden, then seems to catch himself and looks toward me with a grimace. He doesn't know she's staying.

"I think that's an excellent idea, Dad." I say softly.

Mom chooses that moment to come in with a giant tray of roast Cornish hens, miniature red potatoes, and honey-glazed carrots. I pop out of my chair to help her serve.

Mom takes a seat next to my father, and I watch her practically hold her breath as Edmund takes his first bite.

"Exquisite, Mrs. Larkspur."

"Oh, thank you, Edmund," she says.

I muffle a frown. What kind of brownnosing teenager uses the word *exquisite*? He's too smooth. Edmund doesn't act like a kid trying to impress his girlfriend's parents. He acts like a boy who is well practiced in the art of making others see in him exactly what he wants them to see.

Beside him, Arden eats her dinner with her left hand while she continues to grip his fingers with her right. *Fuck.* She's never had a crush like this before. I fork a bit of hen into my mouth—*Mmm. Delicious.*—while my mother asks Edmund about his postgraduation plans.

"Business," he says without missing a beat. "I plan to work for the family business—follow in my mother's footsteps as they say."

"I haven't met many young people who know what they want to do at your age," I say to him.

He frowns. "There aren't many Fausts, I suppose. I think it's different being a leprechaun. There are expectations."

I don't hear the snobbery in his tone as much as I feel it. Gods, I wish Seven were here. I bet he'd know a lot about the Fausts.

It's just after seven thirty when Arden and Edmund stand up from empty plates.

"Thanks, Grandma," Arden says. "We have to go."

Edmund offers a practiced but charming smile. "We have tickets for Wonderland Theater."

"Oh? What are they putting on?" Mom asks.

"*A Midsummer Night's Dream.*"

"You've never seen that one until you see it put on with actual pixies and a satyr as Puck," I say, excited for Arden to have this experience despite my reservations about Edmund.

"I'm looking forward to it." Arden moves to collect her and Edmund's dirty plates, but I wave her off.

"Never mind that. I'll clear."

I walk them to the door and watch Arden stride

toward the center of town on Edmund's arm. I close the door behind them with a sigh.

When I turn back around, Grandma is right behind me, so close her nose is almost touching mine. "Fucking gods!" I jump, my fist going to my chest.

"Sorry," she whispers. "I didn't mean to scare you, but there's something you need to know."

"What?" I'd noticed how quiet she'd gotten at dinner. She knows something.

She looks over her shoulder, but the hallway is clear. My parents are still in the dining room. "That boy is Alicia Faust's son." She widens her eyes as if that should alarm me.

"I gathered that. I know he's rich, but—"

She grabs my arm and squeezes. "Sophia, Alicia Faust is the one you saw Seven talking to at graduation. Alicia was once *engaged* to Seven Delaney."

CHAPTER

FOURTEEN

I blink at Grandma like a cursor on a computer that's trying to process its last command. I try to say no! and what now? at the same time, and somehow it comes out "Snow, what?"

Grandma gets my meaning. "The dark-haired woman I pointed out to you at graduation... While you were gone, Alicia and Seven were an item for a while. They were matched at that big leprechaun thing they do in the summer."

"The Gilded Gala?"

"That's the one."

My skin prickles at the news. No one but us knows about Arden, but what are the odds her son would take an interest in her? I don't believe in coincidences. I smell a rat, although I can't think of what possible cheese it might be after.

"How long ago was this, Grandma?"

She rubs her chin. "Well now... I'd say at least five years. Maybe six."

"Did the relationship last long?" Do I really want to know? Probably not. But I ask anyway, like I'm prodding a sore tooth.

"About a year, I think," Grandma says. My heart clenches. "Oh, she always seemed more enthusiastic about the relationship than he did."

"What makes you say that?" It wasn't like my grandmother regularly ran in the same circles as leprechaun society.

"The *Hatter*. In every picture, she's gazing up at him adoringly and he's staring at the camera with a wooden smile and dead eyes."

That bit raises my spirits. "How did it end?" Barreling into the ground in streaming flames, I hoped.

Grandma grinned from behind three fingers that warned me of impending salacious gossip. "Well, I heard from Nancy Buttercup who heard from Auria Singh that Alicia grew tired of waiting for Seven to propose and bought herself an enormous diamond ring. Then she let it slip that they were engaged. Only Seven had never agreed to marry her. She probably assumed the social pressure would be enough to force him to go along with the ruse and tie the knot, but he didn't. Instead, he broke it off. Although he never humiliated her by coming right out and saying what she did, they attended the Yule ball separately and she was no longer wearing the ring. She was forced to give a statement to the *Hatter* that the engagement was called off for personal reasons just to get them off her back."

"Holy shit." I laugh a little too joyously. That was better than I was hoping for.

"I might still have a copy of the *Hatter* where they broke the news if you want to read it for yourself."

"Uh, no, thanks. Frankly, I'd love to forget it ever happened."

Grandma purses her lips, her eyes narrowing knowingly on me. "The question is if Alicia has forgotten, or if it will become an issue. I'd just hate for our sweet Arden to step on a land mine with that one. She has such stars in her eyes for Edmund."

I sigh. "About that, did anything strike you as odd about that boy?"

She snorts. "Leprechauns always strike me as odd."

"I mean he's very precocious and smooth-talking for a teenager."

For a moment she thinks about that, then says softly, "Seven was the same way when he was that age, Sophia. You just didn't notice because you were blinded by your own stars."

Flabbergasted by the assertion, I try to think back. Certainly Seven was always charming, especially when it came to parents and teachers, but it was as if it was expected of him, being who he was. I chide myself for my stupidity. Of course Edmund has the same expectations. He represents the Armon/Faust family line, and his mother has probably groomed him from birth to be as smooth as butter and as sweet as honey in any social situation. *Fuck.* I have a new appreciation for what my parents went through with me and Seven. How could you ever know for sure if a leprechaun's feelings were true when their entire lives were on display as the social royalty of our species?

The sigh I heave is laden with worry. "What do you think I should do?"

She toys with the lacy fringe of one of her elbow-length sleeves. "I'd never tell you how to parent your child, Sophia, but if I were Arden, I'd want to know this information so that I could prepare myself. If you're not comfortable talking to her about it, I could let it slip sometime when she was within earshot."

That would be the easy way out, but I owe Arden more than that. We've always had the type of relationship where we could talk about anything. "No. I'll tell her myself."

Grandma pats my hand and returns to the dining room.

AFTER A QUICK TEXT TO SEVEN TELLING HIM I'M THINKING OF him. I pack up some leftovers along with a bottle of wine to take to River and head to the safe house. The house is dark when I get there. I knock, but when no one answers, I let myself in through the unlocked door. It takes me a hot minute to make my way through the house and find him on the back porch, staring up at the stars. His horns reflect alabaster in the moonlight.

When he looks at me, he doesn't smile.

"I brought you dinner," I say.

"Already ate. I'm a chef. I don't need you to feed me."

"Okay."

The silhouette of his head sways. "But thank you for thinking of me," he says in a softer voice. "If you wouldn't mind, put it in the fridge?"

"Of course." I turn to take it inside but pause. "Is something wrong?" It's a stupid question. Everything about this situation is wrong, and both of us know it. I'm just not used to him directing his disappointment at me.

"Do you think I'll ever get out of here, Sophia?"

"Of course. I'm going to find who really did this and prove your innocence," I say softly.

He scoffs. "But will it matter? Godmother has a scapegoat. She's wrapped this murder up into a tight little package. So convenient."

"Too convenient." It's crossed my mind before, but I'm not ready to guess what it might mean.

"Now you see what I see," he grumbles.

"I'll make her release you. I'll go public with the murderer. I won't give her an option."

He sighs heavily. "I believe you'll try. I just hope you don't end up in here with me, or worse... in Ashgate."

He turns his face, and his eyes glint in the moonlight. In all the time we've been friends, I've never seen River cry. In fact, I can count on one hand how many times I've seen him without a smile on his face.

"I'm willing to take that chance." When he doesn't say anything for a few minutes more, I add, "I took care of Jinx yesterday. He's looking good. I think he's going to survive this."

That makes him laugh. "He's probably taken over the place. I'll come home to his wife and kittens nesting in my bed."

I shrug. "Probably. He seemed like he was enjoying the place to himself."

He stands and strides toward me. "Thanks for doing that for me. I'm not sure what I'd do without you."

"While I was there, I noticed lipstick on one of the glasses next to your bed."

"Hmm. I can't say anything about that."

"I know. But I also found a purple coat near the door. That coat had custom-made buttons that are almost exclusively used on garments worn by leprechauns."

"You don't say." He steps closer, and I can see his

face. He's smiling, his eyes taking on a surprised twinkle.

"Your third is a woman and a leprechaun. That's who you were talking to right before the murder. And I think maybe she's the one who cleared the sidewalk. And the person who murdered Adam Barker, perhaps they took advantage of that."

His eyes narrow. "That's a good theory."

"But you can't confirm or deny it."

He shakes his head.

"That's okay. I think I'm right. I also found this." I pull the rock from my pocket and hold it up in the moonlight.

At first he just stares at it as if he's trying to figure out what it is; then he opens the door for me and ushers me inside, flipping on the kitchen light to get a better view. "You found it! That was in the victim's hand."

I nod. "Why do you think he'd be clutching this rock?"

"I have no idea."

"Neither do I, yet, but Seven says Adam Barker was a geology professor who came here to give a presentation to a Bailiwick's class on formations specific to the Appalachians. I'm going to go to the school tomorrow and ask around, see who invited him and how the presentation went. Maybe there's something we're missing."

River takes the stone from my grip and weighs it in his hand. "It's heavy for its size."

"I thought the same thing."

"I wonder... Have you thought about having it analyzed? Maybe whatever it's made of will give us a clue."

Smart. "I bet if I take it to Elderflame University, someone there could tell me what it is." I turn and slip the food I brought into the fridge. An idea comes to me just as I'm closing the door. "What if it's not what's in the rock but the spell on it? Barker was human... maybe he got his hands on a stone that makes up the wards around the park."

River scratches his cheek. "Do you think someone on the outside wants in?"

I shrug. "I'm not sure. Even if they could deconstruct the magic, which humans can't because they're human, what would they hope to accomplish?"

"An undetectable way in and out," River says simply. "Maybe the murderer is a thief."

Possible, but the idea still isn't coming together for me. "I'll get someone to analyze it."

We stand there in the tiny kitchen, the weight of the past week settling on our shoulders. "I am going to figure this out, River. I'm on it."

He glances down at his toes. "I'm not meant for this kind of life, Sophia. I appreciate you coming. I do. Without you, I'd be out of my mind. I just need to be back in my restaurant. I need to see the people I love."

He leans a hip against the counter. "Do you think...? Can you at least tell Patrick that I'm not in Ashgate anymore? I'd hate for him to try to visit me there only to find..."

"Yes," I say immediately. "I'll find a way to let him know."

"Good." He scrubs his face with his hands. "I bet when you were on your way to confront Chance Delaney over that pixie's murder, you never expected it would lead to this. I know when I heard you'd caught him, I believed it was over."

River is one of the only people in Devashire who knows Seven and I were behind Chance's capture. The public believes Godmother is to thank for the raid and his arrest. Fine with me. I never wanted to draw any more attention than I had to.

"Actually, we didn't think he'd be there, at the cabin. Seven suspected we'd find something inappropriate, something he was trying to hide, but we were convinced someone was blackmailing him over a fetish. No one was more surprised than us when Chance walked in."

"I thought you caught him at his hunting cabin?"

"We did, but he was supposed to have a meeting that afternoon. He wasn't supposed to be there."

"Hmm. What tipped him off?"

I blink at River. It's been a long time since that fateful night, and I blocked out some of the details. I had to in order to feel safe and to heal. But now his question makes me look back on that night with fresh eyes. When Chance caught us in the dungeon under his cabin, he was dressed in a suit and tie... dressed for the office. Seven confirmed he was supposed to be in a finance meeting at that hour. So how did he get to the cabin so quickly, and how did he find out we were there?

I think I know the answer to the second part—we tampered with the fairy ring in the front yard. We thought we'd dismantled his protective wards, but the one we could see must have been a decoy for one we couldn't.

How he got there as fast as he did is still beyond me. The man was incredibly powerful, the luckiest fae in Devashire aside from Godmother, but that didn't mean he could teleport. That trick is beyond even Godmother's abilities as far as I know. So how did he make it to the cabin so quickly?

"You know, I'm not sure," I tell River honestly. "I've been so busy recovering from that night and trying to get you out of Ashgate, I never even thought to ask Godmother."

"Understandable."

I jump when my phone rings. Hoping it's Seven, I yank it from my back pocket, then frown when I see it's a call from Evangeline. "I have to take this. It's my new boss."

"Go ahead," River says softly, then adds with a chuckle, "Tell Evangeline I said hello."

"I wish I could. She's been worried about you."
Everyone misses River, but his freedom is predicated
on maintaining the illusion that he's still in Ashgate. I
might be able to trust Patrick with a vague version of
the truth, but I can never risk telling more people.

He gives me a nod and points toward the living
room, leaving me alone to take the call.

"Sophia? Are you there? I can hardly hear you."
Eva's voice sounds shaky, as if she's been crying.

"I'm in the mountains. The reception is bad."

"What are you doing in the mountains?"

I hesitate.

"Sophia? Sophia, are you there?"

"Visiting a friend."

"Oh... I..." She sobs on the other end of the line.

"What's wrong?" I ask. "You sound upset. Has
something happened?"

For several moments, she seems to hesitate. She
starts and stops but can't get the words out.

"Where are you?" I ask.

"I'm at Seven's apartment," she says. "He's back.
You need to come right away."

"Well, let me talk to him." I can't understand why
Seven wouldn't have called me himself.

"He can't right now, Sophia. Oh gods, this would
be easier to explain in person."

I am already jogging for the door. "I'll be there as
soon as I can."

CHAPTER

FIFTEEN

I reach Seven's building just after ten, where a security guard I don't know—the place is crawling with them—ushers me up to his penthouse. Evangeline lets me in, looking even worse than the last time I saw her. The circles under her eyes are even darker, and she locks the door behind me before pulling me into a hug.

"What's wrong? Where's Seven?" I ask, extremely worried now.

"He's in bed." A tear trickles from the corner of her eye. "I found him, badly injured and barely breathing, in my office. I don't know how he got in there. I've already called a doctor."

Without so much as a word to Eva, I run for the bedroom, suddenly unable to breathe. All my thoughts turn to Seven. I burst through the door and it's as if someone has punched me in the gut. All my breath rushes from my lungs, and my knees threaten to give out.

He looks dead. His complexion is almost gray where it's not covered in blood. His white shirt is soaked with red. He's still in his suit, but the dark material is torn and discolored with scuffs as if he was dragged behind a truck on a gravel road. I climb onto the bed and start examining him close up.

"How long has he been like this?" I ask Eva.

A sob cuts through the room and she answers, "Since I found him. Jericho helped me get him here."

"Why didn't you take him to the hospital?" I ask, annoyed.

She looks at me like I'm an idiot. "We have a private family doctor. I've already called him. He's on his way."

Of course, like everything in their family, discretion is key. After we battled Yissevel, I spent weeks in the hospital but Seven recovered here. That's how the Delaneys work.

"Help me get him out of this suit. I'm going to clean him up." It will be easier for the doctor to examine him anyway.

With Eva's help, I roll him onto his side and ease his arm from the sleeve of his jacket. I wince when a sickening pop comes from his opposite shoulder, and I quickly roll him onto his back again.

"Fuck, I think his shoulder dislocated." For a moment I just stare at Seven, his shallow breathing, pale skin, frail body. "Oh my god, he's negative, Eva. Why is he still negative?" For a fae, luck is like a bank. We only have so much stored up, and if we overdraw our account, the forces of the universe take the luck back from us by cursing us. When we're negative, walking across the street could be deadly. We attract bad luck and bad circumstances.

"I don't know," she says. "I gave him some on the way over here."

"Well, do it again!" I bark at her.

The look she gives me is positively offended, but her expression morphs quickly from defeat to determination. I feel her luck rise in the room like a great feathered beast. It's fiery, like her brother's that always reminds me of a dragon, but feminine. Instead of wrapping around me like a hot, muscular serpent, what brushes my skin is like a duster warmed by the sun. It soars through the room and fizzles as it reaches her brother. She moves closer and places her hands on him.

"Sophia... there's something wrong. I'm sending luck into him but it's just... dissolving. It's like... It's like..."

My blood turns icy in my veins. "Blue iron."

Carefully I feel his wrists and ankles, looking for manacles like the ones FIRE restrained me with when they captured me, but Seven's limbs are unencumbered. His breath rattles in his lungs, and I quickly unbutton his shirt to give him more air.

"Those fucking evil bastards," I say when I see a row of stitches on his chest. Under the stitches is a raised section of flesh in a misshapen square.

"Gods! Is that what I think it is?" Eva yells.

"Bring me a knife from the kitchen. Quickly! And a clean towel."

She runs from the room and returns with a paring knife. Good enough. I don't hesitate but slice the stitches open and dig my fingers into the wound. Seven doesn't flinch or moan, and I try not to think about what that means. My fingers clamp around a stone, and I drag it from his flesh, feeling all my energy drain away as I do. As soon as it's out of him, I fling it across the room and catch my breath. My luck bubbles up again in my veins.

"They sewed blue iron into him?" Eva shouts incredulously. "What kind of psycho would do a thing like that?"

"I don't know, but if I find out, I'm going to kill them." I press the clean towel to the wound and run my hands over every inch of his body, looking for more. I don't find any. "Eva, try giving him luck again. It's the only way to know that it's all out of his system."

That enormous, fiery bird rises over me again and sinks into Seven as her hands come to rest on his arm. The effect is instant. He draws a deep breath into his lungs and then cries out, fisting the sheets. For a second, his eyes are wild; then they fix on me.

"Sophia? Thank the gods." One arm flops around my neck and pulls me to him. He presses his lips to my forehead.

"What happened, Seven?" Eva is pacing now, her luck fluttering around the room. "For fuck's sake, there was blue iron sewn into your chest!"

He looks at her for the first time, then reaches over to grab her hand. "There's something I have to tell you. It's bad Eva. It's so bad." He tries to sit up, and fresh blood pours down his shirt.

"Fuck. Hold still." I press the towel to his chest again. "The doctor will be here any minute. You need that wound cleaned and probably stitched."

He closes his eyes for a long beat. "This can't wait." When he opens them again, I'm sure his luck is coming back because they're glowing bright emerald. His gaze shifts to Eva. "Dad made a deal with Rayrcore for... stones, something he was getting from Devashire, a valuable mineral. Rayrcore made it extremely clear to me that his imprisonment is no excuse for not delivering the goods."

"What mineral?" Eva spread her hands. "Rayrcore supplies us; we don't supply them."

My head is spinning. "Back up. Who is Rayrcore, and what exactly do they supply you with?"

Eva flashes me a pitying look. "Rayrcore is who Seven just met with. They're an American mining conglomerate run by Alex Hearst. They provide us with rare earth metals, which we use in a variety of our products—anything that can run on a battery, like our slot machines for example."

I shake my head, completely confused now. "And your father was bringing stones to them? What kind of stones?"

"Something called malivite. They claim they've *paid* for a delivery of this stuff. I'd never even heard of it."

"Wait, so your father has a secret mining operation happening somewhere in Devashire, and because he was arrested, he wasn't able to deliver the goods?"

"So it seems," Seven says.

I pull the stone from my pocket. "This was in Adam Barker's hand when he was murdered."

Eva reaches for it and turns it between her fingers. "Is this malivite? I've never heard of it either."

I squint at both of them. "Isn't mining in Devashire illegal? I thought Godmother put a stop to it a hundred years ago because of the environmental impact."

"She did," Seven says. "She knows our bread and butter is getting humans in the door, and none of them want to be breathing in dust from mining activities. They come here for the natural surroundings and for the fun. That's why Rayrcore took it upon themselves to kidnap me rather than take this to the authorities. They wanted to show me in no uncertain terms what would happen if I don't keep supplying them. I just can't figure out how their payment to us slipped by me. There should have been a red flag raised if they paid us for something we never delivered."

Eva's face pales, and she sits down on the edge of the bed. "They did pay us."

Seven grunts with the effort of turning his head to look at her.

"It was the day you found out about Dad—the meeting with the accountants. Dad was supposed to attend, but I filled in for him at the last minute. He grabbed me right before the meeting and said he had to go. That was the day Godmother arrested him. In that meeting, I noticed a large payment from Rayrcore. No one could explain it, and we tabled it to ask Chance when he was back in the office. He was never back in the office. I've been so busy I forgot about it."

Seven runs a hand down his face. "Well, Rayrcore remembers."

The same niggling questions surface in my brain as when I'd talked to River earlier. "How did Chance get to the cabin so fast that day? We arrived at your father's place at the same time he was scheduled to meet with the accountants. If he was in Evangeline's office right before the meeting to ask her to take his place, how did he get to us, an hour outside of Elder-flame, so quickly?"

Seven sighs. "The same way I ended up in Eva's office tonight. There's a secret passage through Dad's old office."

Eva and I stare at Seven disbelievingly. "You came through a secret passageway?"

"We need to go to the casino. There's something —" He tries to push up on his elbows and collapses flat on his back.

I place a hand gently on his shoulder. "You're not going anywhere. You were negative, Seven. You had blue iron sewn into your chest. And I'm pretty sure you have a dislocated shoulder."

He groans. "We don't have time for this."

Evangeline slips her hand into his. "You're home now. That's what's important. I'll fill in until you heal."

He closes his eyes and shakes his head. "You don't understand. They still have Saul. And if we don't bring them what they want in seventy-two hours, they're going to kill him."

It's all I can do to keep Seven in bed. I'm as worried about getting Saul back as he is, but he can hardly sit up. We both know we'll need him in tip-top shape to have any hope of doing what we need him to do. Thankfully the doctor arrives. He's an ancient-looking leprechaun who goes by the name of Felix Bonheur. I don't want to leave Seven's side, but Dr. Bonheur insists. Evangeline ushers me from the room and into the kitchen where she puts on water for tea.

"Sophia, I need you to do something for me," Evangeline says, not meeting my eyes. Something's been bothering her for days.

"Just ask already, Eva," I say flatly. "This has something to do with the real reason you wanted me to come to your office the other day, doesn't it? I feel like you've been meaning to ask me something, but you haven't."

Now she lifts her head and meets my eyes. "You've got to tell Godmother about what's happened here tonight. Rayrcore has to be behind the murder even if we don't have proof yet. You need to lie to her. It's wrong to leave River locked up in Ashgate when we all know he didn't do it." She fists her hands on the counter.

I study her for a moment, her agitation, the dark circles heavy beneath her eyes. Her luck rises in the room, those hot feathers brushing against my skin. It's a bird. No, a *phoenix*.

"He's not in Ashgate," I say softly. I could get in big trouble for this, but if what I suspect is true, she'll keep my secret. "He was moved, but you can't tell anyone. If anyone finds out, they'll send him back."

She reaches across the counter and takes my hands in hers. "Please, Sophia, where is he? Is he okay?"

My throat tightens at the pleading in her voice. "Why are you so concerned about River, Evangeline?" I ask softly. "You know, I've never seen you near River's until the morning of the murder. At the time, I thought you were there for PR purposes, but you got there awfully fast for someone who lives in Elderflame and works in After Dark."

The teakettle whistles, and she slides her hands from mine to pour the water into the teapot with the loose tea. "Do you take it with sugar?"

"Milk." I continue to stare at her, but she refuses to meet my eyes. "You've been worried about River's fate since the moment of the murder."

No response.

"You haven't been sleeping or eating." I eye the way her collarbones protrude where they can be seen inside the vee of her blouse.

"Tell me where he is. Please." She still refuses to look at me.

"Your luck takes the form of a phoenix. I recently learned that River has a phoenix tattooed on his shoulder. Is that a coincidence, Eva?"

This time she raises her gaze to meet mine and there's fire in her emerald-green eyes, the same possessive fire I sometimes see in her brother's. The room grows warmer as her luck circles it, and she says through her teeth, "How exactly do you know what's tattooed on the back of his shoulder?"

Reaching out, I take her hand and squeeze. "I know you can't tell me directly about any relationship you have with River, but tell me this: are you missing a purple coat?"

Our gazes lock, and tears slip from her eyes and

carve down her cheeks. "Please, please tell me he's okay."

"He is. But Eva, you've got to break the bargain with him. You can prove he didn't do this thing."

She sobs openly now, her entire body trembling. "No one can find out. A leprechaun with a satyr is scandalous enough. Two satyrs... I will never live it down. No one will ever take me as a wife after that."

A bad taste floods my mouth. "But it's his life, Eva. If you care for him at all, you have to know that his life trumps any fear you might have about the truth getting out." There's empathy in my voice but also a slight edge of accusation.

She gasps as if I hit her, and her eyes rove wildly around the room. "You're right." She runs a hand down her face. "Maybe I can convince Godmother to keep it a secret."

"For a price, I'm sure you can. But right now you must go to him. You must break his bargain with you so that both of you can help us free him."

"But where is he? How did you get him out of Ashgate?"

I cross my arms over my chest. "I told Godmother I was their third. I said I was you."

She gasps, her fingers flying to her lips. "But—"

"Yeah, she's holding it over my head like an acid bomb. One slipup and my reputation, what's left of it, is toast. I don't need to tell you how unfortunate that would be for Seven and me."

"Fuck, Sophia, I'm sorry. I never meant for you to do that. How... how did you even know?" Her voice comes out breathy on that last part, and her cheeks redden.

"I didn't know it was you if that's what you're asking. Both Patrick and River kept their bargain." Not that they had a choice. A bargain can't be broken, not without killing the fairy who breaks it. And although we are experts at finding loopholes in our deals, River is too upstanding of a person to try. "I went to visit River in Ashgate, and he told me there was *someone*. I knew that someone couldn't come forward, so I pretended to be you. Godmother accepted it and moved him to a safe house."

"It takes all participants involved to break a bargain made by three." She sounds breathless.

"You'll need to find Patrick, then bring him to this address." I pull out my phone and show it to her. "You should go now, before you lose your nerve."

Her eyes widen and she grabs her phone, her thumbs flying as she enters the address. "Thank you, Sophia." She squeezes my hand. "Thank you."

Dr. Bonheur chooses that moment to waddle into the kitchen. "Now, now, no need for tears!" he says when he sees Evangeline's face. "Your brother will be as good as new in a day or two. I've loaded him with enough luck to be sure of that and taken care of those nasty wounds. Nothing to worry about but making sure they don't happen again!" He holds up a hand before Eva or I can say a word. "I don't want to know." He reaches into his bag and withdraws an invoice. "My bill."

I glance at the paper. The header reads PIPES AND THINGS REPAIR AND REPLACEMENT. The line item simply says HOUSE CALL with an amount in the five figures. Discretion is key, Eva had said. If someone found this, they'd never know Seven had seen a doctor.

Bonheur gives as both a little wave and then heads toward the door with his big black bag. Once the door is closed behind him, I move for Seven's bedroom.

Eva grabs my elbow. "Don't tell Seven, okay? Not now. He has enough to worry about."

"Okay. But Eva, I've spent a lot of time bluffing over the years, and the truth is always better."

She holds up her phone with the safe house address, hugs me, and all but runs for the door.

CHAPTER

SIXTEEN

B y the time I return to Seven's side, his hair is wet from a shower and he's standing in front of his closet in nothing but a pair of green boxer briefs. The blood is gone but there are cuts and scrapes marring the muscles of his back, although they all seem to be healing now. When he hears me come in, he turns to look at me and I notice a gash under his left eye. Nothing is worse than the line of black stitches up his sternum though. I cringe when I see it.

"What are you doing out of bed?" I ask. "You need to rest."

"I need to go to Ashgate and confront my father about what he promised Rayrcore. Where is this malivite mine? How much am I supposed to bring them?" He's thumbing through a row of slacks as if he's trying to decide which to wear or which will hurt the least when he puts them on.

"It's the middle of the night. Ashgate is locked up. You won't get in until the morning."

He pauses for a second, staring aimlessly into his closet. "Right. We'll go to Dad's office instead. There's got to be something on his computer, some clue to what I'm supposed to do." Seven glances over his shoulder at me. "They didn't believe that I don't know what Chance promised them. I think they thought I was working with him, that we were swindling them."

I close the space between us, and it's a good thing because when he turns back to his closet, he stumbles. I wrap my arms around him from behind, steadying him. "It's late. You're in no condition to face this right now. It can wait until tomorrow."

He heaves a sigh and leans back into me. "They have Saul, Sophia."

"I know. Aside from Godmother, you are the most powerful fae in Devashire... when you're healthy. I don't know how they captured you—"

"It was an ambush."

"It won't happen twice." I grip his shoulder and place a kiss on the bare skin of his back. "Rest. Recover. A plan will come to us tomorrow."

He releases the pair of pants he's gripping and hangs his head. "We don't just need to save Saul; we need to stop Rayrcore. I don't know why they want this malivite, but it must be incredibly valuable if they're willing to kill for it. This isn't going to end with one shipment."

"I don't think so either," I say. "The night we discovered what your father was doing, the last thing he said to me before he passed out was that the murders were part of something far bigger than him. He alluded to the same thing when I interviewed him in Ashgate. This Rayrcore thing, it has to be related, and it wouldn't be a jump to connect it to the murder either."

He shakes his head. "I don't know. I can't put it together, and as hard as I tried, they wouldn't share much about it while they were... b-beating me." His voice cracks slightly, and I hug him tighter from behind, pressing my cheek into his back. It's all I can do not to lose it and melt into a pile of tears over what they did to him, but the last thing Seven needs is to have to comfort me right now.

"I'm here. You're okay," I say confidently.

He places a hand on top of mine on his chest. "Thank the gods."

"Please, Seven, let's lie down. We can talk about all this in the morning. Once we're rested and you've had something to eat, we can make a plan. Things will be so much easier when you're well. I promise."

He turns in my arms and presses his forehead to mine. "Will you stay with me? I don't want to be alone."

No way can I leave him tonight. Not after what he's been through. I pull my phone from my pocket and stare at the screen. I don't like to lie to my family, but can I tell them the truth? Yes. Yes, I can.

I text Mom and Arden.

ME:

Getting late. Staying overnight so I don't drive home tired. See you tomorrow.

ARDEN:

Have fun. Going to a movie with Edmund after school, but I'll see you for dinner.

MOM:

You're working too much! Take care, darling.

I heart both text messages, shaking my head.

"What's wrong?"

"Nothing," I say. "I'm staying. My mother didn't even question me about it."

"That's a good thing, right?"

"Yes. Sometimes I think I underestimate my family. I still think they're going to treat me like I'm seventeen. It surprises me when they don't."

"I always liked your family." He smiles wistfully. "When I was there at your house, sometimes I didn't want to go home."

"Well, it wasn't always perfect, but I know when we go public, we can count on their support. They respect my choices and treat me like an adult. Of course, that also means I have no one to blame for my choices but me, and that's a little scary."

He sighs and sinks onto the bed, looking exhausted. "I really wish your choices were the scariest thing we have to worry about."

"Me too." I help him under the covers, then excuse myself to visit the kitchen. A few minutes later, I return with a club sandwich, a sliced apple, and a big bottle of juice.

Seven props himself up against the headboard and groans. "Thanks. I haven't eaten since yesterday."

My insides sink at the thought of what he endured, but I put the tray on his lap and try not to dwell on it. He lifts the sandwich to his mouth and closes his eyes as he takes a bite.

"Hey, I'm spending the night!" I announce again.

His shoulders soften, and he slants a crooked grin. "We established that."

"I just wanted to hear it out loud. By the way, I thought of something while I was in the kitchen," I say. "Your cleaning lady…"

He nods, then bites into the sandwich again.

"When does she come? It's probably not good for her to find me in bed with you, and I plan to be in bed with you."

He grins around what's in his mouth. "Has the day off tomorrow."

I smile in relief and inch toward the bathroom. "Good. You eat that. I'll shower."

It's a testament to what bad shape Seven is actually in that he doesn't offer to join me.

After a long, hot shower and finding an unused toothbrush in a bathroom drawer, I climb into bed beside a sleeping Seven, dressed in a pair of his sweatpants and an old Van Halen T-shirt I dug out of his dresser. I'm happy to see there's nothing left on his plate and the bottle of juice is empty. I snuggle into his backside and wrap my arm around him. He's bigger than me, and this would be easier if he were spooning me rather than the other way around, but right now, after what he's been through, I think he needs it more.

"I love you," he mumbles.

I'm not sure he's even awake. His breath is even and his eyes stay closed.

"I love you too," I whisper. And then I drift off to sleep.

I WAKE WARM AND CONTENT. THE LIGHT THROUGH THE window sheers is silvery, and a glance at the clock on the bedside table tells me it's early. Barely six a.m. Sometime during the night we've switched positions and Seven is wrapped around me, his hand tucked under my shirt and splayed across my abdomen. His lips brush the back of my neck, and I hear him draw in a deep breath.

"Are you smelling me?" I ask through a grin.

"You're awake?" He lifts onto one arm, and I turn my head to kiss him. "Smelling you comforts me. A day ago, I wasn't sure I'd ever smell you again." His eyes turn stormy.

"What exactly happened, Seven?"

A dark cloud moves across his expression. "They jumped me and Saul the moment we stepped out of the car at their offices. I wasn't focused on protecting us. I never thought I needed to be. I'd dealt with Hearst before, but I guess my father was involved with a lot more behind the scenes than I ever knew about. I was in blue-iron cuffs before I knew what hit me. They asked me where the malivite was and then tore apart our car looking for it. When I told them I didn't know what they were talking about, they didn't believe me. Claimed Lucky Enterprises had taken their payment and the shipment was late. Accused me and my father of underhanded business practices. Filthy fae, they called us. You saw what they did next. They did the same to Saul. They only returned me because I promised I'd talk to my father and come back with the shipment. Saul was their insurance."

"Shit." I shake my head. "You're lucky to have made it out of there alive. We'll get Saul back. We will. We'll find a way."

He rolls me under him, settles between my thighs. "Facing it... Experiencing that kind of pain and wondering if I'd ever make it back to you... Sophia, I don't want to keep us a secret anymore. You are as much family to me as Eva and of course Arden—the three of you are the only family I have left and the only thing I thought about when I was having blue iron sewn into my chest." His voice turns raspy, and he swallows hard against the horrific memory.

I take his face in my hands. "Then I have good news because I don't want to do this anymore either. Arden made her decision. She wants to stay. She's already applied to Elderflame University. She's only waiting to tell you before she announces it to everyone else."

His face lights up with joy, and his eyes grow wet. "We're going to be a family. A real family. I never believed it could happen. I knew she'd make the right choice though. She's a brilliant girl, just like you. She must have realized it was better staying here and living her truth than hiding what she is from the world."

"That and she's dating a boy," I say. "I'd like to think it's more living her truth than boy, but you know teenage hormones."

Seven's entire body stiffens in my arms. "She's dating a boy? Since when?"

"Since before graduation, although I just found out recently. He came to dinner Friday night. Actually, I wanted to talk to you about him because—"

"Who is it?" he asks tersely.

"Edmund Faust."

Seven scrambles off me so fast I get a chill. "No."

"Huh?"

"Tell her to break up with him, now. Forbid her from seeing him ever again." His jaw clenches.

I give a low, throaty laugh. "Oh, my sweet summer child. It's very clear to me that you have never, in fact, raised a teenager, especially a girl. Telling Arden, who is going to be a legal adult in less than a year and a half, to break up with Edmund, whom she says she's in love with, and forbidding her from ever seeing him again is the surest way for her to instantly become pregnant by him and never speak to us again. It's practically a law of nature. You don't want to go there."

He settles back on his heels. The wound in his chest is already so much better, and some other scratches and abrasions I remember from last night are almost completely healed. Being a leprechaun definitely has its perks.

"There's something you should know about the Fausts."

"That you were once engaged to Edmund's mother? My grandmother told me."

A muscle in his jaw twitches like the memory is horribly uncomfortable. "I was never engaged to her, Sophia. She told the *Daily Hatter* we were engaged to try to manipulate me into marriage."

"My grandmother also mentioned speculation about that," I say softly.

"We'd dated, casually, for a short period." He

waves a hand through the air. "You'd been gone a long time, and I was lonely—"

"You don't owe me an explanation."

"We were the talk of leprechaun society because if our houses merged, the empire we could create would be unprecedented. The Fausts rule transportation in Devashire, and we have manufacturing and adult entertainment. You can imagine the opportunities. It was my father's wet dream. He would have married her himself if she would have had him."

"Sounds like you had other plans."

"I wasn't interested. Not only was I not attracted to her, the idea of marrying someone only for the potential they offered to increase my wealth and power made my skin crawl. It's not who I am. I didn't love her. The more I got to know her, the less I even liked her. She's shrewd and completely focused on growing her empire. When I told her I would never marry her, she threatened to increase our shipping costs by sixty percent."

"She tried to extort marriage out of you? Psycho!"

He nods. "I told her she could do that, but then I'd be forced to go to the *Hatter* and reveal that she'd bought herself the diamond on her finger and that I'd never proposed. She decided to let it go."

"Fuck, that's messed up! Wait, but I saw you talking to her after graduation. It looked friendly."

"She wanted to know why I was there. Edmund

was graduating, but I didn't have a child in the ceremony."

"What did you tell her?"

"That as a member of the school board, I like to attend to wish the best to the new class. It's not unheard of for me to be there."

"That's right. I forgot you did that."

"Still, she saw me sitting near you and speaking with you. I have a hard time believing that Edmund is an apple that has rolled far enough from the tree to be interested in Arden without any other ulterior motives."

I release a heavy sigh. It *is* suspect. "But Edmund doesn't know what she is. He doesn't know she's your daughter. What could he be using her for?" I shrug. "As far as he knows, she's a half-human pixie hybrid and a shopkeeper's granddaughter."

Seven scratches the side of his jaw and snorts. "She suspects I love you. We talked about it back then, when you were gone. Maybe not directly. I mean, I didn't share intimate details with her, but I talked about you. You came up in conversation. She suspects. And after the kiss and the job at the casino, I'm sure she's speculating that I still have feelings for you. She doesn't know that Arden is my daughter, thank the gods, but that doesn't matter. Getting close to Arden gets her close to you, and if she can get dirt on you, she can manipulate me."

"That's devious. She'd actually use her own son for something like that?"

"Most certainly."

I sit up and cross my legs in front of me, trying to center myself. Everything I've ever done, since the moment I found out I was pregnant with her, has been for Arden's benefit. I left Devashire to protect her from a society who would have pressured me to abort her. I stayed in America so she could have a normal human childhood. I came back to Devashire to protect her from the consequences when I was arrested. I would do anything for Arden, but she's not a baby anymore, and to keep doing things for our children that they can do for themselves is dysfunctional. My job as a parent is to make sure she can fly, to prepare her for leaving the nest, not to make her dependent on it.

"Arden is a smart girl. As clever as any teenager I've ever known. And she's strong and experienced in ways that most kids never have to be because they weren't raised surviving in a world where their very existence is against the law. She can handle herself with Edmund."

Seven works his jaw back and forth. "He's a leprechaun, Sophia. Enough luck can make her feel like she's in love."

"Yep. But you've taught her what luck can do. She knows what it feels like."

"What if he tries to manipulate her? What if he uses her?"

"She'll figure it out. And when she does, we'll be there to help her negotiate the fallout."

"We have to warn her." He rubs his palms on his thighs.

"We will. We absolutely will. But only as a side conversation, not like we're forbidding her or telling her what to do. The fact is, when we go public, when we tell people she's ours, she'll have to deal with the fallout on her own. We'll have each other to lean on, but we won't be able to protect her from it. Not completely. We have to start trusting that she's not a baby. We can help her, we can be there for her, we can try to show her the truth, but we can't make her choices for her."

He nods slowly. "I hate it, but I think you're right." He crawls across the bed to me and kneels in front of my crossed legs. "But if he hurts her, I'm going to cause every capillary in his body to rupture simultaneously. I won't kill him, but I will make sure he suffers." There is nothing flippant about his tone.

I grin. "Agreed. We'll take the little pissant out if he hurts her."

He kisses me soundly.

"When do you want to leave for Ashgate to interrogate your father?"

He stares down at me. "When you talked to Chance, did you think he gave you anything of value?"

"No. The riddle he spewed hasn't helped us at all. I think the torture he endured at Godmother's hand and

217

the isolation has damaged his mind. Plus he asked to see you, made me promise to request that you go. Knowing Chance, that means he hoped for an opportunity to get his hooks into you. He tried to kill you before. Who's to say he'd be honest with you now?"

"I agree. So what if there was a way to deliver what Rayrcore wants and get Saul back without talking to him?" Seven has an idea, and the twinkle in his eye tells me it's going to be good.

"I'm listening."

CHAPTER
SEVENTEEN

S even holds a golden acorn, identical to the one he
gave Arden, between his thumb and forefinger,
its shell glinting in the fluorescent lights. He's
handling the charm as if it's the One Ring. I almost
expect him to murmur "my precious."

We're standing in his father's office in Dragonfly
Casino, preserved as if Chance just moved out yesterday. A sleek desktop computer rests artfully in the
corner of the desk with a pen and a notepad on the
blotter in front of it. Bookshelves laden with profes-
sional-looking tomes line the walls, noteworthy sculp-
tures breaking up the sets of expensive leather
volumes.

Seven's brought an oversized briefcase from his
place, and he sets it on the desk in front of us, then
pops the top open.

"You gave one of those to Arden for her graduation. What is it?"

"A wish," he says solemnly.

"A wish? Like a genie-in-a-bottle-type wish?"

"Sort of. This is an acorn from a tree no longer in existence, one that had roots they say reached all the way to the cauldron, that mystical place from which it's said all fairies came. It will magnify the luck of any fairy that wields it, and with enough focus, the results are very nearly magic. The man I obtained this from claims that Godmother used one hundreds of years ago to increase her capacity for luck and power."

"Wait, have you told Arden about this? Does she know how dangerous it is?"

He nods. "Graduation night. I pulled her aside before I left your parents' house. She knows."

"Gods, Seven. Next time ask me before you hand our daughter a live grenade."

He snorts. "You can't deny she might need it, given the circumstances."

I can't argue with that logic. "Is that the plan then? Make yourself so strong you can charge into Rayrcore and tear Saul from their clutches?"

He smiles but shakes his head. "What Godmother did was extremely dangerous. This little charm packs big magic. Wish too big and it will drain your luck dry trying to fulfill that wish. Many have died, wishing beyond their capacities."

"Wait, Seven, why haven't you used this to break Godmother's hold over you?" How could he not have considered that first?

He frowns in my direction. "I have another one I've held back for that purpose. If I get desperate enough, I'll try it. But yes, I'm afraid. Breaking a fairy bargain without being released from it is said to be impossible. It's very probable that it will kill me before it works."

"So what's your plan with this one?"

"I think this situation calls for a bit more delicacy. Hand me that malivite."

"Would this be a bad time to remind you that we are only assuming this is malivite?" I pinch above the bridge of my nose, a headache threatening. "River confirmed this was the stone clutched in Adam Barker's hand when he was shot, and it's logical that the stones Rayrcore is asking for are the same as this one. But we're making a mental leap there. They could be entirely disconnected events."

"I'm feeling lucky," Seven says with a wink, then grows serious. "The timing... I don't believe in coincidences. We are taking a risk but an educated one, and every moment matters if we want to get Saul back alive. Besides, I have a hunch that Hearst might not know what malivite looks like anyway."

"Huh?"

"I've been racking my brain, trying to think what motivation he would have to withhold the details I asked him for about the stones while he was torturing me. It occurred to me that he might not know. My dad was a master at giving just enough information to sell something. He used to tell me, 'Make no promises, Seven. Let them assume the promises. They can't hold you to assumptions.'"

"It doesn't matter if it's malivite or not, as long as he thinks it's malivite."

"Mm-hmm."

"Here's to educated guesses." I hand over the piece I recovered from where Adam Barker was murdered. He takes an ordinary rubber band from Chance's desk and wraps it around the stone, then places it inside the case. He pauses, the acorn resting in his palm. "You have no idea how much it pains me to use this charm. I only had three to begin with, and they're absolutely priceless."

"We could try Ashgate," I propose. "Or search your father's records."

He shakes his head. "I want to give them enough to get Saul back but not enough to use the malivite for whatever nefarious purposes they're planning. This is the only way to do that. Once Saul is home and safe, we can take our time figuring out the details."

"Then make your wish and let's do this." My palms are sweating, and I hug myself against a sudden chill.

Acorn in hand, he closes his eyes and his lips start to move. A wind picks up in the room, swirling around us, sending my hair thrashing against my face. Goose bumps erupt across my skin, and my stomach turns over with the gathering power. Under it all, I feel Seven's luck rise around us, only the fiery dragon that usually accompanies his use of luck is now enormous. I can barely breathe because it takes up every spare inch of space, and still I sense the room itself can't contain it. His luck is as big as the building, maybe bigger.

Clank. Clank. Clank. I peer into the belly of the case, in awe as the malivite reproduces, a stone sounding against stone with each additional piece that pops into existence. It spills into every corner, then reproduces until the case is full.

Seven opens his eyes. "We have our malivite."

I pick up one of the pieces and turn it in my fingers. It is identical to the original—same color, weight, and size. Seven fishes the original stone from the lot, still marked by the rubber band. "How long will the illusion last?"

"Forever. They're not an illusion. They're real."

I gape at the case as he closes it. "I thought the point of using the wish was to not give Rayrcore malivite."

"It is. There's only one actual piece of malivite in this case. The rest are look-alikes. Pretty gray stones with the chemical composition of concrete."

"Do you think they'll fall for it?"

Seven gives me a wry grin. "I think we're going to get lucky."

His phone chimes, and he peeks at the screen. "Hearst got my message. He's meeting me in twenty minutes." He lifts the case and heads for the bookshelves at the back of the office.

"I'm coming with you." No way am I letting him go back there alone.

"Bad idea. These people are dangerous."

"Exactly why you need backup."

His fingers find a latch at the back of the frame, and the bookshelf swings open to reveal a small elevator, barely wide enough for two. He opens the cage and steps inside. The shelf starts to close.

As fast as I can move, I slip through the narrowing crack and press my chest against his, shoving him to the back of the compartment. The cage closes, and the bookcase seals us in. We begin to descend.

"Sophia..." Seven's cheek presses against mine. His breath softly brushes my ear as he says, "I want you to stay where it's safe. I couldn't stand it if anything happened to you."

"You know what? I can't remember the last time I was truly safe. But I can remember when I was happy. Now. Right here with you. If the choice is without you but safe or with you and in danger, I'll take my chances."

The elevator stops and the door opens. We're in a concrete vestibule. I exit the lift and find myself in a tunnel. We must be in the secret underground garage, but this section appears to only be accessible through Chance's old office.

"This is how they brought you back?"

"Not exactly." He leads me away from the exit, through a tunnel just big enough for a single car. It's a long and poorly lit walk until our surroundings transform. We reach a section that looks positively ancient. The ceiling is arched here and decorated with stone gargoyles and arcane symbols. I sense the ward before we reach it, like prickly burrs scraping my skin.

"It knows my blood. Take my hand." Seven's luck rises around us, and the prickly sensation fades. He leads me under the arch.

I'm in a chamber that would be at home in an archaeological dig. Stone walls carved with ancient runes surround us, and in front of us, a giant mirror stretches across one wall. I squeeze Seven's hand, temporarily struck mute by the revelation. The silver undulates as if it's merely a pool and fish swim just under the surface. But those aren't fish, they're souls, and this mirror is no reflective surface, it's a portal.

"How?"

Seven swallows. "I don't know."

"And it leads to Rayrcore?"

"The garage under Rayrcore," Seven says.

But my mind can't reconcile that. "But Chance must have used this to get to his cabin the afternoon we confronted him. He had a mirror there. I saw it.

Godmother said she delivered it to the hands of the guardians."

Seven's brow creases. "This is how they brought me back... but you're right. I don't know how these silvers work. The one we traveled through was a passageway between Devashire and Shadowvale, and we assumed that portal only went between those two places. Maybe they can be used to travel between any two mirrors?"

"I've never heard of such a thing."

He raises an eyebrow. "Why would we? The guardians own that knowledge."

"I don't like this, Seven. How do you know this can take us where we need to go and won't dump us somewhere else?"

"I don't. I'm hoping to get lucky."

I glare at him.

"There's no reason you can't stay here, Sophia. This is dangerous."

"We're in this together," I say firmly.

He sets down the malivite and lifts a long, hooked staff off the wall. The moment he does, symbols ignite across the stone bordering the silver.

"What language is that?" I've never seen anything like it in my life.

"Interesting. *That* is ancient leprechaun, and it says, 'Where the mind lies, there shall ye go.'"

"So you just think about where you want to travel and that's where it takes you?"

"Let's hope."

He dips the staff into the silver and stirs, muscles bunching with the effort. The silver swirls slowly at first and then picks up speed until it seems to shatter into a million spinning stars, a galaxy trapped in the spin cycle.

With a last grunt of effort, Seven casts the staff aside. I get an eye-popping view of it flying back into its cradle before he grabs my hand and pulls me and the stones into the tunnel. My feet hit a squishy floor as Seven lifts the stones from my grip and breaks into a sprint, tugging me forward. We're surrounded by galaxies of shimmering silver, stars that cascade on either side of us while whispers of the dead drift through the air around us. Unfortunately, I can clearly see them growing closer to our heads with every step. The tunnel is getting smaller!

Seven's luck tingles through my hand, and a rush of energy fills me. Ducking, I move faster. I see the light now too. It's dim but flickering like a candle in a dark room. We leap through the narrowing portal and land in a squat on a rough-hewn stone floor. The same breathlessness and disorientation I'd experienced before floods me, but Seven still has my hand and his luck bolsters me. I pant through it.

"You're late, Mr. Delaney," a raspy voice says.

I raise my head to see an elderly man in a black trench coat, his face deeply lined in a way that suggests he's never genuinely smiled. He bares his teeth and they're stained indigo—he's been drinking blue iron. *Fuck.* Our luck won't work directly on him. Beside him, three brutish-looking men with equally blue smiles surround Saul, whose skin is more bruised than not. He's unconscious and barely breathing.

"For a moment, I thought we might have to send your friend back to you in pieces."

CHAPTER
EIGHTEEN

"Hearst," Seven says through his teeth. "I have what you want. Give me Saul."

"Show me." Hearst points his chin toward the case.

Seven places it in front of him and enters the code to unlock it. As he lifts the lid, he slips his hand inside. He's finding the real malivite, slipping the rubber band off. He does it all so seamlessly. Hearst has no idea what he's dealing with when it comes to Seven. He's not his father. Yes, he's as powerful, but Seven has a heart, and that will always make all the difference.

He tosses the piece to Hearst and then turns the case around to show him the rest of the stones. Hearst pulls a magnifying lens from his pocket and inspects the stone.

"That's more than we agreed upon," Hearst says. "There will be no additional payment until our proof of concept."

I desperately want to know what that the concept is, but I keep my mouth shut. We're so close.

"Consider it an act of good faith," Seven says. "To make up for the misunderstanding."

Hearst nods. "Am I to assume then, that you'll be taking your father's place at the helm on this project while he's indisposed?"

Seven nods slowly, deliberately. That's right, don't say a word. Don't give him anything that might lead to a bargain. "Now give me Saul."

Hearst waves at his three goons, and they unchain Saul and dump him unceremoniously out of the chair.

I run to him and squat at his side, inspecting him for implanted blue iron. I don't find any, but the injuries at his wrists and ankles tell me he's been cuffed and chained with it. "He's clean."

Seven closes the case and pushes it across the stone toward Hearst, then joins me next to Saul.

Hearst lifts the case, a dark chuckle rumbling from his lungs. "Pleasure doing business with you, Delaney. I look forward to a *revolutionary* future."

Only when he's gone and we're alone in the room do I ask Seven, "What the hell does that mean?"

"I have no idea."

Saul groans.

"I'm going to have to carry him, Sophia. Do you think you can stir the silver?"

"There's only one way to find out." No part of me wants to remain in this room, which I realize with a start is in the United States. If Agent Donovan knew I was here, he'd have me strapped to a table in a rehabilitation center in no time. I shiver.

Lifting the staff from its hook, I plunge it into the silver the way I watched Seven do it and try to stir. Nothing happens. It's like trying to stir concrete. I pour on a little luck and throw my back into it, pushing with my legs. Slowly the staff starts to move. Very slowly. I circle it down and around, the push turning into a pull that reminds me of a rowing machine. I repeat the process—push, push, push, pull, pull, pull. My face breaks into a sweat, but the staff is moving faster now. Again and again, I stir until the silver itself gains momentum, carrying my strokes along with it.

"Now," Seven says, "concentrate on returning us the way we came."

I toss the staff aside and bound into the swirling stars, looking back only to confirm that Seven is following me, Saul over his shoulders in a fireman's carry. I race forward, mind picturing the room under the casino. It feels like I'm running into a hard wind. Every step is harder than the last. I'm sure the stars are going to collapse on my head before I can reach the other side when Seven pushes me hard from behind. I dive out of the tunnel and roll across the stone with a pained grunt.

Seven and Saul collapse beside me. The tunnel snaps closed behind us. I lay flat on my back, staring up at the stone ceiling. My head is pounding, and I'm covered in scrapes and scuffs. Seven doesn't look much better, and Saul is out again, barely breathing.

"What do you think Hearst meant about you taking over the helm?"

Seven taps the back of his head against the stone. "No clue, but it looks like I'll be visiting my father in Ashgate after all. I have questions, and he's the only one with answers."

THANK THE GODS THAT BY THE TIME SEVEN AND I ARE STRONG enough to stand, Saul has come to enough to carry some of his own weight. We put his arms around our shoulders and help him through the wards. Seven calls Jericho to pick us up, and we race him to Elderflame Hospital.

It's late by the time he's safely in a room. Besides being a mass of bruised flesh, Saul's got three broken bones: a shin, a clavicle, and an arm. The doctors are able to revive him long enough to tell him he's safe, and then he passes out again. We stay in the room while they set his bones, then hook him up to an IV drip of saline fortified with liquid luck. Eventually the doctors request we leave so he can rest.

"Is there someone we should call for him?" I ask Seven.

Seven rubs the back of his neck. "His mother. But I'll have to check with Human Resources for her contact information. Excuse me." He raises the phone to his ear and then pads toward the privacy of the stairwell.

I stand there, staring through the glass window into Saul's room, listening to the machine's beep and acknowledging the level of evil it must have taken to turn a leprechaun the size of Saul into the broken, black-and-blue blood bag in front of me. Gods, he looks like hell. But then we all do. My cuts and scrapes are many and healing slowly.

Still, any of us might be in that bed if things happened differently. Someone might have died. Life is short, even for us fae. I think about Arden then, about how our time together is sifting through our fingers. How things will have to change. How I won't be able to climb into bed with her like we used to and watch cheesy movies late into the night. I stare and stare at Saul, this man I don't know well but whom I liked a great deal, who'd guarded me and drove me places and shared about his own simple leprechaun life to make me feel better.

My hands start to shake. All the saliva dries up in my mouth, and my throat tightens. I feel an emotion building in my chest, and I know that if I give in to it, the barbed seed of regret will barrel up my throat. I swallow it down, tears flowing, and make up my mind not to waste a single minute more.

Seven returns, still looking at his phone in his

hands. "She's on her way. I told her we were in an accident. I didn't know what else to say."

I launch myself at him, wrapping my arms around his neck and weeping into his chest.

"Shhh. Shhh. Sophia, what's wrong. What happened?"

All the words I want to say get twisted up in my brain, and the only thing that will come out is "I'm so tired."

He rubs my back. "Of course you are. We need to eat and rest. We haven't had anything since breakfast, and it's almost eight o'clock."

That must be why I'm not healing. I'm exhausted and hungry. But what I'm feeling right now is far more than all that.

Seven tucks my hair behind my ear. "Let's go back to my place and I'll fix you something."

I shake my head, clinging to him like he's the only thing keeping me from drowning. "No."

"No?"

He takes me gently by the shoulders and eases me off him so he can see my tearstained face. Out of the corner of my eye, I see a nurse give us a judgmental look, but I don't care. I might never let go of Seven again.

"Where do *you* want to go?" he asks me. "I'll take you anywhere. We can go to River's or one of the restaurants in Elderflame. Wherever you want. I'll clear the place out if you want me to."

I take a deep breath and look him in the eye. "I want to go to my parents' house, and after we eat, I want to tell them the truth."

"Tonight?" He looks down at our arms, covered in bruises and abrasions, then at my rumpled dress.

"What are we waiting for, Seven?" I step in closer and place my hands on his face. A few more nurses pass us and glance in our direction, but he doesn't push me away. "Arden's made her choice. We're here together, and for the moment we're alive and well. I don't know what the future holds. I don't know what's going on with your father or Hearst or anything else. All I know is, we've only got today, and I think it's time we told my family the whole truth. They should know before we announce it to the world."

He breathes a heavy sigh of relief, then pulls me into his arms, kissing me sweetly. "Finally. Yes. Tonight is the night."

Warmth spreads across my torso and grows so large that it turns the corners of my mouth up. I'm so happy I almost can't process it. My lips part as more tears start to fall.

He takes my hand, threading his fingers through mine. "Come on. Let's go relieve Jericho. I'll drive. We don't know exactly how this will go."

I nod. As we start walking to the car, I cough into my hand, and I can't stop the delicate purple seed that follows. Seven looks down at it curiously.

"You probably think its gross, but sometimes I can't control it."

He shakes his head. "Not gross. It's a pixie thing. It's part of you. I was just wondering... what emotion is it?"

I close my fist around the seed and give him a shaky smile. "Hope."

CHAPTER
NINETEEN

The moment we set foot in my parents' home, we are bombarded by love. I've texted ahead to say Seven would be coming with me and to be prepared because we're a little beat up. Mom meets us at the door.

"Oh my," she says, glaring at our wounds with a worried frown. "Should I fetch the first aid kit?"

"No. We've come from the hospital. Nothing is bleeding, anymore," I say. "But we're both starving. Do you have anything left from dinner?"

She administers two careful hugs. "Who do you think you're talking to, Sophia? No one leaves this house unfed." She ushers us toward the breakfast nook where she has sandwiches and cookies waiting.

"Oh, Mom, thank you." I actually tear up as I bite into a ham and cheese.

"There's lemonade there too, although you two look like you might need something stronger."

"Definitely," Seven murmurs around a bite. "Please, Mrs. Larkspur."

She nods once, darts into the kitchen, and comes back with a bottle of vodka still frosty from the freezer. I pour a shot into my lemonade and then into Seven's.

"Are you sure you don't need anything else? Bandages? Painkillers?" she asks softly.

"No," I assure her. "We're fine. Just scraped up a bit."

"Good. Then Seven, I'd like you to tell me why my daughter looks like she's been in a fight and why you didn't protect her." An unmistakable edge has crept into her voice that makes both of us sit up straighter.

"It's a long story, Mom, and we only want to tell it once, so you can invite Grandma and the rest of them in here."

My grandmother pops out from behind the door to the living room as if she's been waiting there listening and beams like she won the lottery. "I thought you'd never ask!"

She smooths the skirt of her metallic blue gown and tucks herself into the chair across from Seven, resting her chin in her palm.

I narrow my eyes on her. "Do you actually still live in Sunnyville?"

"It's where they deliver my mail, darling. Now, you were saying?"

"Wait. I want to hear this." Dad enters the room from the kitchen.

"Where's Arden?" I ask.

"Out with Edmund again. I think they were going skating in Winter Wonderland," Dad says.

A wave of nostalgia hits me as I remember what it was like to go ice-skating or sledding in the small section of Wonderland where it always snows but is never cold. I haven't been there since I was a child. I hope Arden loves it.

"All right. I'll talk to her later," I say softly. Arden already knows Seven and I are a couple, but I don't want my family to feel bad that I'm just telling them now, so I leave it at that.

"But you're going to tell the rest of us now, right?" Grandma asks enthusiastically.

"Yes." I turn toward Seven, but he motions with his head as if to say *it's your family. You do the talking.*

Across the table, three pairs of eyes stare at me expectantly. I take a deep breath and just say it. "Seven and I are together again. We're going to take our relationship public. And he's Arden's father."

Grandma's gasp fills the room, but my parents' silence is more concerning. I start to explain. I tell them about Godmother and her bargain with Seven and how none of us knew until Arden and I returned to Dragonfly. I talk about working together and the kiss being real, and how what happened at the Yule ball was all Chance's doing. I only stop when it's clear I'm vomiting words, some of which don't even make sense anymore.

I close my mouth. We all stare at each other, silence cloaking us in its weighty blanket.

Seven clears his throat. "I love your daughter," he says to my father. "And your granddaughter. I want to present them both to leprechaun society at the Gilded Gala, Sophia on my arm as my date and Arden as my daughter and debutante. With your blessing, of course."

My parents say nothing. I think they're speechless. But my grandmother's face goes deadly serious. It's the first time I've ever seen her look worried since I've been back.

"Do you know what you're getting yourselves into going public?" she asks. "I like you, Seven. I've always liked you, and I've suspected for a long time that there was more going on between you two than you were letting on. Sophia's feelings for you have been clear to me since you were children." She gives a raspy laugh. "But relationships like yours aren't a common thing in Devashire. I don't have to tell you that. People will talk. People will always talk. But revealing a serious relationship at the Gilded Gala? It's going to be a nuclear bomb. The gala is televised around the world! The *Daily Hatter* will want interviews. The gossip columns will all comment on it. Social media will overflow with vitriol. Sure, you'll have some support-ers, your bravery might be celebrated at first, but many more will hope to see your relationship fail to prove it's unnatural... Impossible."

"It's not impossible," Seven says bitterly. "I love her. I've loved her since we were six years old."

Grandma nods, her eyes going teary. "Yes, you have. Sometimes wars are worth fighting, and if you choose to take up your sword on this, I'm behind you all the way. I'm an old woman. I have very little to lose. But make no mistake, both of you, this will be a war. You, Seven, are attempting to elevate a pixie to your status, and if there's one thing that has been treated as sacrosanct among leprechauns, it is their higher status. Your contemporaries will fear that your relationship won't be the last. They'll fear an erosion of wealth to the lower classes, a loss of privilege and prestige. Fear can turn people into monsters. Do what you must, but sharpen your weapons. The beasts will come."

My father finds his voice. "Betty is right. I don't think anyone at this table is surprised by your relationship." His eyebrows lift. "But you have to know going public will change everything. For all of us."

His words force an icy weight of anxiety in my chest. "You're right. It will affect you too. I can't help that."

"Unless you kept it a secret," Mom says. "Why not continue as you have? Now that we know, we can help you."

I sense Seven tense beside me, and when I look

over, his jaw is clenched tight. My heart thumps in my chest. I rest both hands flat on the counter, releasing a giant breath. "I'm sorry if this is disappointing to you. I am thirty-four years old, a grown pixie. I've spent the past sixteen years pretending to be something I'm not, living among people who could never truly know me, spending my days wrapped in deception and my nights terrified of being found out. I did that to protect Arden and myself, and in some ways, it protected you as well. I bore the burden of being no one, of living a pretend existence, for so long. Too long. I can't do it anymore, and with Arden staying, it's to her advantage for the world to know she's leprechaun. When that happens, it's going to get hard for us anyway. It won't be that much harder when the world finds out her mother and her father love each other."

"You hope," Mom says.

I nod. "I do. For many things. We can't control what happens. My hopes and dreams may be ridiculous, but I'm going to do everything in my power to make them come true. Grandma called this going to war. I'm willing to fight. I don't want to hide who I am or who I love anymore." I pause for a moment, dreading what has to come next. I stare at a spot on the table as I say, "But I understand if you want no part in it. I can move out. You can distance yourselves from me, deny that you know anything. Eventually they'll leave you alone."

My mom's hand lands on top of mine. "Not for all the luck in the kingdom. We are in this together."

Dad places his hand on top of Mom's. "If we're going to war, I plan to start sharpening my arrows. Gods help anyone who hurts you."

Grandma laughs wickedly. "You know I'm in! I wouldn't miss it for the world. I live for this shit."

Seven leans back in his chair and threads his fingers across his bottom ribs. "Then it looks like you need to pick out a gold dress, Sophia. You're going to the ball."

Grandma nods and murmurs, "Hurrah!"

"There's just one thing I don't understand," Mom says. "Why are you covered in blood?"

THE NEXT DAY, SEVEN AND I DECIDE TO DIVIDE AND conquer. Since only one person can enter Ashgate at a time, he plans to go interrogate his father without me. Meanwhile, I journey to River's house to feed Jinx and then head back to the safe house to bring him more groceries and give him an update on what's happened.

When I knock, no one answers. I knock again, picturing River on the back porch, as lonely and depressed as the last time I'd seen him. I use my key to let myself in.

"Hello?"

A scuffle of sounds comes from the bedroom. The

rustle of bedding. The thump of feet on the floor. Low cursing when something glass is knocked over.

"River?" I call, laughing a little.

A moment later he appears in the bedroom door in a pair of gray sweats and nothing else, his hair suspiciously tousled around his horns. "Sophia, thanks for coming!" He embraces me in one of his warm River hugs and takes the groceries from my arms.

"Is that who I think it is?" I gesture an eyebrow toward the bedroom door.

He smirks. "Who else could it be?"

"Someone you met in the woods and charmed out of their pants."

His laugh is deep and rich. "No. There are only two people in the world I want to charm out of their pants."

My brows inch up a little farther. "Both Patrick and Eva are here?"

He nods. "Just Eva right now. We broke the bargain, then sealed it with a kiss. Patrick left earlier this morning for work."

"You've been 'breaking the bargain' for..." I look at my watch. "A day and a half."

His smirk grows more pronounced. "Mm-hmm."

I don't know what to say, so I mouth, *daaaamn.*

Eva appears a moment later, looking remarkably put together for someone who's spent the past thirty hours or so in bed with two satyrs. In fact, her color is back. Her red hair shines like silk, and her emerald eyes twinkle. She adjusts her navy wrap dress as she clicks across the room to us on a pair of stunning Louboutin pumps. She kisses River on the cheek.

"Hi Sophia," she says shyly.

"Hi." I glance between them both. There's obvious affection on River's face, and I've never seen Eva happier. "So now that the bargain is broken, can you finally tell me what you saw that day?"

Eva nods, growing serious. "I used my luck to clear the area around River's restaurant so that I could speak to him without anyone seeing us. It wasn't hard because so many people were distracted with the graduation. Still, to be safe, we met behind his restaurant. All I wanted was to steal a kiss and tell him I was letting myself into his house to get the coat I forgot the night before. But then we heard the shot and the scream."

River strokes a hand down the back of her head. "I ran around the building and saw a man on the walkway with a bloody hole in his chest. I immediately rushed to him, knelt down, and put pressure on the wound."

"Is that when you moved the gun?"

"I don't remember any gun," River says bitterly.

"And I don't either," Eva adds.

They look at each other as if they've just put it all together.

"But Godmother says your prints were on the murder weapon."

River nods. "She told me that, and I assumed I must have moved it without even thinking when I knelt down. But I don't remember that, Sophia. I never consciously saw a gun until Godmother and her team arrived. I was too focused on the bleeding human in front of me."

A dark pit forms in my stomach. We all know River was framed, but by whom? "The gun was there," I confirm, remembering it clearly a foot or two from River's knee. "Eva, did you see anyone ditch the gun?"

She shakes her head. "When I came around the corner, all I saw was River and the victim, but that's what's weird about the whole thing. I was using my luck to clear the area. So both the victim and the murderer must have been immune to it."

"River, were Adam's teeth blue?"

River snorts. "I don't think I ever saw his teeth, to be honest."

"You think he was on blue iron?" Eva asks.

"Must have been if he resisted your luck, right?" I cross my arms against a growing sense of dread. None of this is adding up. If the murderer left the gun near the body, where did they go so quickly?

Eva nods. "I did notice one other thing, but it's not infallible."

"I'll take anything you've got at this point."

"I *sensed* someone."

"Hmm?"

River puts a supportive arm around Eva's shoulders, and she glances up at him before she continues. "I had my luck up, and I sensed another fae's luck nearby... from the direction of the bank. I sensed there was someone else there, but I couldn't see them."

"What did their luck feel like?"

She sighed. "A spider. Giant and dark. The signature left me cold. The thing is, it might have nothing to do with the murder. It's completely possible that someone just shielded themselves with luck when they heard the shot."

"How strong was it? Another leprechaun could have neutralized your luck just as well as blue iron."

"It could have been a leprechaun, but I didn't recognize the signature. It was strong but different. I'm not sure if that was due to distance or something else."

Strong but different. I shake my head. Maybe a leprechaun. Maybe a pixie or satyr amplifying their luck with a charm. That would be rare, but I'm not ruling anything out at this point.

"I'm still struggling with how the gun got there though. Someone had to leave it behind after the murder." I try to think back to the crime scene and find my memory sketchy on the subject. Godmother was there so fast and cleaned everything up so thoroughly I never got close enough to really inspect the scene. Was there blood spray? In what direction? Is it possible the murderer shot Adam from behind the bank? But then how did the gun get to its spot beside River? I keep coming back to that point, and it's starting to hurt my head thinking about it. Seven was closer. I'll have to ask him what he remembers.

"The one thing all of us know for sure is that River didn't do this. So how do we prove that and get him out of here?"

Eva sighs. "I plan to go to Godmother and tell her what I know."

I cross my arms against a sense of unease at the thought. "Do you think you'll have better luck than I did? I don't think she cares about the truth as much as she wants a scapegoat. Her ego is everything. She'll never admit to a mistake unless there's undeniable proof."

"We've *got* to do something." Eva threads her fingers into River's and slants him a pitying look.

I study them both, desperate for an answer that seems just out of reach. "There are a few details I want to run down. Can you both wait a few days?"

"Depends. What kind of details are you talking about?" River asks.

"Now that I have Eva's perspective, I want to rewatch the security video for more clues. And then I want to do some research into which leprechauns have a luck aura that feels like a spider."

Eva snorts. "How do you plan to do that?"

Eva's phone vibrates, interrupting our conversation. She taps the screen, then turns wide eyes on me.

"Why is my brother texting me about finding you an outfit for the Gilded Gala?"

"What better place to meet a few leprechauns?" I grin.

Her mouth drops open. Luck is a strange and wonderful thing.

CHAPTER

TWENTY

O nce Evangeline came down from the surprise that I was attending the Gilded Gala on Seven's arm, she was quick to offer her help with styling Arden and me for the event, which, as it turns out, is a far more complicated endeavor than what I expected.

"It's not just that it has to be gold, you two. This year's event is a masquerade! Everyone's outfit will be designed to represent a historical or literary figure. It will take a hell of a lot of luck and influence to have anything ready on time. People have been planning their apparel for months. Some since the last gala!"

I glance at Arden, but she's glued to her phone. Texting Edmund, no doubt. I haven't had a moment alone with her in days. She's been with him every waking minute.

"Are you sure we'll be able to find something appropriate?" I ask.

She flashes an adorably mischievous grin. "Seven has made sure of it."

Jericho parks in front of a glass tower in Elderflame, and Eva leads me up the elevator to the twenty-fifth floor where a svelte black satyr with gracefully polished horns and a bespoke suit meets us at the door. He's a beautiful man, not just handsome but pretty, with perfect skin and enviable posture.

"Ms. Larkspur, I presume. Valentine Sullivan at your service."

Valentine bows slightly at the waist, and I am struck again by his grace and keen fashion sense, at the way the fabric of his suit reacts to his movement. It's breathtaking, like the man is wearing a silk waterfall.

"Thank you for helping us on such short notice," I say.

A smile dances across his face, bringing out dimples in his cheeks. "You must know that Mr. Delaney is a very good customer. What he wants, he gets. It appears he wants the two of you dressed for the gala, and I have strict orders to make sure every eye is on you."

Eva slides her hands into her pockets. "I'm not sure my brother understands what goes into a gala gown. We'll be happy with anything you can do for us."

Valentine snorts and couples his perfectly manicured hands. "Not what I can do but what I have done. Follow me."

"Arden!" I elbow her in the arm and gesture for her to put her phone away.

"It's Edmund. We're just making plans for dinner. I'm supposed to meet his mom," she whispers as she falls into step behind Valentine.

I close my eyes for a beat. I've put off this conversation far too long. "About that, there's something I need to tell you—"

"Here we are," Valentine says, gesturing toward three chairs as music starts to play. I lower myself into one of them. "We'll start with our sweet Arden. My designers and I stayed up all night preparing three prototypes for you. Come in, girls."

Three gorgeous young pixies stride into the room, only they've used their illusion to make themselves look exactly like Arden. They approach, turn, walk away. One is in a mermaid gown designed to give the impression of a golden toga, another in a dress with bell sleeves and lace that belongs on an eighteenth-century British queen, and the third wears a delicate, sleeveless wrap dress cinched at the waist by a thick band of gold metal. Two gold bracers cover her forearms, and an ornate golden mask depicting leaves and branches with two golden stag horns rises from her temples. A coordinating bow and quiver of arrows completes the outfit.

Valentine gestures proudly at the three. "I give you

Persephone, Queen Anne of the humans, and, my personal favorite, Artemis, goddess of the hunt."

"Holy crap," Arden says softly. "Is that really what I look like from behind?"

I chuckle. "Yes, and everyone should be so lucky. What do you think?"

She stares, open mouthed, at each model. "I can't stop looking at Artemis. Can I try it on?"

Valentine makes a show of taking her hand and the hand of the Artemis model and leading them both to a set of changing rooms. They disappear inside.

"I love when my patrons are so easily suited," Valentine says. "Now, Ms. Larkspur, you were a bit more difficult. I wanted to capture the femininity of your pixie blood but also the inner fire and courage that allowed you to survive so long outside our world." He claps his hands, and I watch three more models walk into the room. They look exactly like me, and I suddenly understand why Arden found this unsettling.

The first outfit is made to resemble armor but in a formfitting dress. It comes with a helmetlike mask with wings along the side. "For you, to fortify you against what promises to be a trying evening, I give you a Valkyrie."

"Oooh," Eva says. "You could be a warrior."

"I don't feel like a warrior," I say honestly.

The next model strides forward, dressed in another toga-like dress with a mask to make her look like an owl. Valentine spreads his hands. "Athena, goddess of wisdom."

I smile. It is beautiful but not really me.

The next model takes my breath away. The lining of the strapless princess dress is midnight-blue silk, but it's covered in a layer of tulle embroidered with tiny cascading gold stars, each with a tiny diamond sewn into its center. An asymmetrical, gold filigree laser-cut mask decorated with diamonds perches delicately on the nose of the model. But the best part of the ensemble is the crown of dark crystals on her head, illuminated by hidden lights.

"Oh," I say, hand splaying across my chest. "That's beautiful."

Eva gapes. "Valentine, you have outdone yourself."

"Titania, Shakespeare's queen of fairies, here displaying her rule over the stars. I believe it will suit you."

I stand. "I'd like to try it."

Valentine's smile lights up the room. Twenty minutes later, Arden and I stand on a small platform in front of a large three-way mirror, expertly pinned into our dresses and assessing our new looks.

"What do you think?" I ask Arden. She is a convincing goddess, the highlights in her auburn hair drawn out by the gold metal mask.

"I love it. But Mom, you look stunning. I still can't believe you and Seven are back together again, but any man alive would stop in his tracks if he saw you."

I smile at her. I've spent a little luck to make my hair darker and my teeth whiter to complete the look, but honestly, the dress itself is so flattering I don't have to do much.

"The dress is designed to accommodate your wings," Valentine says. "I confess, I've rarely had opportunity to design for a pixie, but I am pleased with the results."

I pivot on my gold stilettos and smile down at Eva. "What do you think?"

"I think fifty percent of the attendees at the Gilded Gala are going to be hot and bothered by the two of you, and the other fifty percent are going to have a jealous meltdown. You *must* have that dress, Sophia."

I release a deep breath and look toward Valentine. "How much do I owe you?" I'm sure I can't afford these dresses, but maybe I can rent them for the night.

Valentine spreads his hands. "Mr. Delaney has already taken care of it, Ms. Larkspur. Now, if you don't mind changing, I'll have the dresses tailored and brought to the address of your choosing by the end of the week."

I MEET SEVEN BACK AT HIS PLACE THAT NIGHT. HIS FACE lights up when he sees me. It's easier now that my parents and Arden know about our relationship, and I happily throw myself into his arms.

"Thank you for the dress," I whisper.

I feel him smile against the side of my neck. "I can't wait to see you in it."

Luck coils around me, and I inhale sharply at the pulse that sizzles in my blood. But I shake my head and push him away. "Uh-uh. If we start this, we'll be distracted for the rest of the night."

He looks at me through his lashes, his tongue grazing his bottom lip. "Sounds good to me."

I place a hand on the center of his chest. "First tell me how it went with your father."

With a groan, he turns from me and mumbles something about needing a drink. He pours himself one at the bar, then holds up an empty glass in lieu of asking me what I'd like.

"Vodka and tonic."

He fixes me the drink and hands it over.

"Did you get him to talk?"

"The problem wasn't getting him to talk." Seven sips his bourbon. "The problem was that what he said made no sense, and when he said it, he was entirely naked and writing on the walls in his own blood."

I scowl. "I had a similar experience. So he didn't tell you anything about Rayrcore or where the malivite mine is?"

"He told me that it was my holy duty to bulldoze the wall and free the unseelie."

I squint at him. "What now?"

"Exactly what he said. 'Walls. There are too many

walls, Seven. Too many rules. Tear it all down. Let the strongest survive. We are the strongest.'" He does an uncanny imitation of his father's voice, and I shiver at the accuracy.

Blinking away my confusion, I ask, "And this has what to do with Rayrcore?"

He snorts. "Absolutely nothing. I learned nothing about the mine or the malivite. I recorded our interaction if you'd like to watch it. There's an especially poignant moment where he takes a piss in the corner of his cell while he's talking to me."

"Eww. No, thanks. I trust your assessment."

He takes another long drink. "How'd it go with River?"

I straighten, feeling all the blood drain from my face. "There's something I have to tell you. Only maybe I shouldn't. It isn't really my story to tell. But it does relate to this and to you and I did find out here, while you were in with your doctor."

He sits down in the chair across from me and runs his fingers through his hair. "I give you full immunity. I will not shoot the messenger."

"It's not that... It's just..."

Seven arches one brow at me. This is important. Sorry Eva, I need his help if we're going to save River and that means he needs to know now. "Your sister was the third," I blurt.

His eyes narrow to slits. "Third what?"

"Eva was the one with River the morning of the

murder. She's the one who made the bargain and why River couldn't say her name. She's broken the bargain now and is prepared to tell Godmother the truth to free him."

Seven's eyes widen. He crosses an ankle over one knee. "My sister is having an affair with two satyrs?"

I nod slowly. "River and Patrick. More than an affair, I think. I met with Eva and River today, and they seemed happy. I believe they have genuine feelings for each other."

Seven's lips press together. "I'm not sure what to think about that."

"Maybe you should talk to her about it."

"I plan to." He swallows hard. "While I'm processing that bombshell, did either of them have any clue about who actually murdered Adam Barker?"

"Not exactly, but Eva said she felt someone's power, probably a leprechaun. Their luck signature was a massive dark spider. She sensed them standing behind the wall of the bank. Do you know anyone who fits that description?"

Threading his fingers, he tenses, leaning forward in his chair. "Maybe. There are a few people who have dark insect-like energy."

"You were there before I was. Did the blood from the victim spray away from that direction?"

He thinks for a minute, then rubs the back of his neck. "You know, the only blood I remember was all over River."

"But the man was shot."

"Godmother cleaned up that crime scene so quickly. It's possible she hid the blood. Equally possible the bullet didn't go all the way though him."

"If that's true, it means we have further proof that River is innocent. The gun was found next to him, but a shot at close range would have gone through the victim."

"Maybe he shot Adam from a distance and then ran to his side with the gun."

"Why would anyone do that?"

"I don't know. I'm just preparing you for what Godmother might say. She's going to use any excuse not to free River."

"If the shot was taken at a distance, it's highly likely the murderer is the fae whose luck manifests as a spider. I don't know how the gun got to River's side, but I do know there's something here. We're close. Can you look at Godmother's records and see what the coroner found out? If the bullet entered at an angle that supports it being fired from behind the bank, we'll have even more evidence to free him."

"I'll do one better. I'll check the surveillance video for that side of the bank. Maybe we'll get lucky and whoever tampered with the security system was so focused on the body they forgot the cameras around the bank."

I inhale sharply. "No. Even if they did remember to wipe those cameras too, that proves they were covering something that happened there, which also proves River's innocence."

Seven nods, then leans his head back on the chair and stares at the ceiling. "We should go down to the security office now and review the video."

He's dressed in slacks and a work shirt, although his suit jacket and tie are strewn across the back of the sofa. The neck of his shirt is open, and I can see the scar where the doctor stitched him up following Rayrcore's torture. He's barely healed, and it's clear the events of the day have wrung him out. "You look exhausted, Seven. We have time."

He sighs. "We don't. There's a murderer on the loose. We should check on Saul. See if he's awake. Maybe he heard something about Rayrcore's motives while he was being held captive. And we haven't even touched on what we should tell Godmother about this mess. She's going to want a status update soon."

I stand. "All of that will still be there in an hour."

Seven closes his eyes. When he speaks, his voice is strained. "I know you don't want to hear this, Sophia, but you should really think twice about this weekend. All this shit, it isn't going away once we go public. Godmother still *owns* me. People are going to harass us. If they find out about Eva, the entire Delaney family name is going to be smeared across the gossip columns." His throat bobs on a hard swallow, and a muscle in his jaw twitches. "You should get out now. What if you change your mind about me? What if your feelings change but it's too late because you've already been caught up in this gilded machine I was born into?"

"What if I leave you when you're at your most vulnerable?"

His body clenches like I've hit him in the gut, and his eyes pop open. I've poked a sore spot that needs to be poked. His mother abandoned him to his abusive father, but I'm not them.

"I'd forgive you, Sophia. I couldn't blame you. I really couldn't." A dark cloud passes over his expression, his fingers digging into the arm of the chair. I've never seen a man drawn limb from limb, but he's doing a fantastic impression. He might come apart at any moment. "My family is a fucking mess. This thing with Godmother is a curse. Leprechaun society is a scourge. I love you too much to see your life ruined because of me. I love you enough to let you go."

My heart gives an anguished thump at the thought, and I cross the living room to stand between his knees. Nothing is going to tear me from this man, not even him.

I lean over and place my hands on his thighs. "There's a problem with that plan."

He looks at me with an intensity that seems to cut straight to my soul. "What's that?"

"I love you. And see, I know what it's like to live with you and without you, and I choose with you even if that means we have to build a castle with a moat and we only lower the drawbridge for nice people who are supportive of our relationship."

"A castle?" He gives a breathy laugh.

"Yes, a castle is what we need. I'll be like Cinderella with her prince at the ball every night for the rest of my life."

"You know what they never tell you about Cinderella?"

Lots of things. I've been pondering the failings of fairy tales for some time now, but I'm curious what he thinks, so I ask, "What?"

"They never talk about how the townspeople treat her once she marries the prince. She has to rule over her wicked stepmother and stepsisters, who probably gossip about her all over town. After the wedding, when the glass slippers are packed away, you've got to wonder what happened to her. She wasn't born to be a princess, and being royalty isn't always what it's cracked up to be. What if meeting the prince wasn't the answer to a wish but a curse?"

I smile down at him, my beautiful, damaged, and selfless man, and I tell him the conclusion I've come to about these tales. "They do tell you the end of the story, Seven. *They both live happily ever after*, and it's not because it's easy or that Cinderella magically knows how to be a royal. It's not because there are no bumps in the road. They live happily ever after because they're together, and in the end, that's all that matters. Life will always be hard. People will always be cruel. But love and family, it's priceless."

His hands sweep under my skirt and land on the back of my thighs. "I don't deserve you."

I unzip my dress, step out of it, and kick it to the side. "No, you don't," I say through a smirk. I lower myself to my knees and reach for his fly. "But I keep you around for your giant cock."

"Sophia... I'm serious—" His words are choked off by a distinctly male sound as I make short work of his button and zipper and take his dick in my hands. He's already hard, looking down at me with a soul-deep vulnerability. I wonder how long it took him to work up the courage to try to convince me to leave him. I wonder how long it will take me to convince him I'll never go.

I tighten my grip around the base of his shaft and slowly swirl my tongue around the head. His thighs clench and his stomach tenses beneath his shirt. It's a power trip. I work my fingers lower to play with his balls, then leisurely lick from base to tip, adding a swirl of my tongue over the crown again where I know he's most sensitive. His breath quickens, but he doesn't move. I do it again, adding the slightest bit of suction at the tip.

He groans. "Gods, Sophia..."

I stare up into his eyes as I take one more languid lick and then suck him deep into my mouth, repositioning myself until he's all the way to the back of my throat. This time that sound turns into a growl. His fingers claw the back of my head, gathering my hair into his grip so he can watch me. *Good.*

Taking him deep again and again, I suck harder, move my tongue up and down his cock. His grip tightens at the back of my head, and then he finally starts to move, thrusting hard and quick into my mouth. His luck rises in the room, tingling hot against my skin, between my breasts, between my legs. It draws my nipples to tight peaks beneath the silk of my bra.

"You're fucking mine," he says between thrusts, his voice taking on a commanding edge. "Your hot little mouth will never touch another cock, you understand?"

I suck harder in answer and groan as he hits the back of my throat. I'm so hot and wound up I reach between my legs and play with myself as his luck rushes through me. The sight must be enough to push him over the edge because his grip on me tightens and he erupts inside my mouth without warning.

I swallow everything he gives me, my own pleasure building as his luck fills me with hot, vibrating energy. He only lets go of me when I've taken all he has to give. Tugging on my hair, he pulls my mouth off his cock and I pant up at him, eyeing him wickedly.

"Whose are you?" he demands.

"Yours." I wipe my thumb under my bottom lip and spread my knees wider on the carpet. "Always."

He makes a strangled sound, then pushes me until my back hits the carpet. My panties are off in a heartbeat, and the next second, his tongue is licking up my center. Only it isn't just his tongue—hot currents of luck are buzzing inside me like the world's best vibrator. One hand splays across my lower abdomen as the other joins in on the fun. He works one long finger inside me, then two, rubbing circles in just the right place, his breath hot against my clit.

A storm is gathering inside me, low and heavy in my torso. I pant through the intensity, arching against his mouth. "More."

I grab his head and press him into me. He doesn't disappoint.

The orgasm rips through me like a stroke of lightning, but it doesn't stop. His luck chases it, driving it higher. My head is tipped back and I'm blinded by pleasure when he enters me, pitching me over the edge again. His fingers dig into my hips, holding me as he thrusts into my clenching pussy.

"Don't forget you chose this," he grits out. "There's no going back."

I wrap my arms and legs around him as he empties himself into me again, and my body decides to reward me with yet another mind-blowing orgasm. I'm so high I think I might never come down. Slowly, like two feathers dropped from a height, we both return to earth.

"Fuck, that was intense," he says, rising so he can look at me.

"Yeah, it was. And I loved every minute of it."

"Good, because I predict it's going to happen frequently in the future."

I reach up to toy with a strand of his hair. "What makes you so sure?"

He strokes the side of my face. "We're going to need something to do in our castle."

TWENTY-ONE

On the night of the Gilded Gala, I emerge from Seven's room dressed in my perfectly tailored gown and carrying my mask. Valentine was right— this may be the only dress that could make me feel confident tonight. I feel like a queen and I stand up straighter, the weight of the crown light on my head.

Seven stops in his tracks when he sees me, his eyes trailing over me. "Gods, Sophia, I have half a mind to tell Jericho we won't need the car after all." He steps in close and grips my chin, running his thumb just under my pouty red lips. "The things I'd like to do to that hot little mouth."

"You'll smear my lipstick." I give him a wink.

"Oh, if that's your concern, there are plenty of things I can think of to do to you that don't involve your mouth." A firm, hot tingle runs up my inner thigh and settles between my legs.

"Seven," I say breathlessly, my hand rising to hold my crown in place as my knees threaten to give out. "Control yourself!"

The tingle stops, and he brushes a hand down his sleeve. "For now."

"You look incredible by the way." He's opted for a velvet tuxedo in midnight blue that matches the bodice of my dress, with a white vest and tie. Understated by Gilded Gala standards, except that all his trimmings are gold. His watch, his cuff links, the buttons on his shirt, and—most importantly—his mask, which is entirely gold and includes a helmet with two impressive horns. "Loki seems appropriate. You're about to pull the trick of the century."

He slants an impish smile. "You picked up on that, huh? Perfectly choreographed leprechaun society is about to go down in flames and topple into chaos. I think we should try to enjoy it. Loki and Titania seem perfectly appropriate. Thank you, Valentine." He smiles and leans forward to place a kiss on my cheek.

We pull apart when the door to the guest room opens and Arden strides toward us, looking like the living, breathing manifestation of Artemis. She's left her auburn hair down in loose waves that gather at her shoulders, but her makeup is exquisite and Valentine's filmy gold dress hugs her body like a whisper.

Seven groans.

"What's wrong with you?" Arden asks.

"Just wondering why I trusted Valentine," he says through his teeth, eyes rolling.

I chuckle. "He thinks you look lovely, Arden."

A tight smile spreads his lips. "Yes, lovely. Are you cold? I can fetch a sweater."

"Not even a little bit," she says through a laugh.

"Did you bring the wish?" he asks, smile fading.

"Yeah." She moves her hair aside to expose the gold acorn at her throat. "Although, based on how powerful the two of you say it is, I hope I don't have to use it."

I run my fingers over the coin at my neck. "It's only for emergencies. Rayrcore isn't going to be happy when they discover we've tricked them, and this is a very public event. We'll be exposed. Seven and I will both feel more comfortable if you have it with you."

Seven slides his hands into the pockets of his jacket. "It just amplifies your luck with a little magic, Arden. It works the same as we've practiced. Focus your intention, hold it against your skin, and the wish will do the rest. Only if you need it, and keep the wish small so you don't drain yourself."

She cracks her neck. "We're really doing this then? I'm going to be introduced as a leprechaun tonight?"

I look between the two great loves of my life and nod. "We are."

Moments later, we're all in the back of Seven's car, headed for the hotel.

As sure as I am about going public with our relationship, my stomach is a ball of nerves. "All right, I'm a little excited for this, come what may. As long as we're together as a family, it will be all right."

Arden shifts in her seat beside me. "I guess this is a good time to tell you both that I've already broken the news to Edmund."

I stiffen. "You did what? I thought we agreed we were all keeping this a secret before today?"

"I couldn't have him find out at the gala." She spreads her hands. "We're in love. What kind of person would I be if I sprang this on him in that setting?"

All levity drains from Seven's expression. "Does his mother know?"

She shrugs, her emerald eyes flashing. "I told him not to tell anyone, but I mean, it's possible." She folds her arms. "What's the big deal anyway? Everyone is going to know in about ten minutes."

Seven sighs. "It probably doesn't matter, Arden, but you need to understand that Edmund's mother and I have a history."

She nods. "You used to be engaged to her. She told me."

I widen my eyes at her. "What exactly did she say?"

Arden shrugs. "Just that she knew you worked for Seven and that she and Seven had been engaged in the past until you both decided to break it off. That's it."

Both decided. What a creative memory Alicia has.

"Be careful with her, Arden. She's not what she seems," Seven says.

Arden bristles. "Mrs. Faust has been nothing but nice to me, and I like her. I want to be with Edmund, and that means getting along with his family. Whatever went on between you, it's in the past, right?"

There's an edge to Arden's voice, and I watch Seven's jaw harden against it.

The sound of cheering grabs our attention, and we all look out the tinted windows. Thanks to special approval by Godmother, Jericho is able to drive us right up to the edge of the rainbow carpet.

"We'll talk about this later," Seven says.

Arden shoots him a look that makes it clear the conversation is over as far as she's concerned.

"Arden," I say quickly. "There's more to this than you think. The Fausts have a history."

"We're here," Seven says. "Masks."

I tie on my Titania mask and help Arden to do hers. The door opens. Mask in place, Seven steps from the vehicle to a roar of cheers and a storm of flashing lights.

Voices scream, "Seeeeveeen! Seeeveeen! Oh my gods, he's Loki!" Crowds of women wave at him from behind the velvet rope. He holds out a hand to me.

"Here we go," I whisper to Arden. I place my fingers in Seven's and use a little luck to gracefully slide from the limo, unraveling my wings as I do so that they are on full display.

The cheering stops but the camera's don't. I smile up at Seven, and we take a step forward. The murmurs in the crowd grow louder as Seven holds out his other hand to Arden. She emerges from the vehicle, careful to straighten her bow and quiver as she takes Seven's hand and steps between us. Jericho closes the door behind us, and then the three of us walk the rainbow carpet, arm in arm, toward the building.

The walk feels long with every eye boring into us. I concentrate on the entrance. Black balloons have been strung together to make the hotel entrance look like the side of a cauldron. There's nothing subtle about it. We are pieces of gold, sliding down a rainbow into a pot of gold.

"Seven!" a woman calls from up ahead. She's standing beside a camera with a *Daily Hatter* badge on the side. "Who is that with you?"

Seven pauses and turns to her, a smile spreading across his face that perfectly fits his Loki costume. "This is my date, Sophia Larkspur, and our daughter, Arden."

We start to walk again as the murmurs rise to a fever pitch, and the woman from the *Hatter* elbows her way through the crowd to keep pace.

"Sorry, but did you say Arden is your daughter?"

Seven stops again, and we all smile for a picture. "Yes," Seven says clearly. "Arden is my and Sophia's daughter. We are a modern family. Now, if you'll excuse me."

We walk again as the crowd goes absolutely wild. We're surrounded by a sea of recording cell phones and snapping lenses, people crying out questions.

"Why are you dating a pixie?"

"Did you pay for Sophia to leave Devashire because of the baby?"

"Why are you legitimizing Arden now?"

All the questions are aimed at Seven, as if Arden and I are mere accessories on his arms.

Eva arrives alone behind us and waves to the crowd. Her dress is evocative of *The Little Mermaid*, making stunning work of her red hair, but no one is even looking in her direction aside from me. They don't stop screaming questions at us. A few charge the barrier, and the security guards have to intervene. We all take a deep breath when we enter the antechamber inside the front doors.

"Wow, that was scary," Arden says, one hand pressing into her stomach. "Did you see how they were shoving the security guards?"

"Stay close," Seven says. "It's going to get worse before it gets better."

An usher directs us up a flight of stairs to a balcony overlooking the gala ballroom.

A sharply dressed leprechaun with a clipboard glances at Seven. "Mr. Delaney, pleasure to see you again. The master of ceremonies wishes to know how you would like to be introduced?"

"Seven Delaney with Sophia Larkspur and, introducing for the very first time, their daughter, Arden Delaney."

The man lifts his head in alarm, frowning at my wings, and glares at Seven as if he smells something bad. "Are you certain, sir?"

"Is there a problem?" Seven's luck barges into the room, the dragon energy spreading its wings. Everyone within a ten-foot radius feels it. Behind us, Eva grins as the landing grows increasingly quiet.

"No, sir." The man taps his earpiece and whispers Seven's instructions into it, then repeats himself... twice.

"Very well, sir. Please proceed forward. The MC will announce you, and then you may descend to the main floor." The man's gaze drifts down his nose at me and Arden, and then he moves on to Eva behind us.

Fingers thread with mine, and I glance down to see Arden taking my hand. For the first time, she looks truly nervous. Her chest rises and falls abnormally fast.

"It's okay," I whisper. "We're together. It's okay."

"Edmund said he'd support me." She glances down at the crowd below. "Do you think he will?"

"If he doesn't, he's an idiot."

Seven takes a step forward as they announce the couple in front of us. Arden releases my hand to take Seven's arm again. I do the same, and we step to the center of a brilliant gold staircase with a plush red runner down the center.

All eyes turn up at us, the masks on the crowd below making them appear less seelie and more monster under the candelabra. A hush falls over the gala.

"Seven Delaney with guest Sophia Larkspur and, for the first time ever, introducing their daughter, Arden Delaney."

Gasps rise from the crowd and we begin our descent, step by painfully slow step. Behind the masks, some of the faces show signs of disgust. Others fascination. And still others are unreadable, as if they are calculating how this strange turn of events might benefit or challenge them and are keeping their options open.

My gaze falls on Edmund, who's dressed as one of the three musketeers. I have to hand it to him—he's the only one smiling, and he's watching Arden as if she's the only source of light in a dark room. He approaches as we reach the landing.

"You do know how to make an entrance," he says, his gaze flicking over the three of us. "Arden, would you care to dance?"

Arden looks at me and then at Seven, who also looks at me. *Fuck.* I'm not entirely comfortable with her being out of my sight in this mob, most of whom seem increasingly angry. *Come on, Sophia, think.* I put myself at the poker table. My heart slows. I look at the choices in front of me, and then I trust my gut.

"Seven and I will go with you. I'm always up for some dancing." I slip my hand into Seven's.

Edmund leads Arden through the ballroom to where a satyr orchestra plays, with us right behind them.

When we reach the dance floor, Seven pulls me into his arms. "Smart move. I didn't think she'd take it well if we said no."

"Absolutely not, especially considering he was the only one with a smile for us when we entered the room." We turn three times and continue our waltz. Seven has to lift me to keep from tripping over my feet. "You're very good at this."

"I've done it every year since I was fifteen," he says dryly. "But never with such an attractive partner." His eyes flick to where Edmund is teaching Arden the steps. "I should have taught this dance to Arden."

I look over my shoulder at her. "She seems to be enjoying herself. I wouldn't worry about it."

"How?"

"How what?"

"How do you not constantly worry? All I've done is worry about her since the moment I found out she was mine."

I meet his eyes—deep, fathomless pools of green— through the holes of his mask. "The truth is, I do worry, or at least I start to. But then I remember that she's my daughter and I've raised her to be savvy about life, to make good decisions but also to know when she's made a mistake and own it."

"You've done a phenomenal job with her. I should trust in that."

I give him a soft smile. "It was you also. Many of the lessons I taught her were things I'd learned from you."

His lips part, but he remains silent.

"Poker, of course. When to bet and when to fold. How to bluff. But also that friends and lovers can come into our lives from unexpected places. That sometimes society is wrong about what should or shouldn't be. That sometimes people might hurt you but that the fight isn't over if you can get back up again."

"I never meant to hurt you."

"I know, but the lesson is the same." I glance back at Arden and watch as she spins across the floor in Edmund's arms. "Your daughter is a survivor. Never underestimate her. She has too much of you in her to be taken advantage of."

He pulls me closer, his nostrils flaring as he inhales slowly. "It's the part of her that comes from me that I'm worried about. Or need I remind you that Godmother still has her chains around my neck thanks to the fool I was at her age?"

"And here I am publicly announcing my love for you. I must be an equal fool. Maybe we *should* be afraid for her." We turn three times, and I spot Arden and

Edmund again by a table of drinks. She looks like she's enjoying herself.

"Tell me, Cinderella," Seven says, "now that you've made it to the ball, is it all you imagined it would be?"

I lean in close and say in the most seductive voice I can muster, "Oh, I made it to the ball last night, and I found every inch of it worth the effort."

Seven makes a choking sound, his eyebrows lifting. A rush of luck bubbles through me, and I miss a step. He lifts me and sets me on my feet again.

We stop dancing, and he leads me to the drink table opposite the one where Edmund and Arden are now talking with Edmund's mother, Alicia.

Seven's expression sags when he sees her. "Is it too early to call it a night?"

"I have until midnight with these crystal slippers." I glance around the room again. "Besides, I'm just starting to enjoy myself. Not as many people are hatefully glaring in our direction as before. I think the shock has worn off. Oh wait. That person looks overly interested."

"That's Fredrick Graceling. He's provost of Elderflame University and rumor has it quite the playboy. I've caught him staring at your ass since we took the floor."

"How charming," I say sarcastically, glancing back at the bearded leprechaun dressed as a wizard. "Although he is quite attractive for a man whose sole purpose is to smoke a pipe and tell others they're going on a quest."

Seven smothers a laugh. "Be nice. He's coming this way."

"Delaney, will you introduce me to your lovely friend?" Graceling flashes a warm smile.

"I can do the honors myself. Sophia Larkspur. And you?"

"Fredrick Graceling."

"Are you sure your name isn't Albus or Gandalf?"

He breaks into a low chuckle. "This one is clever, Seven. Wherever have you been hiding her?"

"In my poker room. She teaches there five days a week," he mumbles.

But Graceling doesn't even hear him. He's studying me, his gaze lingering where my dress meets my skin. I feel his luck rise and circle me like a massive gray owl. "Delaney, do you mind if I borrow Sophia for a dance?"

"Sophia can decide that for herself," Seven deadpans.

Graceling extends a hand to me and I take it.

"It's your feet," I warn him, loud enough for Seven to hear. I catch him chuckling behind Graceling's head.

We begin to dance. Graceling is barely older than Seven but far less nimble on his feet. I try my best to follow his lead.

"The Titania costume suits you," he says. "You

might as well be the queen of the fairies for how much attention you're commanding tonight."

"It's not hard—just grow a set of wings."

He gives a light laugh. "I find it refreshing honestly. We at Elderflame have long thought it was time to break the gold ceiling on this gala."

"Oh? It's a wonder I'm the first one then."

"I know what you're thinking, that I sit in my ivory tower talking about it when people like Delaney and yourself do it, but what you don't know is that I've invited a number of pixies over the years and all have refused me. No one wants to open themselves up to the possible backlash."

"Then I'm proud to be the first."

He spins me around and I feel his thumb stroke along my spine. A glance toward Seven and I know he hasn't missed it. The look he's giving Fredrick could bend a silver spoon in half.

"I wonder, are you and Seven exclusive or are you here together to support your daughter, Arden?"

"Exclusive," I blurt. "Extremely. We are as serious about each other as two people can be."

"Hmm. A sad day for me then. One less beautiful fish in the sea."

Stars and lightning, he did not just say that. I stop myself short of rolling my eyes. I focus on Seven and the death glare he's giving the back of Graceling's head.

"Anyway, there's something else I wanted to

discuss with you, and it has to do with your dear Arden."

"Oh?" Now he has my full and complete attention.

"I wanted to give you the unofficial news that I approved Arden's admission to our premed program just today. She should receive a letter of acceptance this week."

I grip his shoulder excitedly. "That is wonderful news. Thank you, Fredrick."

"My pleasure. She's a wonderful candidate, and I know we won't be disappointed in the decision."

"Do you mind if I go tell her?" I slow my feet, and we grind to a stop.

"Are you sure your mind is settled on Delaney?"

I slant him a consoling smile. "Forever and always."

He gives a disgruntled huff. "Well then, please." He removes his hands from me and wanders off toward a group of women dressed as muses in the corner of the room. I whirl around, searching for Arden. This is shaping up to be one hell of a night. She's going to flip when she learns she's in!

I cross the room to the drink table where I last saw her talking to Edmund and his mother, but she's not there anymore. I whirl and scan the dance floor. Not there either. Nor do I see either of the Fausts.

Seven is still staring at me like he wants to tattoo MINE across my chest, so I put him out of his misery and join him again.

"Does it bother you that I danced with another man?" I trace my fingers along the edge of his velvet jacket, my knuckles brushing his abs through his shirt.

There's heat in his eyes when he looks at me. "Yes. If he wasn't a leprechaun and we weren't in polite company, he'd have had a very hard time of it. One blast of luck and he'd have fallen on that pointy hat of his."

"Oh, you are grouchy tonight. He was a very nice man—"

"He touched your back."

"He told me Arden has been admitted to Elderflame."

"He did?" Seven's lips twitch upward.

"That was what he wanted to tell me and to welcome me to the gala. Apparently he's an advocate."

"Hmm. A good thing I didn't shove his hat up his ass then."

"Where's Arden? I want to tell her the good news."

"She was right—" Seven's head snaps around to where we both saw her last, but she still isn't there.

"I looked there and the dance floor. I can't find her or Edmund. I can't find Alicia either." I dig my phone out of my purse and text her. "She's not answering my texts."

I feel his luck rise around us.

He takes my hand and leads me toward the back of the room. "Come on."

"Let's not get too worried. She's probably just in some corner somewhere, making out with Edmund."

Seven flashes an annoyed look in my direction and tugs me behind him. We circle the first floor and then the second. I start to worry when I feel Seven's luck burn hotter against my skin. "I can't sense her, Sophia."

"Wait, I just remembered something." I pull out my phone again and navigate to the Find Phone app. We set it up a while back in case one of us forgot their phone somewhere. I locate Arden's. "Seven? This doesn't make sense. It says she's at the casino, but isn't it closed tonight because of the gala?"

Seven's phone rings, and I watch all the blood drain from his face as he brings it to his ear.

"Seven, why is Arden at the casino?" I ask again.

He slides the phone back into his pocket and pulls me toward the elevator. "Because she isn't at the casino, she's under it. They have her."

TWENTY-TWO

W hen your kid is in trouble, time stops. Everything in you focuses on one thing—doing whatever it takes to get her back. Right now I understand how those stories about mothers experiencing an adrenaline rush and lifting a car off their trapped children might be true. I'd burrow through a wall if I thought it would help right now. There is no morality. I have no boundaries. I will do anything to get her back.

We descend into the tunnels, and Jericho arrives with the car. Seven takes over behind the wheel and tells him to go home for the night, and then we're racing toward the casino.

"What exactly did Alicia say to you?" I ask him.

"They have Arden and if we want her back, we both need to come to the mirror. This has to be about Rayrcore. I wouldn't put it past Alicia to be one of the people working with my dad. She's exactly the type of power-hungry tyrant he'd trust with something like this. I'm just not sure exactly what she wants from us."

"That bitch is going to pay, Seven."

"Yeah, she is."

Seven is driving fast enough to make me nervous we'll collide with something in the narrow passageways but not nearly fast enough for my taste. We arrive outside the tunnel, and I practically dive from the vehicle. I start running for the mirror, then realize I can't get through the wards without Seven.

He's right there behind me, his eyes glowing emerald, his luck growing larger by the second, like a great sleeping dragon waking and unraveling toward its enemy. We've reached the archway, and he doesn't even pause. He grabs my hand and yanks me through.

The wards are a sharp prickle against my skin, and then we're in that ancient room again, panting and slick with sweat. We're not alone. Alicia Faust stands with the staff in one hand and a phone in the other. She holds it up to show me the screen, a picture of Arden and me with the penguins at the zoo several years ago. That's Arden's phone!

"She's not hurt," Alicia says loudly and clearly. "But she will be if you don't do exactly as I say."

Seven's luck snaps at her, an angry beast, but her dark eyes spark and another presence enters the room. A large, dark spider.

"It was you," I say breathlessly.

Alicia pretends I'm not even there. "Hurt me and they hurt her. Do you understand?"

"I understand," Seven says.

I don't understand anything, but I'll do what I have to to make her take me to Arden.

"Follow me." She stabs the staff into the silver and starts to stir.

I glance at Seven. She's vulnerable while she stirs the silver. We could easily take her right now. But I see in his eyes the same concern as my own. I know in my gut she's not bluffing. Only Alicia knows where Arden is, which means she's the only one who can direct the mirror. And if Rayrcore is behind this and they're treating Arden like they did him and Saul, we can't risk not doing exactly what she says.

The portal opens, and Alicia leaps into the tunnel of falling stars. Seven and I clasp hands and dive in after her. It's more disorienting this time than before, and I wonder if it's because I'm the third in and it's Alicia's consciousness that's directing us. I put my trust in Seven. When we finally topple out the other side onto a stone floor, I feel like I've had the wind knocked out of me and I roll into a ball on my side, hugging myself.

Stone, yes, but not the same as before. I run trembling fingers over the floor, surprised, confused. I lift my face, still half-expecting to see Rayrcore's garage and stare up at a man whose face I only know from textbooks and stock photos.

The only way to describe him is golden and filled with light. His hair is white and his skin sun-kissed where it peeks outside his tunic. He's a tall, large man. But it's the crown of stars that halos his head that tells me exactly who he is.

"Welcome to Thistlebend Castle."

We're in Shadowvale?

"King Kieran," Seven says through his teeth.

My mind races like a swirling top, but my instincts lead me to Arden. She's there, chained but otherwise unhurt, although it's clear she's been crying.

"Mom?"

"I'm here, baby!" I scramble to my feet, but the two unseelie monsters who guard her step in front of her and stab their spears in my direction before I can reach her. They're at least seven feet tall with black skin drawn taut over horrific, wolflike forms. Wolflike if a wolf was shorn of all its hair, stretched and twisted. They stand on two legs but look like they run on four.

"You have what you want. Let my son go," Alicia demands. I notice Edmund then, across the room, chained and guarded in the same way Arden is. Arden is staring at him, but he keeps his gaze locked on the floor.

Kieran waves a hand in the air. "Give her the boy. He's done the task appointed to him and earned his place."

One of the black creatures releases Edmund, and

he runs into his mother's arms. The two move for the mirror, but Kieran raises a hand.

"Stay where you are, Alicia. We're not done here."

Seven trades a deadly look with Alicia, and I send my own dagger-filled stare after his. If I ever get out of this, I'm going to make her and her brat pay.

"Release Arden as well," Seven demands.

"Whether Arden walks out of my castle or is carried out in the bellies of my hounds is up to you, young Delaney."

"What do you want from me?" Seven's eyes flash, and I sense him holding back his power. Kieran is rumored to be as formidable as Godmother. She bested him, which is why he's here, but she's the only one who ever has as far as I know. Seven is wise to tread lightly.

I inch toward Arden, hoping Seven is enough of a diversion that I can reach her.

"Stay right there, Ms. Larkspur," Kieran says, pointing at me. "I'm afraid everyone in this room is now part of this. I will need your cooperation as well."

"If you want my cooperation, let me go to my daughter!" I blurt.

"All in good time. I'm sure you're wondering why I went to such great lengths to bring you here, and it's time you understood exactly what role you will play in the future of Shadowvale." He turns to the hound creatures. "Bring them."

Bony black fingers seize my shoulders. I try to

make eye contact with Seven, but I'm pushed forward into a dim hallway. Arden is in front of me, and I notice for the first time that they haven't taken her bow. I wonder if it's operational or just a costume prop. Either way, Kieran must not see it as a threat to allow her to keep it on her person. Still, if I could get my hands on it...

The hounds herd us along until we reach a large balcony overlooking Shadowvale. I blink against the orangey light of sunset. When my eyes adapt, what I see beyond the walls of the castle confuses me more than anything that's happened today.

"You're mining malivite here?" Seven is beside me again, and he looks as confused as I am.

Kieran glowers at us. "It's sad really how detached you were from your father's vision, Seven. Allow me to bring you up to speed. Shadowvale is a source of a unique mineral." He holds up a segment of malivite between his thumb and forefinger, similar to the one I retrieved from Adam Barker's murder scene but bigger. "This stone is as dense as lead but far more interesting. You see, it shares properties with both rhodium and neodymium to the extent it can replace those minerals in manufacturing. What I'm holding here is so concentrated an ounce of it is equivalent to a pound of those other elements."

Beside me, Seven shifts with his astonishment. "No wonder Rayrcore wants it."

I can't help myself. "Sorry, what do rhodium and neodymium do?"

Seven turns to me. "They're rare earth elements. They're used in electronic devices and car engines. We use them in our slot machines."

"Rare earth isn't exactly rare," Kieran says, "But it is essential and problematic to mine in your world. We are the solution to that problem. We are going to mine, sell, and ship malivite to Rayrcore from Shadowvale. You, Seven, and Lucky Enterprises are going to be the conduit for that transaction."

"Is that what this is all about? You need me because I own the casino now," Seven says slowly. "Once my father was arrested, I inherited the property the portal is on. You want me to power the portal so you can get the malivite from here into Rayrcore's garage."

Alicia laughs. "You self-important twit. I have access to the tunnels too and can open a portal without you. We need you because Lucky Enterprises' manufacturing subsidiary has the established business relationship with Rayrcore. If you don't carry this through, it could raise a red flag with Godmother or FIRE."

"That's it? This is all about selling malivite? But why did you kill Adam Barker?" I ask.

"We didn't," Alicia says.

"I know you were there." I don't bother explaining how I know that. No reason to bring Eva into this.

She nods. "I *was* there because I was working with Adam. I'd provided him with some malivite, and he came to Dragonfly Hollow to share the results of his analysis with me, results I planned to share with Rayrcore. Someone shot him before we could connect."

She's telling the truth and I glance at Seven, but he just shakes his head. If Alicia didn't kill Adam, who did? Kieran had no reason to want him dead.

Seven struggles against the hound creatures' grip, but they only hold him tighter. "Okay, you have me now. Just let Arden and Sophia go."

I glance over to see that Arden's eyes are rimmed with red. She's staring at Edmund. I've never seen her so heartbroken. The hounds that guard her barely have to do anything because she's barely there. A ghost among us.

You're going to be okay, I mouth to her. Her next breath trembles in her throat, her tears flowing freely, but she offers me a nod.

"They are as much a part of this now as you are, Seven. We are all in this together, for the good of our kind," Kieran says.

The good of our kind. What a crock of shit. He sounds like *Chance*. Connections spark in my mind as I stare out over the balcony at the creatures pulling carts and carrying axes into the tunnels below. The mine reminds me of something from a Tolkien novel, spiraling into the ground with endless activity, only it isn't orcs doing the work. It's goblins

—unseelie fae who are, I've read, normally uncooperative.

"How did you get goblins to work in your mine?" Even as I ask it, the hair on the back of my neck stands on end because I know whatever he's done, it must be dark.

Seven darts a glance toward me and then at the mine, and I see the moment it registers on his face.

Kieran responds with a wicked smile that makes my skin want to crawl right off my body. "I'd heard you were a clever pixie, Sophia. No wonder Valentine dressed you as Titania. You would make a fine queen. You already see where this is going, don't you?"

Beside me, Seven has gone terminally silent. I wonder if Kieran knows how worried he should be right now. The last time I saw Seven look like this, he was bringing down Yissevel's house around him.

"I could guess, but I don't see any prizes for being right. Why don't you save us all some time and tell us," I say dryly.

"Such a smart mouth." He focuses on my lips.

Seven gives a low growl beside me. "What are you up to, Kieran? If you want my help, you need to tell me all of it."

Kieran turns to face the mine and rests his hands on the balcony rail. "Delivering malivite through the silver is only the beginning. For too long Shadowvale has been cut off from prosperity because Godmother didn't have the vision to allow it to grow into what it could be. The goblins are working for me because I've promised them they will be rewarded when we bring down the wall and meld this realm with earth."

My eyes widen. "You're a madman. If you bring down the wall, the unseelie will never respect the peace we have with the outside world. There will be chaos. Once the unseelie start feasting on humans, the only outcome is war."

Kieran nods. "A war we should have fought over a hundred years ago. After the humans' Civil War when Johnson tried to force us from Devashire, I wanted to release the unseelie and put the colonizers in their place. Only Godmother believed a peaceful solution was the most profitable. She gathered enough support among the seelie elders to banish me to this realm. And what has become of you who live on the other side of the wall? Relegated to jesters for human pleasure."

"You were wrong then and you're wrong now." Seven shakes his head. "Devashire is more successful than ever. Our gross national product exceeds that of Germany, and we have power and presence economically in every major industry in North America. Humans flock to our tourist attractions. If the seelie had done it your way, there would be nothing left to rule. The unseelie would have ravaged the States. We'd still be living in forests of claws and teeth, hunting for our meals and battling each other for survival."

Kieran turns his focus on me. "What do you think

about that, Sophia? How are things in Devashire for you? Is what Seven says true? Has posterity blessed all fae equally?"

I swallow and answer honestly. "No. Of course not. Leprechauns have benefited the most from Godmother's arrangement, but—"

"And what about walls? Have walls worked out well for you as a pixie? The barrier between Devashire and the United States proved especially problematic for you, did it not?"

"Yes, but—"

"Did you enjoy being treated as a thing? Being told it was illegal for you to live on land that was once ours? Wouldn't you prefer to come and go as you please? To be treated as an equal to the humans that you now serve? And what about the barrier between you and Seven? That's a different sort of wall, isn't it, Sophia? Oh yes, I know all about you and your relationship." His eyes dart to Alicia, who is still holding her son protectively. "Do you enjoy being considered a lesser class than your lover? Do you think they'll allow you to marry? Is it fun for you to think that Godmother and her laws will determine your future with the man you love?"

"Stop it," I hiss through my teeth. My head pounds, and I'm not sure if it's because he's crazy or because he has a point. It's unsettling, and I find my mind racing from his words.

"The citizens of Shadowvale feel the same way

about their captivity as you feel about yours. And yes, it is captivity. If there are walls, there is captivity. You understand, don't you Sophia? You understand in a way that Seven never can how tearing down all the walls, all the borders, all the barriers, is the only fair and equitable future."

"You don't know what you're saying," Seven says.

"There the leprechaun goes again, speaking for you. Stealing your voice."

"I don't need anyone to speak for me," I snap. "What I need is for men like you to listen to me. It is true that walls have consequences and sometimes barriers need to be torn down, but that's where the truth in what you've said ends. A fair and equitable future for the fae is not one where there are no walls and no rules, because in that scenario I'd be dead. It is no secret that pixies are a delicacy to the unseelie."

Kieran shrugs. "Nature must take its course."

"Who decides what is nature and what is brutality? Will it be you who rules over the chaos, Kieran? There has always been a fairy king and queen, hasn't there? Someone has to rule. Someone has to settle disputes. If I remember my history correctly, you came into your position by killing the king before you."

"The strong survive, Sophia. I am the fairy king, and I will rule the kingdom that is to come, alongside Hearst, who has made preparations to help us take back North America in exchange for exclusive rights to this." He gestures at the mines and the goblins toiling below us. "Hearst sees the writing on the wall and is willing to bow to my rule. As I have served as the ruler of this unseelie kingdom, believe me, I am strong enough. Look how even the goblins do my will."

"Then there are still walls. You're still above everyone else. It's true that I wish things could be different between Devashire and the United States and maybe the unseelie should be represented as well, but the answer is thoughtful and controlled change, not war and complete chaos. Not sitting back while an army of goblins feasts on hapless humans."

He shakes his head, and the hounds holding me grip my arms harder. "I expected better of you. I thought you of all people would see that this is how it has to be."

Alicia straightens. "I told you, Kieran, she's dangerous and uncooperative. Throw her in the dungeon. It's the only way you'll ensure Seven's compliance."

Seven struggles against the hounds holding him, his power rising until I can feel its heat on my skin.

"Careful, Seven." Kieran touches his thumbs and forefingers to form a triangle in front of his chest and I watch in horror as the dragon of energy beside me is turned inside out and then fizzles like a snuffed candle. Seven slumps in his captors' grasp.

"What did you do to him?" Arden yells.

Kieran approaches her and pinches her chin. "Don't they teach your age anymore that the king and queen of the fairies have dominion over all fairy powers? I can give them and I can take them."

"Leave her alone," Seven grits out beside me.

I try to reach for him but the black hounds hold me firm.

"Oh, your daddy does love you, little leprechaun hybrid." He brings his face close to hers, and my heart sprints in fear for her. I don't like the way he's touching her. I don't like the way he's looking at her.

"I am the king, little Larkspur, and you've wandered into my realm."

"You tricked me into coming here." She says it to Kieran, but her eyes lock on Edmund, who is pouting like someone stole his puppy.

Kieran laughs. "It doesn't matter how you got here, little girl, only that you are here. And now you are mine, just like your mommy and daddy."

I glare at Edmund, wondering how he lured Arden here. The lie he must have told her. Lies. Kieran has been playing us this entire time. I close my eyes and steady my breathing. This is a game, and I'm Sophia Larkspur. I could rail against Kieran touching Arden and threatening her with the dungeon, or I could remember what I do best. I can play the game. What cards am I holding? What's my position at the table? What's already been played?

"You're right, Kieran," I say, shaking my head as if waking up from a deep sleep. "The wall must come down." My voice is firm and completely convincing.

He turns to look at me, eyes narrowing. "I see it now. What you say is true. It's a gamble but the only way forward for our species."

"Sophia, you can't mean that!" Seven cries, and he's almost as convincing as I am, although I can always tell when Seven is lying.

"I do, Seven." I look up at Kieran like he's a juicy hamburger and I haven't eaten in four days. I use the slightest bit of luck to make myself more enchanting. "Is it possible to take down the wall? How do you plan to do it?"

I don't look directly at Arden, but as I stare at Kieran, I casually touch the coin around my neck, the dark charm that Seven gave me as protection. It's my table talk, my signal to her to remind Arden that she has a wish. I can't tell her how to use it. I barely understand how to use it myself, and knowing exactly what to wish for in this situation has me perplexed. It occurs to me that this is where the rubber hits the road when it comes to all the things I told Seven about parenting. I raised her to be strong. I raised her to make good decisions. I let her make her own mistakes. Now she's our only way out of this. I have no way to tell her what to do without calling attention to her charm and possibly blowing our best chance out of this. I have to trust that Arden will find a way to save us.

Kieran studies me for a moment and then blessedly leaves Arden's side to approach me. "I understand now what you see in her, Seven. She does have an unusual fire."

Out of the corner of my eye, I see Seven hang his head as if in defeat, but I feel the slightest spark of his luck beside me. He's readying himself.

I drop my chin, turning my face slightly toward Seven. "It's the only way we can truly be a family."

Kieran grins like a shark in bloody waters. "Listen to reason, Seven. Join us. Take your father's place in the new order."

Beside me, Seven goes perfectly still. "What do you need us to do?"

"Thousands of years ago, the wall was erected by the Light Bearers, the predecessors to guardians, using Odin's magic, the magic of the gods. I've spent a century studying that magic, preparing a way to take it apart. The gods are fickle, and this ancient magic has an ancient antidote. All it takes is blood sacrifice, one powerful enough to appease the gods."

"Dark magic," Seven murmurs.

"Ancient magic was dark." Kieran looks out over the mine. "When our kind ruled this world, our luck was stronger and our society traded in bargains and blood. We will unlock those secrets again. And the first step is to kill the guardians."

"What? All of them?" I ask.

"Edmund and I will do that deed," Alicia says, although sniveling Edmund seems less than enthused about being chosen for the task.

"Excellent." Kieran turns back to Seven. "You will open the portal. The sacrifice must be made inside it, where the blood will drip through the stars and into the hereafter."

"Who exactly is being sacrificed?" Seven asks.

I swallow, a nagging suspicion unsettling me.

Kieran lowers his chin. "I think you know the answer to that." His eyes dart to Arden. "The rarest fairy blood of all our kind resides in that girl. No god would refuse it."

"No!" Edmund cries, backing away from his mother. "You promised you wouldn't hurt her!"

"Quiet, boy!" Kieran snaps his fingers and Edmund's mouth disappears. He claws at his face as his mother tries to calm him down.

"Kieran, my son!" Alicia snaps.

"Shall remain quiet now. Why should he cry when our hybrid waits like a lamb for the slaughter?"

Gooseflesh covers my skin and my blood has turned to ice, but I say nothing. Seven doesn't either. We both know words won't help us now. I look toward Arden, willing her to use the wish. She's eerily calm in a way I've never seen her before. Only... I *have* seen that calm in her father and in myself. Oh Kieran, you do not know what you're in for.

"I have questions," Arden says softly, her hand pressed into the base of her throat, palm over the gold acorn.

"And I will answer them. It's the least I can do to say thank you for your sacrifice," Kieran says.

"Will you, as king of the fae, play a part in the spell to bring down the wall?" Arden asks.

He nods. "I will. It can't be done without me. I will snuff the magic and then use your blood to neutralize it permanently."

"Because you're king of the fae," she says softly. "It can't be done without you."

"That's right," he says proudly.

"My teacher at Bailiwick's said that many people believe Godmother trapped you here because if she killed you, another fairy would rise to your position, possibly someone she couldn't defeat. So it was safer for her to keep you alive."

"Clever theory. Although I'm stronger now. I believe Godmother will be unpleasantly surprised when we bring down the wall and I pay her a visit."

Arden's gaze darts to me and then to Seven, where it lingers, almost apologetically.

"*Fuck,*" Seven utters under his breath. What does he know that I don't?

Fingers clutching the acorn in the hollow of her throat, Arden says clearly and with intention, "I wish my father was king of the fae."

TWENTY-THREE

A rden's luck snaps out of her body, but unlike before, it's no cute, lovable raccoon. The acorn amplifies her power into a primordial beast that expands to the size of the castle and roars, blowing back my hair in a gale-force wind.

Kieran raises his hands, forming a triangle with his thumbs and forefingers, and tries to absorb the excess energy. His magic glows orange as a sunrise, but it is nothing compared to Arden's. She grinds his power beneath the heel of the wish.

I raise my arm to shield my eyes from the intensity of the clashing magic. Seven draws me into his chest. "Whatever happens, Sophia, I love you. I have always loved you."

His words scare me as much as the flames of power licking at my skin. It feels like we've been thrust into a kiln. A flash between our bodies draws my attention, and I see the coin around my neck glowing bright. The charm! I spin around, my back to Seven, shielding both of us as much as possible. Seven ducks his head, making himself small behind me as the blast grows in intensity.

Kieran is a glowing ball of fire. He is an orange sun, an exploding star, a detonated bomb.

The hound creatures in the room are the first to go, their bodies incinerating to ash before my eyes. Suddenly Edmund screams. His mouth has returned, which must mean Kieran's power is waning, but the blast coming off Kieran is frying the boy and his mother. Alicia shields him with the giant spider of her luck, but it isn't strong enough. They run for the hall, but it's too late. They both collapse near the exit, their skin blistering, then burning off altogether. I watch them gasp one last time before they stop breathing.

Across the room, Arden's eyes glow like emerald fire, the wish protecting her from the fallout. Her luck feels boundless but not targetless. Every ounce of it is directed at Kieran. The rest of us are simply collateral damage.

The king's face sags and his arms flop to his sides. I stand up straighter, my arms wrapped around Seven behind me, panting in the heat of this magic. It finally wanes, coiling back in on itself. Kieran's knees give out, then the rest of him, flesh and bone. He melts into a puddle of blue liquid, his crown of stars splashing down in the center. It dissolves as if in acid, sizzling until it's gone. A cool breeze blows through the room, and I draw a deep breath.

But behind me, Seven pulls away, grunting in pain. I whirl to find him doubled over. "Arden, stop!" I yell. "It's hurting him."

Her hands are fisted at her sides and she sways on her feet. "I'm not doing it! I want it to stop, but I can't."

I wrap my arm around Seven, trying my best to protect him from whatever is happening. He's leaning on me, hard. I can't let him go. I keep one arm around his waist and hold the other out to her. "Come to me, Arden."

But she can't seem to move.

"Go," Seven growls and shoves me.

I rush toward Arden and reach her just in time. Her eyes roll back in her head, and she tumbles into my arms. I collapse onto my knees from her weight but save her from the worst of the fall. Cradling her, I rock her gently. She's barely breathing.

"You're okay. I've got you. I've got you."

Tears slip down my cheeks and fall on her too-hot skin. I place my fingers on the side of her throat, but her pulse is a weak tap against my fingers.

"Come on, Arden. Fight. You are going to be okay. Just hold on." I wish to every god above that I could give her my luck. My chest hurts.

"She's negative," a deep voice with the hollow tone of a cavernous space says above me.

I glance up and find Seven standing over us, only it's a version of Seven I've never known before. A gold crown of stars hovers over his toffee-colored hair like a halo, and his glowing emerald pupils are ringed in silver.

"Let me give her my luck."

"Seven?" my voice cracks.

"Yeah, it's me, Sophia." He reaches down and takes Arden by the arms. When his luck rises in the room, it's clear something has changed. His dragon is no longer red but gold, and it's massive, at least twenty times larger than before. Long moments tick by. It might be seconds, minutes, hours. Time has no meaning when your child is unconscious in your arms.

Finally her body takes on a golden glow and her lips part on a gasp.

"Oh, thank the gods." I draw her to me, but when her eyes pop open, she reaches for Seven.

"Dad?" It's the first time she's ever called him that, and my eyes burn with emotion. Their hands intertwine. "I'm sorry. I didn't know what else to do."

Seven closes his eyes and the crown disappears, its energy sinking inside him. A line from Chance's poem comes to mind: *He who carries his crown within his bones.* He'd meant Kieran. *Mirror, mirror* had meant the portal. *They whose hunger has grown and grown* must have been referring to Rayrcore and their ravenous appetite for rare earth, and *she whose hatred is cast in stone* was Alicia, who'd hated Seven since her fateful purchase of her own engagement ring. He'd told us the truth after all.

Seven's eyes shift to a normal color again. "It was the only thing you could have done, Arden. If you had wished he was dead, his power might have gone anywhere, even to one of the goblins."

He doesn't say it might have gone to Edmund, but we all must think it because Arden's eyes slip to the boy's body. She starts to sob.

"He must have drugged me. The last thing I remember is having a drink with him and his mother and suddenly feeling woozy. They promised to take me outside to get some air, but instead took me to the mirror. I think I passed out for a while, and then you were there. I wanted to use the wish sooner, but my brain was too foggy to know what to do. I—"

"It's all right, Arden," Seven says. "You did the best anyone could do. It's over."

She sits up between us and hugs her knees to her chest, the tears coming in waves now. I draw her protectively against my side. Seven lowers himself to sit on her other side and puts his arm around her shoulders.

"I really loved him," she says.

I look down and see that the red ribbon is still tied around her wrist. It all makes me want to scream.

Seven and I look at each other, then each grab a side of the ribbon and pull. It breaks, and I cast it aside.

"He didn't deserve you," Seven says.

"But did he deserve to die? I did that." Her eyes drift toward the body, her sobs shuddering.

I hug her tighter. "Edmund made the choice to deceive you. He made the choice to drug you and help abduct you. You didn't do that to him, Arden. Kieran did. But Edmund put himself in Kieran's orbit. He said yes to all this."

She nods and presses her forehead to her knees.

Seven's expression turns dark. "Does this change how you feel about staying in Devashire?"

I bristle and brace myself for the worst. It's too late to go back now. Everyone knows who and what she is.

But Arden shakes her head. "No. I want to be here, with my family." She threads her hands into both of ours.

"Truly?" I ask.

At first she doesn't answer, just stares at her toes and releases a long, shaky breath. "Bad things happen everywhere," she says slowly, "but I think friends and family are the only way to weather the storm. I need Dragonfly Hollow. I need you, Mom, and Dad and Grandma and Grandpa. This place has meant more to me than any of the places we lived in America. It's not that it's better or worse, just different, and it's home."

I kiss the side of her head.

"Can we go now?" she asks.

I look at Seven. There's so much to discuss. Is it safe for him? Once Godmother finds out that he's the new king, will she try to banish him like she did Kieran, or worse, try to control him using their bargain? Does he have an obligation to Shadowvale and the unseelie there? What should be done about the mine and Rayrcore?

But the look he gives me tells me everything I need to know. Our problems will always be with us. There will always be some heavy weight regarding his company, our relationship, Arden, and now his position as fairy regent. But when we're tired and we've had enough, sometimes it's time for the prince and Cinderella to just go back to the castle, roll up the drawbridge, and enjoy being a family.

He rises first and helps us both to our feet. "Let's go home."

CHAPTER

TWENTY-FOUR

I t's early the next day when I make my way to
Godmother's Tearoom and ask the pixie behind
the hostess stand to speak with her. I've come alone on
purpose. Both Seven and I agree that him being in the
same room as her at the moment is a bad idea.
Because of their bargain, if she senses what he is, she'll
never let him go. Our only hope is to take advantage of
the moment, when no one but us knows what
occurred.

I'm shown back to her office and take a deep fortifying breath outside her door before being ushered
inside. Dressed in a sophisticated yellow gown,
Godmother looks like a queen, sitting behind a delicate curved-leg desk, signing something with her long,
feathered quill.

She barely glances my way before saying, "Sophia

Larkspur, to what do I owe the pleasure of your inter-ruption?"

I sit down in one of the dainty chairs across the desk from her. "It's time for you to release River from the safe house."

Now she raises her dark gaze and stares at me. "Have you solved the murder then? Will you be giving me the name of the true perpetrator to arrest in River's stead?"

I pull out my phone and queue up the security video. "I can give you a name, but I'm not sure you'll want to arrest them."

"Why not?" She folds her arms.

"Because *you* shot Adam Barker."

Godmother flashes a stern look in my direction and then laughs. "Is this some kind of joke?"

"No. No, I'm not joking. You knew that Alicia Faust was supposed to meet with Adam Barker that after-noon. He'd promised to bring her the results of his analysis of the malivite being mined in Shadowvale. You knew all about malivite and its promise for industrial applications because you wrung the truth out of Chance when you arrested him. I watched you torture Chance, but it didn't occur to me just how much he shared with you that night. But when I visited him in Ashgate, it was clear you'd broken his mind as well as his body."

"You're boring me with this nonsense, Sophia," Godmother says. "I was giving a speech to the graduating class at the time of the murder, in front of half the town."

"No, you weren't. The shooting happened afterward, as the crowd was filing into the tent for the after-party. You disappeared in the commotion and then reappeared to get Seven after the murder. You shot Adam so that he couldn't confirm the properties of malivite to Alicia, and you intentionally did it from a distance and from the direction she was standing. Your true intention was to frame Alicia for the crime, but you didn't count on River. He was in the wrong place at the wrong time with the wrong sense of responsibility to the victim. Although you planned for people to see the direction of the shot and to link the murder back to Alicia, another leprechaun had cleared the area, which meant you had no choice but to pin the murder on River. After all, you needed someone to blame."

"Your analysis is far from accurate, but I'll give you this—if you can prove Alicia was in the vicinity of where the bullet originated, she is a major suspect and I will arrest her immediately."

I shake my head. "Alicia didn't shoot Adam Barker. She was scheduled to meet with Adam. She wanted him alive. She needed the information and the sample he carried to take to Rayrcore. But you knew that already."

She waves a hand in the air. "Preposterous. It's an

outlandish theory. What motivation could I possibly have to instigate a death in Dragonfly?"

"You thought framing Alicia would stop her and Kieran's plan now that Chance was out of the picture. The fact that Alicia had tampered with the security cameras so that her meeting with Barker wasn't recorded was an added boon. But you forgot one thing. There's security everywhere, and Alicia didn't manipulate the cameras surrounding the bank."

I press Play. Alicia comes into focus on the side of the bank, striding toward the rendezvous point. The pop of a gunshot goes off, and she cows against the building, looking for the source of the bullet. Then the video changes. A different camera, a different angle. The scene repeats, but there in the corner of the screen is Godmother with a shimmer of purple around her. The pop doesn't seem to surprise her at all.

"So I'm standing beside the bank and Alicia. That doesn't mean I shot a man."

"The noise originates with you, Godmother, and although we can't see the gun, you don't react to the shot. It's almost as if you expect it. But if we watch these side by side, we can see that Alicia turns her face toward you when the gun goes off. The shot originates with you."

Godmother leans back in her chair and couples her hands. "You're confused." Her tone is laced with malice. "Let's call Alicia Faust in, and she can explain her behavior on that video."

"That will be impossible. You see, Alicia Faust and her son Edmund are dead. Tragic accident. But I think the people of Devashire would be interested in this video, which is why I've given it to a friend to share publicly if we can't come to an agreement today."

Her power rises in the room, setting my teeth on edge. When she speaks again, her voice is low and her stare intense. "I think we can agree that Alicia Faust shot Adam Barker. River will be freed, and a statement will be prepared explaining that she and her boy were killed trying to escape authorities. You will deliver the bodies to me, and then you are free of your obligation to me."

"Excellent. Now what about Seven?"

"What about him?"

"You must release him from his bargain as well."

"No."

"I have information about Kieran. Information you'll want to know. But I won't share it unless you release him."

"What about Kieran?"

I remain perfectly silent and just stare at her for a beat. "Your bargain with Seven is one-sided. You can break your hold over him at any time. That's what you need to do now if you want me to stay and share what I know about Kieran and his plan to attack you and Devashire."

"Kieran is banished," she says through her teeth.

"Still, when I saw him last night, he was very clear

about his strategy." I pull out the piece of malivite I brought back from Shadowvale and toss it onto her desk.

Eyes wide, she probes me lightly with her power and I let her. I haven't told a single lie. I let her taste the honesty in my claim.

She drums her fingers on the desk, and I toy with the coin around my neck. She doesn't even bother to threaten me with force. We both know it won't work.

"Fine. I will release Seven from our bargain. Now tell me what you know."

"First release him."

She lowers her chin and glares at me. "You're testing me, Sophia, and I'm very close to transforming you into a ferret and tossing you out of here by the tail. I promise you I'll release Seven as soon as you tell me what Kieran told you."

"And I have your word on that?"

"Yes," she says emphatically, her expression full of annoyance.

I lean forward. "Kieran has found a ritual that can take down the wall and meld Shadowvale to earth. He plans to set the unseelie free. He's garnered help from the goblin kingdom and has been mining malivite to exchange with Rayrcore for their help. When he strikes, you're going to feel it from every direction." I shake my head.

For the first time, Godmother looks nervous. She taps the heel of her foot on the floor, her expression going suspiciously blank. "When is he planning this coup?"

"I'll tell you, but first release Seven."

She hesitates. I stand and start walking toward the door.

"Fine!" she grits out. She snaps her fingers, and silver threads appear around her. She cuts one with her fingers.

I pull out my phone to text Seven, but one pops in from him before I have a chance.

> It's done. OMG, Sophia, you did it.

"Now tell me!" Godmother booms. Her magic stabs at my skin. The coin around my throat glows brighter, repelling it.

"Kieran is dead," I say, adding an exaggerated shrug. "So there will be no attack. Toodle-oo!" I wave my fingers.

"Sophia!" The walls shake with her anger, and I hear the pounding of footsteps that I am sure come from her security team.

I pivot. "Yes?"

"You're sure he's dead?" Her eyes narrow.

"Positive. He threatened Arden and so we killed him."

"Do you know who the new king is?"

"Whoever the magic calls, I assume." I force my face into a careful mask.

"You could have told me he was dead straight-away. You cost me my leprechaun with your scheming. I should have you taken to Ashgate for this," she says through her teeth.

"But you won't," I say. "Because now that you can't control Seven, you need us as allies. And despite what you might think, Godmother, I believe that you are the best person to lead Devashire, and so does Seven. And maybe someday Kieran's replacement will surface, and then you might need us to secure your reign. You want Seven in your corner. Trust me on this. And you won't have that if I'm in Ashgate."

She leans back in her chair and threads her fingers. It's with some measure of disgust that she says, "Very well. I'll expect you and Seven to keep that promise. Now please show yourself out."

CHAPTER

TWENTY-FIVE

Six months later...

"Grandma, when did you get here?" I lean against the side of the couch, watching my grandmother knit a gigantic misshapen blanket from fuzzy white yarn.

"Oh, a few minutes ago. Your mom invited me to dinner before the Yule celebration."

"Oh, is that tonight?" I knew it was coming up, but Seven and I have been so busy I didn't realize what day it is. After my conversation with Godmother, River was freed and returned to his life running River's Tavern. He's still seeing Eva and Patrick, and although there's no bargain between them anymore, they've successfully kept their tryst a secret. Seven and I are the only ones who know.

Although Seven was freed from Godmother's hold

over him, we still had to deal with the fallout from going public about our relationship at the Gilded Gala and the announcement that Arden was our daughter. At first the commentary was insulting. The *Daily Hatter* ran headlines like PERNICIOUS PIXIE HOOKS DRAGONFLY'S MOST DESIRABLE BACHELOR and WILL SEVEN DELANEY COME TO HIS SENSES ABOUT FLIGHTY AFFAIR? But as time went on and we continued to appear in public —affectionately in each other's company—people became curious about our relationship.

We agreed to an exclusive interview with Fairly Goodweather for the *Daily Hatter* that was recorded for their YouTube channel. Over the course of three grueling hours, we answered every question Fairly sent our way. Seven admitted he fell in love with me in grade one when I softened the blow of his mother's neglect. I admitted that I was wrong to leave the way I did, that Devashire would always be my home, and that in a way, the luckiest day of my life was being captured by FIRE because it brought us back together. The interview was heart-wrenching, and Penelope told me everyone in River's Tavern cried during the live showing.

After that, things changed for us. Oh, there were still leprechauns who looked down their noses at me, but we had no trouble getting a table for dinner at even the snootiest restaurants in Elderflame. The humans loved our story so much there was even a middle-aged romance author from the Midwest willing to buy the rights to it. We liked her, so we signed it over for free. My parents sell copies in their shop, the Silver Ember, where they also do a booming business in Sophia and Seven action figures.

Our popularity also spilled over into our business venture. Spots in my poker classes fill the moment we open them now. The demand is so great that we've added two other poker teachers, another pixie and a satyr. Talks have resumed on allowing fae to take poker lessons and perhaps try a tournament in the future.

As for Arden, she started premed at Elderflame University and dreams of becoming a pediatrician. Graceling tells me she's at the top of her class. That's why I'm here tonight and not staying at Seven's. She's on her way home for winter break.

"It is tonight," Grandma says. "And it will be Arden's first Yule ball. You don't want to miss that."

"I wouldn't dream of it... if she wants to go that is. After everything that happened with Edmund, she might prefer to stay as far away as possible. It took her weeks to get over that evening. She hasn't dated anyone else since. I think it still holds bad memories for her."

Grandma's blue eyes twinkle. "Arden is a strong young woman. Smart as they come. I think you'll be surprised how thoroughly she's recovered when she's home again."

"I hope so."

My phone buzzes, and I pull it from the hidden pocket of my plum-colored princess dress. It's Seven's favorite color on me, and he plans to meet us tonight. My heart leaps when I see the call is from Arden, and I bring the phone to my ear.

"Mom?" Her voice sounds shaky, like she's upset.

"What's going on?"

"I need help. You know how to drive a sleigh, right?" My phone vibrates again, and I see that she'd sent me a picture of a sleigh in line for the Yule parade.

"Gods, Arden. What's going on?" *Fuck*, Edmund would have had to rent a sleigh to get the red ribbon he tied on Arden's wrist. Did no one think to cancel it after he died?

"Can you meet me at the edge of the Winter Wood?" Her voice cracks again, and my heart breaks.

"I'll be there as fast as I can fly." I end the call and head for the door.

When I arrive at the Winter Wood, panting and almost crazy with worry, I find Arden waiting for me, dressed in the cobalt princess dress I bought her for graduation. She's standing beside one of the red sleighs in the lineup, but she doesn't look upset at all. On the contrary, she's beaming at me.

"Arden, what is going on?" I ask, more than a little annoyed.

"Get in the sleigh, Mom." Arden laughs and points at a thick fur blanket in the back.

"Why? Honey, I'll drive if we can't get out of this. You can be in the back."

She takes me by the shoulders and gives me a kiss on the cheek. "I love you, Mom. Just enjoy tonight, okay?"

Seven steps out from the shadows, dressed in a deliciously tailored dark suit. "What Arden means is, tonight I'm going to drive."

I can't get my mouth to close as he approaches with a red ribbon in his hand and ties it around my wrist. "Seven?"

"It's long past time we had the night we should have had all those years ago." He kisses me gently, then helps me into the back before lifting himself into the driver's seat.

Arden waves. "I'll meet you in the square." She takes off for the center of the park.

"How long have you been planning this?" I ask him.

He turns on the bench to look me in the eye and gives me a wink. "Sixteen years."

I laugh. "You never fail to surprise me."

"Wait until you see what's in there."

Only then do I notice a small cooler under the edge of the blanket. I open it to find a steaming hot cup of cocoa in a River's Tavern cup. I pop off the lid and see dozens of mini marshmallows and a sprinkle of cinnamon. "I love you, Seven Delaney."

He flashes his most disarming smile. "Good, because that will make this so much easier."

I take a long sip.

The band starts to play, and Seven taps the reins and nudges our reindeer into motion. Snow drifts from the star-filled sky. There's not a cloud above us. This is Godmother's magic. Beautiful.

I wave at the cheering crowd as we drive by, my mind flashing back to the nightmare I experienced sixteen years ago. The memories that flood me are just as painful as they were then, but now they have to war with new memories, joyful ones. I can feel the story I've told myself changing, morphing into a tale of misunderstanding, of redemption, of love and connection, of things working out over time. I let it all wash over me, the good and the bad, and I smile at the sharp edge of emotion it creates in me. The snow on my face makes me feel alive.

By the time we park the sled in the special parking area created for this event, I've finished my chocolate and feel light as a feather, like the past is finally truly in the past. Accepted, part of me, but not any more important than any other moment in our lives. I feel healed.

Seven hops down and helps me out the back, and I throw my arms around him. "Thank you for this."

He presses a kiss into my hair. "We're not done."

Taking my hand, he leads me to the gazebo where a satyr band plays and white lights cast dancing couples in their warm glow. My mother and father are there, as is Arden, who's dancing with River; Penelope, who's swaying with her husband Flick; and Eva, who's taking a turn around the floor with a completely healed Saul, along with a dozen more faces I recognize from Dragonfly. "Are we going to dance?"

He smiles as he leads me up the stairs and nods at the string quartet. They stop playing, and all the dancers pause to look at us.

I turn to Seven to ask him what's happening and find him on one knee. In his hand is a box with a ring. Seven once said there would be a day he'd buy me a ring with a diamond large enough to be seen from space. I can't attest to that, but as I look at the monstrosity he's holding, I question whether I'll get tired carrying it around.

"Sophia Larkspur, for as long as I can remember, you've been my best friend. Then you became my lover, and then when you were gone, the one I thought about when I looked at the moon. Somehow I have you back, and all I want is to be with you forever. You are who I think of when I hear the word *home*. All my life, people have said that I'm lucky, but tonight is the test. Will you make me the luckiest man alive? Will you marry me, Sophia?"

Everyone is watching, but we might as well be standing there alone. My attention narrows like a tunnel until I can see only him.

"Yes," I say. "I guess the rumors are true. You are

lucky, and so am I, because I can't wait to be your wife."

He slips the ring on my finger, and the world starts again amid flashing cameras, claps, and cheers. He pulls me into an embrace.

Seven's power wraps around me with his arms, making me feel safe and loved. He's never told anyone that he's the king of the fae, and he refuses to use his new power for fear of drawing attention to himself. But I know and Arden knows. And I pity anyone who tries to get between the three of us. They won't succeed. Not now. Not ever.

"Would you care to dance?" he asks me.

"Oh yes," I say. "And then we must complete the rest of our plan."

He quirks a half smile. "Our plan?"

"Sixteen years ago we planned to ride in the parade, dance in the gazebo, and…"

He arches a brow as he remembers our plan to lose our virginity to each other, and a wolfish grin spreads across his face. He sweeps me into the middle of the dance floor. "In that case, maybe half a dance."

EPILOGUE

Six years later...

Seven fills a glass with champagne and hands it to me. "Congratulations, Mrs. Delaney."

"Don't congratulate me yet. Not until it's done."

"Everything is going to be fine. I have a feeling." He smiles, and his eyes glint with power. "Today is a very lucky day."

Every day is lucky now that Seven and I are on the other side of our happily-ever-after. We wait on the porch of our country estate. It's not exactly a castle, but the two-story white farmhouse with a bright red door might as well have a moat. It rises at the center of acres and acres of land, the border of which is protected by a ward only the king of the Fae could master. We've been happy here in our getaway from the city, although Seven keeps his penthouse for nights he needs to stay in town.

"There she is," Seven mumbles as a Land Rover weaves up the drive. It parks near the house, and Arden leaps from the driver's seat, her doctor's bag in hand.

"If it isn't Elderflame Hospital's newest resident!" I say proudly.

She beams back at me. "I can't believe you're allowing me to witness this."

She jogs up the steps to us, and we each pull her into our arms.

"This is a family matter, and you are family," I tell her.

Together, the three of us enter the house and pass through the massive foyer and family room to the kitchen and the antechamber that leads to our garden. A real pixie garden with vines of blooming roses, bushes of hydrangeas, hibiscus the size of dinner plates, peonies, and butterfly bushes. Some of the most beautiful plants have no names, but their flowers are uniquely beautiful, and the scent flavors the air.

Seven is king of the fae, and as such he holds the powers of every fairy species. It wasn't long after we were married that he started producing seeds as a pixie would, and we've planted them here along with mine. There are so many positive emotions in this garden we rarely have to weed.

But the most important plant is at the center of it

all. We make our way there now, to the two spheres of glass, one purple and one yellow, that have grown to the size of large pumpkins.

"Are you ready to meet your siblings, Arden?" I ask.

She nods enthusiastically. Seven and I join hands, then bring our heel down with a careful tap on the yellow fairy glass. Cracks form along the edges, and I easily pull the sections apart. Sap spills into the soil and fog rolls up, obstructing my view, but when I reach inside, I find the chubby body of a baby. I gather it into my arms, stroking back its shock of dark hair and staring into two emerald-green eyes.

"A girl!" I squeal. "Arden, you have a sister." I hold her to me until something nudges my arm. Moving her to my shoulder, I watch as two wings unfurl from her back. "And a pixie!"

"What will you name her?" Arden asks.

I look at Seven and smile. "We decided on Harper."

"Harper Delaney," Arden says before holding a receiving blanket out to wrap Harper in. Together we make a baby burrito and Arden takes Harper from me, cooing down at her sister.

I return to Seven's side, and hand in hand, we bring our heels down on the purple glass. This time Seven reaches through the fog, and when he lifts another child from the birth plant, I notice immediately this one looks more like me with brown eyes and hair.

"Harper has a brother!" Seven says, tucking him against his chest.

"No wings," I say.

Arden steps to his side, handing me Harper, and examines the baby. "He's a leprechaun. You can tell by the pattern of the iris. See?" She gently holds open the baby's eyelid, and I see a gently looping pattern in his iris that is different from Harper's. "That will fade by the time he's a year old."

"I can feel his luck," Seven says, a smile spreading.

"Have you decided on a name for my brother?" Arden asks, pulling another receiving blanket from her bag.

"Everett." I kiss my new son on the head, then stand close to Seven so the babies can see each other and both of us together.

"And just like that, we're a party of five," Arden whispers.

Five. I wouldn't believe there was enough room in my chest for the joy I'm feeling if I weren't experiencing it firsthand. We are a family. A strong one. A real one. There are no lies here. No illusions. No more secrets.

The trouble with fairy tales is they never show you the happily-ever-after. The girl marries her prince, but do they stay together? Does it last? Are they strong enough to withstand the pressures that kept them apart before the magic happened?

I can't speak for Cinderella, but for us the answer is yes. Then again, you might say the five of us are as lucky as they come.

Thank you for reading LUCKY US. If you enjoyed this title, please leave a review wherever you buy books.

Love dragons? Try the TREASURE OF PARAGON. Nine royal dragon siblings, exiled in a violent coup from their native realm of Paragon, discover they are destined to find love and their way home.

Get book 1, THE DRAGON OF NEW ORLEANS free when you sign up for my VIP list! https://www. genevievejack.com/nolafreebie/

Turn the page to read an excerpt of THE DRAGON OF NEW ORLEANS.

EXCERPT: THE DRAGON OF NEW ORLEANS

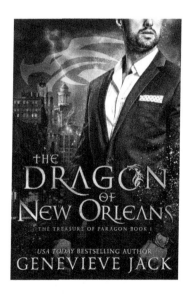

ONE

Gabriel Blakemore was running out of time, which was laughable considering time had never meant anything to him in the past. As an immortal dragon, his life thus far had flowed like an endless river, each new day guaranteed by the last. Not anymore. He thumbed the emerald ring on his finger. Already the curse at its center gave the jewel the appearance of a cat's eye in bright light, a thin black pupil visible at the center of the green. His affliction was spreading.

Hunched over the seventeenth-century Spanish baroque desk in his office at Blakemore's Antiques, he sifted through the stack of papers in front of him, praying for a savior, anyone who had the slightest potential for breaking the curse. None of the candidates seemed powerful enough. He needed more options.

Anxiously, he tugged at the bond connecting him to his manservant. Richard appeared at the door to his office almost immediately, carrying a stack of papers that he squared on the desk in front of Gabriel. "More for you."

Gabriel nodded at the man. Impeccably dressed, as always, in a pinstripe three-piece suit, Richard had proved a crucial asset these days, researching magical options when Gabriel could not. Gabriel had bought the former slave's freedom in 1799, a wise choice. Not only had Richard become a close friend over the centuries, he'd retained a sharp wit and an eye for detail.

The man dusted off his hands before rubbing his sternum. "You don't need to scream down the bond, you know. I'm in the next room. I want to find a cure as much as you do."

Gabriel grunted.

"Are all dragons as friendly and chipper as you, or was I just lucky to be bonded to the best of them?" Richard folded into the chair across the desk, throwing a lanky arm across its back.

"How are sales today?" Gabriel asked, ignoring the man's gibe. He hadn't meant to cause Richard discomfort, but he didn't plan to apologize for it either. Not when the situation was so dire.

"Strong enough that if we all live another year, we can throw one hell of a party," Richard said. "How's that plan coming along? You find a way for us to do that? Live another year? There must be something here. For God's sake, we live in the voodoo capital of America, the home and burial place of Marie Laveau herself."

A whiff of cinnamon and molasses curled off Gabriel's coffee, and he took a long, steadying drink. "Marie would roll over in her tomb if she knew who was running this city now." New Orleans was brimming with humans claiming to have supernatural abilities. Liars, most of them. Unfortunately, the voodoo priestess who'd cast the curse on his ring was the real thing, and she did not take prisoners. Anyone left with true power in the city was either on her side or too afraid to oppose her.

Gabriel snorted. Three hundred years in this realm, only to be turned to stone by the jealous rage of a woman who couldn't take no for an answer.

The thought made his fingers drum against the desk. Tap-tap-tap. Always in threes. The compulsion to tap was so strong when it hit him, not doing so resulted in pain. Muscle tremors ran the length of his arms and hands. He flipped his thumb against the corner of the paper nearest him, hoping it would curb the impulse.

Richard frowned at his fidgeting. "You should rest, Gabriel. It's getting worse. This is the third time this morning."

"Soon."

"That's what you said an hour ago."

Gabriel pulled the pile of papers toward him. His hands cramped with the effort, and the stack spilled across the walnut desk. He cursed, but the word caught in his throat. A woman's picture had been revealed in the collapse, instantly catching his eye. He lifted the folded newspaper to get a better look.

Enchanting. That was the only way to describe her. He couldn't look away. The woman had eyes the color of deep water and curly black hair as wild as the hint of trouble she carried in her smile. He had the sudden intense desire to kiss away that lopsided grin and further tangle that hair. Where had such an urge come from? A dragon like Gabriel didn't often find himself drawn to human women. He closed his eyes and gave his head a well-deserved shake.

"Who is this?" he demanded.

Richard leaned over the desk in order to get a better look, and Gabriel turned the article in his direction. Richard groaned. "That, my friend, is a long shot."

RAVENNA TANGLEWOOD OPENED HER EYES TO DARKNESS. SHE blinked and blinked again, but the eyelid flutter didn't seem to help. This was new. While she'd slept, an irregular blotch had formed in her vision, partially obstructing her view. Now it painted itself like black ink against the sterile white walls of her hospital room.

A Rorschach test, she thought. What did she see in it? An oil slick. A dark cumulus cloud. A rough joke told by her brain cancer.

Cancer. That fucking bitch.

The aroma of this morning's half-eaten eggs and the tang of antiseptic brought her fully awake. She was in the exact same place she'd been every day for the past three months: the hospice at Ochsner Medical Center in New Orleans. Only the last time she'd drifted off, there wasn't a stain obstructing half her field of vision.

She rolled her head and the dark splotch followed, blotting out the left side of the room. She closed her eyes again, counted to ten. No change. Damn, that couldn't be good.

Through her working eye, she watched her mother sleep in the chair next to the bed; she at least was the same as Raven had left her. A *Cosmo* was sprawled across her mother's lap as if she'd drifted off midsentence. Though now that Raven looked more closely, the lifestyle magazine was wrapped around a disturbingly worn copy of *Surviving Divorce* by Amy Dickerman, PhD. Raven winced. So her father's pronounced absence had come to this. Or maybe it was a preemptive read, a talisman against the inevitable. As far as she knew, her parents had only separated—the burden of her illness giving rise to separate bank accounts, separate bedrooms, separate lives—in that order. Her care had become an act of full-time charity her father could not abide.

As usual, her mom was bearing the parental weight alone this morning, although the chair beside her held her older sister Avery's rosary. When had she dug that thing up? Raven hadn't seen the likes of it since their aunt had gifted it to her for her first communion. Avery had never been the praying type. Leave it to death to bring out the inner Falwell in everyone.

Did she think she could pray the cancer away? Raven snorted at the thought. *Pull the plug.* That's what she'd say if she had a say, and if she were plugged in to anything more than Mr. Drippy, her full-time fluid and drug-delivery companion. So far, she could breathe on her own and swallow, unlike the man across the hall. *Stopped the vent*, she'd heard the nurses whisper.

Lucky bastard.

"Hey, beautiful," Dr. Freemont said.

Raven rolled her head back to center, then slightly to the left so she could see him clearly out of her good eye. Dr. Freemont was a balding, portly man whose gray temples gave away his advanced age. Still, he was more fun than his stodgy contemporaries. She liked him.

"Hey, ugly," she responded, although the words sounded choked off and raspy.

His bushy silver brows sank over his bulbous nose. "What's this about? You're holding your head at an angle. Raven, can you look at me straight on?"

"No," she drawled. "Dark." Every word was like lifting a two-ton boulder from the depths of her skull and carrying it through a labyrinth of synapses to finally hoist over her lips. It was exhausting.

Dr. Freemont placed one hand gently on her head, then drew a penlight from his pocket. He swung it in front of her right eye, then her left, where the light disappeared inside the dark fog.

"Squeeze my fingers," he commanded, touching her right hand. She did as he asked, then wondered why he never placed his fingers in her left, although he'd walked to that side of the bed. Or maybe he had. She could no longer feel that hand.

As Dr. Freemont continued his assessment, she noticed a trend. Her left side wasn't working. Not just her eye, but also her shoulder, her hand, her thigh, all the way to her pinky toe. Numb. Dead. She was dying in halves.

"Why?" she demanded, but she knew.

"The tumor," he said simply. "The pressure in your brain." He kept speaking, but Raven's mind couldn't keep up with his medical explanation. She did catch the word *stroke*. It didn't matter. They wouldn't treat her for it anyway.

"Donate?" she asked.

Half cloaked in shadow, his face turned grim and

he lowered his voice. "Yes. The cancer is only in your brain. You'll be able to donate your organs. It's all arranged." His voice was funny, and she wondered if he was lying. Normally Dr. Freemont didn't talk to his patients much about organ donation, but she'd pressed him about it early on. For her, it was a light at the end of the tunnel. Every time he reassured her of her donation status, her heart leaped a little. She'd do something with this life. Leave a part of herself behind that mattered.

If he was lying, she didn't want to know the truth.

"Long?" she asked. He knew what she meant. How long until she died? They'd been at this for over five years on and off. Through railroad spikes of pain that left her begging for someone to bash her head in. Months of chemo that turned her inside out. There was nothing left to try. There would be no more chemo. No more surgeries. Raven wanted to live, but if living wasn't possible, she would settle for being free.

His pale eyes met hers, and he gripped her fingers on the right where she could feel his reassurance. "Not long now."

Not long now. She tried her best to smile. "Good."

Her mother roused, her magazine-wrapped book falling from her lap and clattering to the floor. "Oh! Doctor. Excuse me. I must have drifted off. How is she?"

When he turned to look at her, his eyes glossier than usual, his face changed. A mask slipped into place, clinical and authoritative. Raven rolled her head on her pillow to see her mother, and the dark splotch swallowed most of Dr. Freemont's head. She couldn't see anything above his shoulders when he answered.

"I would never put an expiration date on your daughter, Mrs. Tanglewood... Sarah. We both know how strong she is."

"Yes, I know. This one came out fighting." Her mother still believed Raven could beat this thing.

She was wrong.

"Raven's comfort measures are working. We'll maintain the course." He straightened as if he might leave.

Raven squeezed his hand. "Do it," she said. It was the best part of her day. She wouldn't let him leave without giving it to her.

He turned an impassive expression toward her, half light and half dark as she looked at him straight on. "I have no idea what you are talking about, Raven." The corner of his mouth twitched.

With whatever part of her face was still working, she sent him the sternest glare she could muster.

Raising one eyebrow, he backed up a few steps and glanced into the hall. "You know, I don't do this for all my patients. Only for you."

She smiled lopsidedly.

He removed his white lab coat, cleared his throat, and glanced again at the door. There was no one out there. Ceremoniously, he wrapped his coat around Mr.

Drippy, holding the neck in place with one hand and gripping the sleeve with the other. He squared his shoulders.

"I get no drip from champagne...," he began to sing, deep and throaty, in the style of Frank Sinatra. He swayed with her IV pole as much as the length of the tubes leading to the port in her chest would allow. "Mere Toradol doesn't move me at all, but morphine and fentanyl too... Yes, I get a drip out of you." He cradled the screen of the IV pole and dipped it below his round belly, careful not to upset the hanging medications. His lips puckered in an air-kiss toward the screen.

Raven couldn't help it. She started to laugh. Her mother did too, which made her laugh even harder. As always, the sight of that normally stiff and paunchy man dancing with her IV pole tickled something deep inside her, something that bitch cancer hadn't ruined yet. She laughed and laughed until her throat constricted like the valve of a pinched balloon.

Her laugh turned into a cough and then a wheeze.

Dr. Freemont stopped singing.

The next moment he was leaning over her, his pale hands gently shaking her shoulders, and she realized she'd been unconscious. Not long, judging by the look on his surprised face.

"Welcome back," he murmured. He was half dark again.

"That's never happened before," her mother said nervously.

"That's just Raven's body telling us she needs rest," he said. "I'll leave you to it." He removed his lab coat from Mr. Drippy and shrugged it on before nodding his goodbye.

"Well, that sounded promising," Mom said after he was gone. "You just need more rest." She stood up and tucked Raven in, her face positively glowing with denial.

Raven adjusted her head so her good eye was pointed at the door. *Not long now*, he'd said.

That was the day cancer stole her laugh. It was the last time the doctor sang for her. The last time she was awake long enough to ask him to. There were flashes of color and light, the feel of anointing oil crossed on her forehead and wrists as prayers were whispered over her, Avery's rosary dangling from her fingertips above her chest, Dr. Freemont's humorless face as he answered her mother's questions. But most of the following days consisted of darkness.

Until, one night, *he* came for her.

CHAPTER

TWO

Death stood at the end of Raven's bed, looming and dark, and she welcomed him with open arms. Open arm. Only her right was under her control. Oh, how she longed to be free of her broken body.

If any part of her had questioned the true identity of her visitor, the skepticism was short-lived. The aura of the supernatural surrounded him. Raven's first clue was his suit, or rather that he wasn't wearing scrubs. An eternity had passed since someone who wasn't a medical professional or close family had entered her hospice room. Her own father didn't come anymore. It was too sad. A lost cause.

Death's miraculous presence aside, there were stranger things about his visit. Her IV had stopped dripping. Mr. Drippy's digital face was frozen, the impossibly full belly of her next drop of morphine hovering by a silver thread at the center of the machine's plastic chamber. She shot a glance toward her mother, hoping for an explanation, but the woman was motionless and rigid, staring, catatonic, toward the darkened hospital windows. The clock had stopped. Midnight.

Raven's time had finally come.

She took stock of the man who must be Death, the new growth of her hair rustling against the scratchy pillowcase as she turned her head. It was the only sound in an otherwise silent room. Under the fluorescent lights, she studied him. This was the one who would carry her home? He wasn't what she'd expected.

Death was a babe.

Dark. Brooding. Heavy boned and unshaven. There was something handsome about him nonetheless, alluring enough for her failing body to send her a flicker of desire, something she hadn't felt in over a year. It was the eyes, black eyes that seemed to burn into her, with flecks of red and mahogany that radiated from pitch-black pupils. His substantial eyebrows were too full to be considered conventionally attractive, but they balanced a generous nose and lower jaw that had no use for frivolity. He was olive-skinned, full-lipped, and big. Really big. Professional wrestler big. Although, based on his sunken cheeks and long, tapered fingers, she got the sense he could be bigger, like he was perpetually hungry.

"Ravenna Tanglewood?" he asked, his voice lined

with charcoal and grit. A Clint Eastwood voice. A burning voice. Was he taking her to hell? A whiff of campfire drifted past her nose as he neared. That was one thing cancer hadn't taken from her, her sense of smell. And he smelled like the fall, like oak leaves and pumpkin pie, like smoke and old print.

"Yes." Her voice was nonexistent, mostly lips and breath doing the work.

"You are *this* Ravenna Tanglewood." He removed a folded newspaper from his breast pocket. The pages crinkled in his grip. He thrust it toward her.

A large emerald ring on his right pointer finger glinted in the light, and she had trouble looking away from it to focus on what he was asking her. Eventually though, she zeroed in on the story he was showing her. It was an article by a reporter from the *Tulane Hullabaloo*. Psychic Student Saves Family. She blinked slowly, confused. Why would Death care about a piece of gossipy journalism?

Before the doctors had discovered her brain tumor, she had experienced a premonition. She'd been doing laundry when a vision of her parents' pub completely engulfed in flames brought her to her knees. Neither her father nor mother took her vision seriously, but for some reason, her sister Avery did. Avery's resulting tantrum led to the purchase of a brand-new fire extinguisher. A few nights later, an inexperienced cook set his apron down too close to the grill and the strings caught fire. Her father reached for the old extinguisher first. It didn't work. Thankfully the new one did, and consequently her father was able to save the pub and the people in it.

It didn't mean Raven was psychic. Dr. Freemont had explained that the tumor in her brain, with its octopus-like tentacles infiltrating her gray matter, was connecting different areas of her mind, making her exceptionally intuitive. She'd subconsciously noticed the expiration date on the extinguisher, and her brain had produced the vision accordingly. It was the cancer, not anything weird or unusual. The newspaper story was a bit of flamboyant reporting by a friend who hoped to use the piece to attract readers to a fundraiser meant to help with her medical expenses, nothing more.

Death tapped his finger against the newspaper impatiently, the massive green emerald glowing like a star. "Well, is this you?"

She licked her lower lip and nodded. He slid the paper back inside his jacket. Exhausted from the effort of responding, she closed her eyes and prayed silently, *Take me. Please take me.*

GABRIEL STOOD AT THE END OF THE HOSPITAL BED, USING every ounce of willpower he had to restrain himself. When Richard had suggested the girl was a long shot, he wasn't kidding. She was more dead than alive, a porcelain doll he was afraid to startle for fear of breaking her. Still, there was something... alluring about her, the same as when he'd seen her picture. Deep within his chest, a primal urge to heal and protect demanded his attention.

He hadn't felt anything like it in his five hundred years. Not for a human anyway. Perhaps the feeling bore a close resemblance to when he found a rare and priceless item for his collection. Yes, that was it.

She appeared nothing like the picture he'd seen. The only way to describe her now was haunting. The bones of her cheeks protruded as if her skeleton was battling her skin for rights to the surface. Ravenna Tanglewood was death, propped in a bed like a body on display. Above thin lips and a gently curved nose, her blue eyes bulged from her skull, dull and rheumy. Those damned eyes were nothing short of pleading. His chest ached. If she refused his offer, it would haunt him the rest of his days.

He stepped closer to her. Was that night-blooming jasmine? The scent was faint, but he could smell it on her skin. "Is it true you were an anthropology major with a minor in history? Honors student?"

A grunt came from deep within her throat, a warm wet trail of saliva coursing down her lower cheek. Her throat contracted and relaxed, but she seemed unable to form words. He hissed. Damn human hospitals. This was torture. What type of creatures left their females to die like this?

He could wait no more. Already the curse on his ring was weakening his magic. His skin felt thick, like he might turn to stone from the inside out at any moment. He tapped his fingers, exactly three times each against his thumb. Tap-tap-tap. Tap-tap-tap. It was the only thing that helped, the only thing that reminded him he could still move. His magic wasn't completely gone. Not yet.

Still, if he was to save her, he must do so soon.

"I see," he said. "I would like to offer you a job, Ms. Tanglewood. It is hard work. You'll have to learn quickly and take the initiative."

She stared at him blankly. He wondered what she must be thinking, if she could think at all. It was possible her brain was as wasted as her body. From what he'd read, she had brain cancer. Even with magical intervention, there might not be enough left in her head for her to consent. And she must consent. He would not bind her if she didn't. To do so would be to divest himself of any remaining honor he still bore in his wasting body.

He approached her bedside and gently laid his hand on her chest. Those too-big eyes locked onto him. Her heart pounded against his palm. Her expression pleaded for death, but her heart begged for life.

"Ravenna, do you consent? Do you agree to work for me?"

Her eyebrows dipped and her chin twitched as if

she didn't quite understand what he was proposing. A tear escaped the corner of her eye. He wiped it away.

"Say yes, little one," he said. "I cannot bear to see you like this a moment more."

Her eyes widened. "Yes," she mouthed.

He smiled weakly. "Praise the Mountain."

As he held her stare, he removed his hand from her chest, the storm of magic brewing within him. His ring glowed brighter as he drew his power to the surface, the dragon within barely contained inside his human form. Opening his jaw wide, he reached deep into his mouth, his large hand wedging itself between his teeth. He heard her gasp as the sound of tearing flesh filled the room. Gabriel grunted. He was likely scaring her, but it could not be avoided. This was part of the transition. The faster she came to terms with what was happening here, the better.

A spurt of crimson blood beaded on his bottom lip as the tooth materialized, clutched between his fingers. He tugged a handkerchief from his pocket and dabbed at the blood, then held the tooth up to the light. It was thin. Pointed. With a long root still bloody from the extraction. Clearly not a human tooth.

"Never gets easier," he murmured.

Beside him, Ravenna trembled. Her arms were covered in gooseflesh. He had to soothe her, to do something to comfort her before she had a heart attack. He closed his hand and drew on the magic of the ring. When he opened it again in front of her mouth, there was no tooth, only a slim white pill.

"Swallow," he commanded.

She must do this now. They were running out of time, her life fading in front of him, his magic sputtering under the weight of the curse. He scooped an arm behind her shoulders and lifted. Her lips parted like a baby bird's, and he dropped the pill to the back of her throat. She gurgled, coughed. He raised her head higher. Her throat bobbed and the choking stopped.

Oh, how beautiful it was shining through her stomach. The red light spread through her torso and to the ends of her limbs, warming her flesh from within. And all the time, she lay helpless against his arm, staring at him with unrestrained wonder, that jasmine scent of hers growing stronger. It made him feel like a god to hold her like this, to know that he'd given her what she needed to heal, to survive.

He watched her chest rise and fall with the first deep breath she'd taken since he'd arrived.

"What did you give me?" she asked, and this time the words were strong and true, more than the breathy whispers he'd gotten before. Good.

His shoulders slumped. The magic had taken its toll. He must get home to rest.

He brought his face close to hers. "Rest. Recover. You're no use to me like this. We are bound now. I will know when you are ready." He pressed his lips to her forehead and lowered her to the bed.

Her mouth worked soundlessly, as if she couldn't find the words for all the questions she longed to ask.

The rhythmic beep of her heart monitor started again, and a drop of morphine fell within the chamber of her IV. As he left her side and the room, he prayed to the Mountain that he'd chosen wisely. Ravenna Tanglewood was his last chance.

Continue THE DRAGON OF NEW ORLEANS for free when you sign up for my VIP list!

ACKNOWLEDGMENTS

Here's where I say thank you to everyone who helped me tell Seven and Sophia's story. I'm going to miss these two. Thank you to every reader who gave them a chance.

Another big thank you to Anne at Victory Editing. Your gentle hand is always a boon for any story and this one was no exception.

To author Sara Whitney, I so appreciate you beta reading this one and helping me put the final curl of whipped cream on top. I can always count on your clever wit to make a good thing better.

And finally, to Deranged Doctor Designs, thank you for working with me on the cover. Every one you do for me is better than the last.

MEET GENEVIEVE JACK

USA Today bestselling and multi-award winning author Genevieve Jack writes wild, witty, and wicked-hot paranormal romance and romantic fantasy. She believes there's magic in every breath we take and probably something supernatural living in most dark basements. You can summon her with coffee, wine, and books, but she sticks around for dogs and choco-late. Her novels feature badass heroines, fiercely loyal heroes, and fantasy elements that will fill you with wonder. Learn more at GenevieveJack.com.

Do you know Jack? Keep in touch to stay in the know about new releases, sales, and giveaways. https://www.genevievejack.com/newsletter/

facebook.com/AuthorGenevieveJack

instagram.com/authorgenevievejack

bookbub.com/authors/genevieve-jack

tiktok.com/@Genevievejackbooks

twitter.com/genevieve_jack

MORE FROM GENEVIEVE JACK!

His Dark Charms Duet

Lucky Me

Lucky Us

The Treasure of Paragon

The Dragon of New Orleans, Book 1

Windy City Dragon, Book 2,

Manhattan Dragon, Book 3

The Dragon of Sedona, Book 4

The Dragon of Cecil Court, Book 5

Highland Dragon, Book 6

Hidden Dragon, Book 7

The Dragons of Paragon, Book 8

The Last Dragon, Book 9

The Three Sisters Trilogy

The Tanglewood Witches

Tanglewood Magic

Tanglewood Legacy

Knight Games

The Ghost and The Graveyard, Book 1

Printed in Great Britain
by Amazon

19285841R00212